The Third Black Beacon Book of Mystery

Want more thrilling anthologies from Black Beacon Books?

The Second Black Beacon Book of Mystery
The Black Beacon Book of Mystery
The Black Beacon Book of Ghosts
The Black Beacon Book of Horror
The Black Beacon Book of Pirates
Tales from the Ruins
A Hint of Hitchcock
Murder and Machinery
Shelter from the Storm
Lighthouses
Subtropical Suspense

www.blackbeaconbooks.com

The Third
Black Beacon Book
of
Mystery

Ingenious Investigators
Dying Messages
Poison and Pistols
Locked-Room Mysteries
Hidden Treasure

**BLACK
BEACON
BOOKS**

The Third Black Beacon Book of Mystery
Published by Black Beacon Books
Edited by Cameron Trost
Cover art by Małgorzata Mika
Copyright © Black Beacon Books, 2025

The Painting and the Password © Cameron Trost
Death Goes Gourmet © Edward Lodi
Webster's Wallet © Robert Petyo
A Veiled Truth © Karen Keeley
Gunning for a Promotion © Jon Matthew Farber
Take Care of Zozo for Me © Christina Hoag
A Study of Death © Teel James Glenn
(First published in Mystery Magazine, October 2021)
Storm in a Teapot © Chris Hook
The Roman in the Fountain © Ron Fein
The Lunt © S. B. Watson
The Adventure of Woodbury Barrow © Cameron Trost

Black Beacon Books
blackbeaconbooks.com

ISBN: 978-0-9756118-0-7

I see you've cracked the cases and caught the culprits in the first two Black Beacon Books of Mystery and you're back for more puzzling crimes to solve. The third volume won't disappoint you with a new selection of original and enigmatic puzzles to both entertain and challenge even the greatest of armchair detectives. Sherlock Holmes won't be here to help you this time around, but Doctor Watson is on call. You'll be working with Oscar Tremont again on two strange cases, and Lena Lombardi is back, with Marmalade purring on her lap. There are plenty of new additions to the cast as well. You'll be introduced to the *formidable* François Genest—who might remind you of Hercule Poirot, match wits with Tillie Kepler and State Trooper Burt Colosso at Steeples Inn, calculate a crime with Dr Leonard Simon, full-time professor of mathematics and logic, and part-time solver of murders, you'll head back in time to the Roman Empire and witness Joshua the Seer catch a killer in Jerusalem, and Dougal Grieve will need a hand helping the constabulary uncover the truth in misty Scotland. Once again, in *The Third Black Beacon Book of Mystery*, your skills as an active reader are put to the test. Do you have what it takes to solve each mystery before all is unveiled? We'll soon find out. Sit back and make yourself comfortable—but lock the doors and windows first so we'll at least have a puzzling locked-room mystery to solve if you're murdered— and join our private investigators, police detectives, and amateur sleuths for the third time in the latest volume from Black Beacon Books.

- Cameron Trost, editor

Black Beacon Books would like to thank our patrons, whose passion for great fiction and independent publishing helped make this anthology happen.

If you'd like to join the team and reap the benefits, subscribe on our Patreon page at: *patreon.com/blackbeaconbooks*

The five patronage tiers are
Shipwreck Survivor, Moonlight Smuggler, Sea Witch, Assistant Keeper, and *Lighthouse Keeper.*

Author Biographies

The Painting and the Password
Cameron Trost

The subject line immediately caught the attention of Oscar Tremont, Investigator of the Strange and Inexplicable. He'd just politely declined yet another request to follow and photograph a husband suspected of cheating, and he was hopeful as he opened this new email.

Assistance Required with Password Linked to Painting

Intriguing indeed.

Like the subject line, the email was in English, but despite the remarkably good syntax, the name in the introductory sentence told Oscar the choice of language was for his benefit.

'Marjolaine Le Guellec,' he whispered, leaning forward and clasping his hands together. He pressed his index fingers against his lips.

Once he'd finished reading the email, he sat back and stared at his laptop. The fingers of his right hand did a jig on the desk. When they stopped, he smiled. At last, a case that promised to get the cogs turning—to provide a real mental challenge.

He put his fingers to the keyboard and paused. First of all, he had to express his condolences on the passing of her father. Tap, tap, tap. Next, he should thank her for coming to him regarding this matter and assure her that he would give the mystery his undivided and immediate attention. *Tap, tap, tap.* Finally, rather than asking her to send a picture of the painting—which she had failed to do—he would suggest he go to her. *Tap, tap, tap.*

Oscar sent his reply, then immediately stood and looked out the window. It was a cloudy morning, not cold, but not as warm as could be expected in July. Distant seagulls glided in and out of view against the grey backdrop and he wondered whether there were any seagulls depicted in the painting—the seascape.

'Why didn't she send me a photograph of it?' he asked himself aloud, his breath fogging the pane. 'She wants to know whether I'm interested. Perhaps she thinks I might work it out and access her father's secret email account myself. But I don't know the address. She didn't even mention his name.'

He stared at the roof of the townhouse opposite, contemplating the slates that were crooked and the ones that were discoloured or covered in moss and lichen. Details. Most mysteries were a question of details and their place within the bigger picture. To solve this one, he'd have to see the painting—to study it in detail and consider its subtleties and incongruities. Madame Le Guellec would have already tried all the obvious words. If there were seagulls on the canvas sky, she would have tried mouette and mouettes. Would she, however, have tried goéland and goélands? He had a hundred questions to ask her.

'Why hadn't her father simply left the password in his will?' he asked, turning away from the window. He brushed a finger across the touchpad of his laptop and the screen lit up again. He was surprised to find she'd already replied to his email.

Can I come to you today? I'm at my sister's in Pénestin and I have the painting with me. I live in La Baule, so you're on my way home if I'm not mistaken. We've tried every word we can think of. We made a list and we ticked each word off as we tried it. Our father always loved a good puzzle, but he went too far with this one.

Oscar took a deep breath and smiled as he released it. That was one question answered. He made an oath, then and there, that whatever happened, he had to make sure Marjolaine Le Guellec uttered the password with her own lips before he did. He might need to lead her and drop hints, but she had to solve this puzzle herself.

He replied, giving her his home address, telling her to come as quickly as possible, and explaining that he hoped to solve her case before picking his sons up from school at half past four. He concluded by requesting she send a photograph of the painting so he could get started immediately.

Two minutes later, he received her reply and opened the attachment. He looked at the picture for a moment, making a mental note of every detail, then went downstairs to make himself a cup of herbal tea.

10

While the water boiled, he ran a list of words she would have tried through his head, visualising them.

Bateau, bateau bleu, bateau de pêche, chalutier.

There was only one fishing boat in the painting, so plurals would be irrelevant. In any case, her father wouldn't have made it so obvious and uninteresting. This was his final *partie*, and he'd have wanted to make it one to remember.

Quai, filet, and *rochers* were all too simple. He swept them from his mind.

The kettle came to a boil and Oscar prepared his tea. He went back upstairs, sat at his desk, and brushed the touchpad again. As he sat there, studying the picture intensely, the aroma of his herbal tea was replaced with briny air and the silence of his house with the sharp crack of sails taking wind.

There wasn't much to the painting, and that made it all the more mysterious. It wasn't crowded. The view was from a port, with two rocky arms stretching out to either side. There was a hint of the quay with crab pots and fishing nets in the foreground, and the blue fishing boat took centre stage. Beyond it, a straight horizon and a cloudy sky. No gulls. No sun.

The only figure was that of a woman standing on the quay, facing the incoming boat.

'There's more to this than meets the eye,' Oscar said to himself. 'What is it? It can't be a tedious jumble of words. This is a puzzle, designed to be solved with wit, not blundering. This was a man who knew his daughters—who'd taught them and inspired them. Had he overestimated them this time? It would be an understandable error for a proud father.'

A boat entering a port. No way of knowing what the catch was like. No name on the bow. Was the password a combination of letters made up from the features in the painting? He swirled the letters in his mind, changing the order, and swapped the first half of words with the second. But all it came to nought. He wasn't on the right track.

He went to sip his tea but decided it was still too hot, so he looked at the original email instead and reread the subject line: *Assistance Required with Password Linked to Painting.*

'Linked,' he repeated. 'Password *linked* to painting.'

11

The body of the email read the same. Her father had made it clear.

He needed to know more. How old was the painting? Who was the artist? Where had Marjolaine's father acquired it? Did it represent a real place? If so, what had this place meant to him? These were questions his client could answer—some of them, at least—and one of those answers would either be the key or be enough to lead to it. Of that, there was no doubt.

Oscar was on his second mug of herbal tea and still staring at the picture when four quick knocks sounded on the front door. It was half past three. He wondered whether he'd be able to wrap the case up before it was time to go to school—in under an hour.

He hurried downstairs and opened the door.

'Monsieur Tremont?'

'Yes, do come in, Madame Le Guellec.'

She was petite and timid, but she wasn't hesitant. She stepped inside, the painting tucked under one arm, and sat herself on the sofa in the living room. Oscar sat in his armchair and she held the painting up for him to see.

'Tea or coffee?'

'No. Thank you. I'm glad you're interested in my problem. My father always loved a puzzle, as I mentioned, but he's outdone himself. We haven't discussed your fee yet.'

She certainly didn't mess about, this unassuming woman in her early sixties with short grey hair and red-rimmed glasses. But there was a hint of craftiness in those hazel eyes.

'If I can solve the puzzle before four o'clock, I'll ask only my minimum consultation fee as listed on my website.'

She nodded appreciatively.

'May I ask what you expect to find in your father's secret email account?'

'I doubt it will be the details of a Swiss bank account. But if I'm wrong, I'm sure my sister will agree to pay you a handsome bonus.'

'Very kind, but let's not get carried away,' he replied, studying the painting. It was just as it had been in the photograph, except now he could also see the frame and the small bronze plaque at the bottom bearing the words: *La femme du marin.*

'Do you know which port it is?'

'No idea. He never suggested it was a real place.'

'Where was the painting kept?'

'In his study.'

'Please describe his study in as much detail as possible.'

Marjolaine Le Guellec frowned and Oscar wondered whether she found his line of questioning annoying, but he soon realised it was a frown of concentration. This was a woman who'd grown up with a father obsessed with mystery and puzzles, and she was used to interaction of this nature. Looking at her—the expression of concentration on her face—Oscar could tell she had loved every moment of it and that solving this last conundrum was like having one final kiss on the forehead from a loving father who had left her. This was his final goodbye, and his final challenge. Once solved, she would be devastated, but she'd be able to mourn him. Left unsolved, she would never find peace.

'Your sister couldn't come?' Oscar asked just as she was about to speak.

'No,' she answered warmly, understanding the impetus behind the question.

'I should have invited her.'

'It's not that. She wouldn't have accepted. I've always solved the riddles for her. It will shake her to the core if I don't solve this one.' She paused. 'I've already failed, I suppose, since I'm relying on you to do that for me.'

Oscar leaned towards her and the ends of his moustache curled as he offered a comforting smile. 'I'm not going to give you the answer—assuming I'm capable of working it out at all. You will be the one who utters the password.'

'Thank you,' she said in a way that made Oscar struggle to fight back tears.

'His study,' he prompted her.

She took a breath and released it. 'It's in Piriac. Our family home overlooked the old port. His study was on the second floor with one window providing a sea view. His desk was placed in front of that window and the only door giving access to the room was at his back. Against the wall to his right were bookshelves and against the wall

13

to his left was a drinks cabinet with this painting hanging on the wall above it.'

'Very good,' Oscar said. 'What kind of books did he have?'

She sighed. 'We're going through them now, my sister and I. Mother passed away years ago. Our relationship with her wasn't the best. She divorced father when we were fresh out of high school. We never really understood why. Anyway, that's a different matter.'

'Perhaps not,' Oscar answered. 'Did your father ever—how to put this, have an intimate relationship after the divorce?'

'We think so, but he never shared that with us. He was in love with a woman before he married our mother. We know that.'

'A woman from Piriac?'

She shook her head. 'She lived in Morbihan.'

'Which town?'

'I don't know. In the gulf. Somewhere near Locmariaquer, I think.'

'A small fishing village?'

'I think so.' Marjolaine raised her eyebrows. 'You're not suggesting—?'

Oscar shrugged, but his cheeky grin said it all. He stroked his moustache pensively.

'Let's not get ahead of ourselves. The books?'

'They were mostly books about history, mysteries, and sailing. He ran the sailing school in Piriac for many years.'

'I would have loved to meet him.'

She covered her mouth and closed her eyes.

'I'm sorry.'

'No,' she said. 'He was our rock. He was an exceptional man. It's entirely possible he would have treated you like the son he never had.'

She didn't fail to notice the dark cloud that crossed Oscar's face. 'Oh, I shouldn't have said that.'

'Not at all,' Oscar reassured her. 'Let me just say that whenever you're feeling down, be grateful for the wonderful years you had with your father.'

She smiled.

'Which passwords have you tried?'

'All of the obvious ones,' she replied. 'Boat, woman, port, catch, and so forth.'

'The title?'

'*La femme du marin*? Of course. That was the first one I tried.'

Oscar nodded.

'You don't have a clue, do you?' she asked. 'You're as lost as I am.'

He raised his eyebrows. 'That's what you think?'

'You're going to have to pick your sons up from school soon.'

'Not until you've gained access to your father's email account.'

She placed the painting beside her on the sofa leaned forward as though getting ready to stand up.

'This painting,' Oscar pressed on. 'Tell me—is it, in your opinion, your father's?'

'Did he paint it? Is that what you mean?'

'It is,' Oscar said.

'Why do you think so?'

'There's no rational explanation,' Oscar admitted. 'It's a gut feeling.'

She looked surprised.

'My interpretation of this painting has changed in the light of what you've told me about your father.'

'The other woman?' Marjolaine practically whispered, barely daring to ask the question.

'The woman,' Oscar said.

'You think she was the wife of a sailor?'

'I'm quite sure your father wanted her to be the wife of a sailor. The fact that this painting is his handiwork doesn't necessarily mean the scene ever really happened, does it?'

'Symbolism?'

'Indeed,' Oscar replied. 'That's one way of putting it. A yearning desire is another—or a passionate love.'

'In that case, the password should have been the title of the painting—or the woman's name!'

'Do you know her name?'

'No, and my father knew I didn't. It can't be the password.' She held Oscar's gaze. 'You've solved the puzzle, haven't you?'

'I don't know yet, but I have an idea.'

'What else can I tell you? What more do you need to know?'

'Your father loved this woman but had to keep it from you. He did that because he didn't want to hurt you. He didn't want his little girls to know that their mother wasn't the love of his life. He loved you more than anyone else.'

She began to cry, but Oscar didn't apologise. This was part of the puzzle.

'Would you like a tissue?'

'No, no, I'm fine. Thank you.'

'I'm sure she suspected it—my mother.'

'There's no question.'

She wiped her tears away and drew a breath.

'It was a passion he had to hide from you, but his other passions were shared freely and fervently.'

She nodded.

'He loved the sea. He loved puzzles. He loved history.'

'That's right.'

'What kind of history?'

'Local history. The history of Brittany.'

'That's what I thought,' Oscar said.

'You're pushing me along but I'm not biting, am I?'

'No, you are not,' Oscar answered, shaking his head slowly, but his expression was all encouragement.

'Do you make everyone feel like they're stupid?'

'Not intentionally, *madame*. I promise you.'

She groaned. 'Your wife must find you intolerable!'

That made him grin. 'Guilty as charged.'

'You do remind me so terribly much of him.'

'I shall take that as a great compliment.'

'He loved our history,' she went on. 'He was a proud Breton.'

'And rightfully so! Do go on.'

She creased her brow and picked the painting up again. She stared at it.

'He had dozens of books on the history of Brittany, and on the topic of folk legends. He had books of Breton poetry as well. He dabbled in the language. There was a Breton dictionary on his bookshelf.'

'*Dispar*!'

Marjolaine laughed. 'Yes, he used that word sometimes. *Without equal—or peer*. That's the literal translation. You speak Breton?'

'I dabble,' Oscar said with a grin. 'I know more Breton than your average Australian.'

'I don't doubt—' She cut herself short and sat staring at him wide-eyed.

He shot her a wink.

'Give me a minute.'

'Take your time,' he whispered.

He waited patiently, but she ended up shaking her head.

'I don't suppose you have a Breton dictionary?'

'*Evel-just*,' Oscar replied.

'You really think this is it?'

'Don't you?'

She closed her eyes and thought about her father, and she nodded. 'Let's do it!'

Oscar jogged upstairs, grabbed his French-Breton dictionary from his office bookshelf, and hurried back down to his client.

She flicked through the pages for a while—back and forth—and frowned every now and then. After several minutes, she took her smart phone and started entering her translation of *La femme du marin*. Oscar watched her intently and felt a shiver of excitement as her frown turned into a smile and a squeal of excitement escaped her.

'You did it!'

She shot him an admonishing glare. 'You did it!'

'None of that now. I merely gave you a little push in the right direction. *Gwreg ar martolod*?'

'*Ya, gwir eo. Gwreg ar martolod* with no spaces.'

'There we go,' Oscar said. 'Case closed and with plenty of time before I pick the boys up from school.'

'Don't you want to know what's in the email account?'

'That's private, isn't it? I wouldn't dare ask.'

'It might be millions in Swiss francs!'

'I doubt it,' Oscar told her as she began reading the sole email her father had sent to the address from his regular account.

She pursed her lips to stop herself from crying.

'My guess is that it's a letter congratulating you on solving this final mystery and expressing his sorrow for what happened between him and your mother. It also gives you the name of the port in the painting and the name of the woman. He assures you that she's a wonderful human being and wants you and your sister to pay her a visit.'

'You are *intolerable*, Oscar Tremont!'

'Thank you.'

She took a chequebook and pen from her handbag. 'Intolerable or not, you will have your fee with a bonus,' she told him.

'That's very kind of you. I wish you all the best, Madame Le Guellec, and I'd very much like to know how the meeting goes. Please drop by again.'

'I will, and I'll bring my sister with me next time.'

That night, when Louise got home from work, Oscar told her about the case.

'It really hit home for you, didn't it?'

'What do you mean?'

'I can tell how much it has affected you,' she said.

'You're talking about my father?'

'Yes, Oscar. Of course.'

He remained silent for a while.

'You're right, Louise, but that's not exactly the relationship on my mind. I was thinking about marriage.'

'What are you saying, Oscar?'

'Could it happen to us? Has it happened?'

'No, Oscar. You're the one. There's no other man in my heart!'

'You're sure?'

'Of course! How can you even ask me that?'

'It just got me thinking. That's all. How can I really know for sure that I'm the man of your life?'

'You're serious? Really? What can I do to prove it to you?'

Oscar rubbed his face with both hands and sighed heavily, but when he took his hands away, he was grinning. 'Well, I guess you could pour me a whisky.'

Louise raised a hand as if to slap him. 'Oscar Tremont, you are *intolerable*!'

Death Goes Gourmet
Edward Lodi

When Chuck Pierce visited Lena Lombardi, he brought with him a bottle of chilled pinot gris and a heavy heart.

'Make yourself comfortable in the library while I fetch glasses and a corkscrew,' Lena said when she greeted him at the door. 'Don't trip over Marmalade,' she shouted as she headed for the kitchen. The orange tabby lay like a lump of melted cheddar on a scatter rug before the fireplace. Chuck stroked the cat, his fur hot to the touch, and gazed into the fire.

Lena returned balancing a tray with the bottle and two glasses. 'To old times,' she toasted when they were settled in armchairs.

'To old times,' Chuck echoed.

'Now, what's this all about, Chuck?'

'Lena, I got a favor to ask.'

Puzzled, Lena nodded encouragement. She and Chuck had been classmates in high school. But in the half century since graduation they'd seen each other only occasionally, usually at cranberry growers' meetings. Both owned bogs. Lena's lay behind her house. Chuck's was clear across town.

'It's my sister,' Chuck explained. 'Janet. You might not remember her. She's five years younger than us.' He hesitated. 'She's hosting a birthday party for me next week.'

Lena sipped her wine. 'That's nice.'

'Well, Lena, I don't know.' Chuck stared at his glass, untouched on the coffee table. 'You see, Janet and I—well, we haven't spoken in twenty years. All of a sudden she phones me saying she wants a reconciliation. We're both getting older, blah blah blah. It's time we made up. To break the ice she wants to throw a party in honor of my seventieth birthday.'

'What caused the estrangement?'

'We never liked each other, even as kids. Janet felt our folks favored me.' He reached for his glass and drained it.

'Janet never married. She's had boyfriends off and on, but they don't stay long. The last one died suddenly five or six months ago. In the meantime she continued living at the old homestead. Never had a career. Waited on tables, that sort of thing. When Pa died she quit working altogether to take care of Ma. When Ma passed on she inherited the house, which was only fair.'

'So, why the resentment?'

'I got the bog, the whole shebang, except, the way our folks left it, it goes to Janet when I die. Janet felt she should've got half right off the bat, soon as Ma died. Hell, Pa had let the bog go downhill the last few years before he passed on. It was overgrown with weeds. I'm the one built it up almost from scratch, poured money into it, made it profitable. You know the cranberry business, Lena. Most years the money from the sale of the crop don't hardly meet expenses.'

'I know only too well.' She got up and tossed a split chunk of oak onto the fire. 'I don't understand your dilemma, Chuck. Like your sister says, you're both getting older. Maybe her health is failing and she wants to mend things before it's too late.' She replenished their glasses.

'I know my sister. She's mean-spirited.' He avoided Lena's eyes. 'In Salem in 1692 an ancestor of ours was hanged as a witch.'

Lena nodded. 'I get the implication. But how do I fit in?'

'Well, Lena, you got a reputation in town for—for—'

'Snooping?' Lena offered.

'Now Lena, that ain't the word I would've used, but yeah, something like that. Janet says for me to bring a guest, anybody I want. She's invited a handful of others, mostly old classmates of ours.' He stood and rubbed his hands before the fire. 'Lena, I don't trust her. She's up to something.'

'You want me as your guest?'

'You could keep an eye on things, make sure she doesn't do anything underhanded.'

Lena made a church steeple of her hands. 'I think I'd like to meet this sister of yours, Chuck. Of course I'll be your guest.'

The party was to be held on Wednesday. On Monday Lena paid Janet Pierce a visit.

Many of the cranberry bogs in Southeastern Massachusetts were built on swamps and shallow ponds once mined for their iron deposits by the Pilgrims and those who followed them. Much of the iron for the muskets and cannons used in the American Revolution came from these mines. Lena was mindful of this colorful history as she drove through the rural countryside.

A sign depicting a plump quail and the words 'Cozy Covey Farm' marked the entrance to the Pierce homestead, where Chuck's sister grew vegetables and herbs and raised quail for sale to upscale restaurants. A gravel lane led through a field of withered stubble to an asphalt apron next to the farmhouse. When Lena stepped out of her car a large German shepherd, chained beneath an ancient ash, greeted her with bared teeth and an ominous growl.

Calculating the length of chain available to the beast, Lena crossed the apron and mounted granite steps. When she pressed the buzzer a bell chimed within. Seconds later the door swung inward. A woman stood in the doorway. Although she didn't bare her teeth, her face, like the dog's, was not welcoming.

Lena introduced herself.

'Mrs Lombardi,' Jane Pierce stated flatly. The chill in her eyes contradicted the smile on her face. 'You're the classmate Chuck's bringing Wednesday.'

'I'm looking forward to the party,' Lena said, struck by how closely Janet resembled her brother. Both had that lean, flinty look often found in old Yankee families—as if the rock-strewn soil, the hardscrabble struggle for existence over the centuries, had altered their genetic makeup. But where Chuck's features were softened by good humor, his sister's seemed chiseled by bitterness and discontent.

'Chuck told me all about your farm,' Lena enthused. 'I haven't eaten quail in years, since I gave up hunting. Do you have one or two I could purchase for my supper tonight?'

'I'm sorry, Mrs Lombardi, I don't have any at the moment. I sell wholesale to restaurants. I only sell retail if I have any to spare.' Her rictus of a smile broadened. 'I'm saving my extras for the party Wednesday.'

'Oh, you'll be serving quail! How nice. I've never had domesticated quail.'

'Mine aren't exactly domesticated, Mrs Lombardi. I don't clip their wings. I feed them foods similar to those found in nature. The difference is, my quail are fatter, without the gamy taste of quail shot in the wild.'

'And there's no danger of breaking a tooth on shotgun pellets imbedded in the meat.'

'There's that advantage to be sure,' Janet agreed as she began to shut the door in Lena's face.

'Do you mind if I have a quick look around?' Lena asked. 'I'm curious to see how things work.'

Janet Pierce hesitated. 'There's not much to see. They're just quail.' She shrugged. 'But go ahead if you wish. Be careful of Bruno. He doesn't like strangers. Forgive me if I don't accompany you. I have work to do.' With that she closed the door.

'Nice meeting you, too,' Lena muttered.

Wary of Bruno, she edged around to the rear of the house, to be met by a chorus of Bob WHITE! Bob WHITE!

The pens holding the quail consisted of wire fencing about eight feet high, roofed with a fine steel mesh to keep quail in, predators out, and spacious enough to give the birds something akin to free range. Lena estimated twenty birds to a cage, the population of an average covey. She counted a dozen cages. The quail, plumper than their brethren in the wild, seemed content with their lot. One pen stood apart. It held fewer birds, no more than half a dozen. These were even fatter than the others.

Before returning to her car Lena took a quick walk along the perimeter of the field. The tomatoes, peppers, eggplants, squash, herbs, had all been harvested. Only stubble remained. Lena noticed a small patch of parsley that had somehow been neglected. There was far too much work here for one person. In spring and summer Janet Pierce must employ a sizable crew.

When Lena arrived home she made a phone call—one which, ever afterwards, she regretted.

'Chuck? This is Lena. I stopped by your sister's this morning.

She's a charmer all right, along with her German shepherd, Bruno. But don't you think you're being, well, a bit paranoid? What harm can come from a birthday celebration? If she has some sinister motive, I can't see it. Anyhow, see you on Wednesday. Yes, yes. Absolutely no gifts. I'm like you. Got more of everything than I'll ever need. But I will bring a card. Bye now.'

The party was slated for one o'clock. Lena arrived fifteen minutes early, but was not the first. An SUV took pride of place on the asphalt apron. A heavyset man in his mid sixties stood at the foot of the granite steps. He waved as she stepped out of her car.

'Hi, I'm Bill Jenks. Janet's closest neighbor. I'm the official greeter.'

'Lena Lombardi. Glad to meet you, Bill.'

He chuckled, then said in a low voice: 'Don't make the mistake of thinking I'm Janet's boyfriend.' He shuddered. 'The only time I see Janet is when she needs a favor. And that suits me fine. She tells me you and the other guests know one another. Classmates of Chuck.'

'Where's Bruno?'

'In his doghouse out back. Pain in the butt, that dog.'

Though a stiff breeze blew in across the field, Lena preferred standing outside to entering the house and making nice with Janet. Chuck arrived next. He nodded to Lena, shook hands with Bill, and sharing Lena's sentiments regarding his sister, stood silent, forlorn.

Rose Pinto arrived, followed by Hilda Jarorski. Several years had passed since Lena last saw either woman. Dark-skinned, with perfectly blended features inherited from African and Portuguese ancestors, Rose had been the class beauty. At seventy she still could cause a male gaze to linger. Hilda, blonde and petite, was noticeable for the length of her proboscis. Age had sharpened it to a beak. And yet, men found her attractive. The last Lena heard, Hilda was working on her fourth husband. Unlike Lena, both women had reverted to their maiden names.

After they embraced, and congratulated Chuck on joining the septuagenarian club, Lena introduced them to Bill.

'What's this party all about, anyhow?' Rose asked. 'Not an attempt at matchmaking, I hope. Chuck, your wife's been gone, what, two years now? Lena, you and I have been widows a long time. Hilda, you still married?'

23

'Actually, yes. I finally found one I can stick to. I accepted the invitation because my current spouse is visiting his sister in Florida. I came out of curiosity.'

'I guess we all did,' Rose commented. 'No disrespect intended, Chuck,' she quickly added.

'I'm as puzzled as you,' he assured her.

'I was drafted,' Bill said, 'so that Chuck wouldn't be the only male present.'

Hilda stared at the house, then turned to Chuck. 'You two have been feuding for years. I find it hard to believe you're actually burying the hatchet.'

'I'm not sure we are,' Chuck replied as he led the way inside.

They found Janet in the kitchen. A bandage bound her right wrist. 'Bruno's so rambunctious. I tripped on his chain this morning and sprained my hand,' she explained. 'I've managed so far, but I'll need help serving.'

She and Chuck finally made eye contact. 'Nice of you to invite me, Sis.'

'It's time, Chuck. It's time.' There was an awkward silence.

Chuck cleared his throat and thanked everyone for coming, then opened his cards, after which Janet led them into the dining room. At her request, Lena uncorked and poured the wine, an estate vintage she recognized as being quite pricey. Hilda ladled quail-and-vegetable soup into each guest's bowl. Everyone commented on how delicious it was. So far, Lena was impressed. Janet seemed to have gone out of her way to heal the rift between her and her brother.

Janet apologized for not offering a salad. 'Chuck never cared for greens. Rabbit food, he called it. Rose, and you, too, Bill, be so kind as to help me with the *pièce de résistance*.'

Rose and Bill obediently followed her into the kitchen and returned, each with a huge platter of roasted quail.

'I've saved two fat ones for Chuck, since he's the birthday boy,' Janet said, sliding two plump hens onto his plate. 'Everyone else, help yourselves.'

The carrots, Brussels sprouts, and baked potatoes, carried in by Bill on platters, were served family style. 'No need for the old boarding-house reach,' Bill joked. 'I'll hold the platters while you dig in. I always thought I would've made a great butler.'

In the course of the meal Lena uncorked two additional bottles of wine, a goodly portion of which she consumed. In lieu of cake Janet served apple pie *à la mode*. Hilda cut the pie and served it, while Rose scooped a generous dollop of vanilla ice cream onto each slice.

That concluded the celebration. Everyone once again wished Chuck a happy birthday, thanked their hostess, and left. Lena made a point of leaving with Chuck, who before, during, and after the meal had exchanged at most a dozen words with his sister.

It had been a strange afternoon.

Even stranger events were to follow.

When Lena arrived home she gave Marmalade the attention he demanded, then took a stroll around her cranberry bog. When she returned to the house the phone was ringing. The voice at the end of the line was faint, the words barely distinguishable. 'She poisoned me.'

'Who is—Chuck? What are you saying? She poisoned you?'

'Lena, I'm sick. I'm weak. I can hardly move. Janet—she poisoned me.'

'Poisoned? But—Chuck, have you called an ambulance?'

'On their way. Tell them—tell them she poisoned me.' She heard the clatter of his receiver striking the floor.

Lena arrived at the emergency room just as Chuck was being wheeled in. When the attending doctors learned she wasn't kin they asked her to leave.

'But he's been poisoned!'

A sympathetic nurse led her to an interview room. 'They think it's cardiac arrest,' she informed Lena, then asked: 'What makes you think Mr Pierce has been poisoned?'

'He phoned me, after dialing 9-1-1. It's a long story. He thinks his sister did it.'

'If you could tell us what kind of poison—'

Lena spent the next three hours in the waiting room. When, finally, the nurse approached her, her heart sank. The expression on the woman's face read Death.

Lena's attempt to elicit information proved futile. Though

apologetic, the nurse refused to discuss details. Frustrated, Lena left the hospital and drove directly to the police station. The sergeant on duty groaned when he saw her, and muttered something under his breath.

'I must speak to Lieutenant Lopes,' Lena said.

Sergeant O'Hara, a beefy veteran approaching retirement age, chose the path of least resistance. 'Just knock on her door, Mrs Lombardi. I'm sure she'll be delighted to see you.'

Seated at her desk, Lieutenant Maria Lopes looked up when Lena entered. 'Mrs Lombardi, I've been expecting you.' Seeing Lena's puzzled expression, she explained. 'The hospital phoned and informed me of Charles Pierce's death.'

'Did they tell you Chuck was poisoned?'

'They told me you believe he was. Suppose you start at the beginning.'

Lena related the events of the past few days. When she concluded she said, 'I blame myself for Chuck's murder. I should've taken his misgivings seriously and discouraged him from attending that party.'

Lieutenant Lopes got up from her desk. A short, swarthy, muscular woman in her early thirties, she wore her hair short and could easily pass for a boot camp drill instructor. 'Mrs Lombardi, we don't know that it was murder.'

'His sister poisoned him,' Lena insisted.

'You can say that to me with impunity, Mrs Lombardi. But remember, there are laws against slander.'

'You'll do an autopsy?'

'It's a matter of course in this type of death.'

Two days later an unmarked police car drove into Lena's yard. She watched through parted curtains as Lieutenant Lopes and an officer she didn't recognize mounted the steps to her portico.

'So it was murder!' Lena exclaimed as she let them in.

'We haven't said that,' the lieutenant said.

'No, but the fact you're here does,' Lena declared.

'Mrs Lombardi, this is Detective Paul Ioanides. He's new to the force.' Detective Ioanides nodded politely. He was tall, dark, and in

Lena's estimation, quite handsome. 'We'd like to ask you a few questions.'

'Of course. Come into the library. Do you mind if I have a witness?'

'A witness?'

'Marmalade.' Lena pointed to the cat who, as was his wont, lay in front of the fire.

Lena's attempt at levity elicited from Lieutenant Lopes a frown not unlike that which crossed Queen Victoria's face when, told an off-color joke, she famously replied: 'We are not amused.' Detective Ioanides chuckled. Lena immediately took a liking to him. 'Can I offer you folks coffee?'

Ioanides looked inquiringly at his boss. Lieutenant Lopes nodded. 'If it's no bother.'

Lena hastened to the kitchen and made a pot of coffee, which she carried with cream and sugar on a tray into the library. She found Maria Lopes seated in an armchair impatiently drumming her fingers against the coffee table, and Paul Ioanides kneeling on the floor tickling Marmalade's throat. Eyes closed, the orange tabby purred with contentment. Lena poured the coffee. The lieutenant drank hers black. Ioanides, having seated himself, added cream and sugar.

Lieutenant Lopes took several pensive sips of the steaming brew before beginning. 'Yes,' she admitted. 'It's possible that Mr Pierce was murdered. What we can say with certainty is that poison was the cause of death.'

'His sister poisoned him,' Lena insisted.

'It could have been accidental. Or suicide. But that's our concern, not yours, Mrs Lombardi.'

Lena bristled but remained silent. Time—with a little assistance from Lena Lombardi—would reveal the truth.

Ioanides took out his note pad. Lopes asked Lena to once more go over the events of the birthday celebration. When she'd done so, the lieutenant said, 'So, you're saying that everyone ate the same food. No one ate anything different from the others.'

'That's right, Lieutenant.'

'At Miss Pierce's request, you uncorked and poured the wine. What kind of corks were they? Natural cork, or manufactured?'

'Manufactured.'

27

'And you saw no signs of tampering.'

'No. I would have noticed. I've had considerable experience uncorking wine, Lieutenant.'

Ioanides smiled. The lieutenant continued: 'So. Mrs Jarorski served the soup, which she ladled from a tureen. Everyone helped themselves to the potatoes and vegetables from platters that Mr Jenks helped pass around. Mrs Jarorski sliced and served the apple pie, and Mrs Pinto scooped out the ice cream.'

'Yes,' Lena said. 'You've covered everything except the quail.'

'I'll get to that later. So—'

Lena scowled to herself. What an irritating habit, to begin every other statement with 'So.'

'—No salad was served.'

'No salad,' Lena said.

'Miss Pierce claimed to have injured her hand that morning, which is the reason why she asked the guests to help serve.' Lieutenant Lopes said this more to herself than to Lena.

'Providing herself with an alibi,' Lena observed. 'She can't be accused of slipping something into her brother's food while serving him.'

'Except possibly for the quail,' Lopes said.

'She selected the two plumpest hens from the platter and slid them onto his plate. If the quail were doctored—'

'You say the quail were served plain. No stuffing.'

'Yes. There was gravy, which we all helped ourselves to from the gravy boat, which Mrs Pinto passed around.'

'And at no time that afternoon were Mr Pierce and his sister alone together.'

'That's right. Chuck had agreed to the party only reluctantly, and wanted the dinner over with as quickly as possible.'

'Oh,' the lieutenant said, a thought evidently having occurred. 'Was any type of garnish provided? For the soup. Or the potatoes or vegetables. Or the quail. Parsley, for example.'

'No,' Lena replied, smiling. 'So,' she went on, knowing the sarcasm would be lost on the lieutenant. 'I gather the poison was a plant. Foxglove? Nightshade? Monkshood? Rhododendron? Mountain laurel? There are dozens of toxic plants easily found hereabouts.'

'Hemlock,' Ioanides offered.

This earned him a hostile glare from his boss. He could expect a reprimand later. Not wanting him to get in further Dutch with his boss Lena kept quiet.

'I'd appreciate it if you didn't make that information public, Mrs Lombardi,' the lieutenant said.

'I'm the soul of discretion,' Lena assured her.

'So. Let's consider the others present. Do you know of any reason why any of them would want to harm Mr Pierce?'

Lena shook her head. 'Chuck was always well liked in school. I never heard Rose or Hilda say a word against him.' She paused. 'I can't speak for Bill Jenks, who I only met Wednesday. He might be in cahoots with Janet, but I doubt it. He seemed to genuinely dislike her. More coffee, Lieutenant? Detective?'

After the police left, Lena sat for a while, brooding. Chuck had come to her for help and she had failed him. She couldn't bring him back to life, but she could bring his killer to justice. For that she needed information. Information readily found on the Internet. Unfortunately Lena, a technophobe who had only recently acquired a cell phone, did not have access to it.

But she knew someone who did.

Phyllis Baker worked at the Assessor's office in the Town Hall. Lena phoned and asked if she could stop by her apartment after work. 'I'm free all evening,' Phyllis said.

'I come bearing gifts,' Lena announced when Phyllis answered her knock.

Phyllis was eight or nine years younger than Lena and at least one hundred and fifty pounds heavier. 'I still have the bottle of wine you brought last time,' Phyllis reminded her.

'Not wine. An invitation. Dinner at Lorenzo's Sunday afternoon. My treat.'

'And in exchange?'

'Information. I need to know about quails.'

'As in bob white?'

Lena nodded. 'And hemlock.'

'As in tree?'

'As in poison.'

'It's what killed Socrates,' Phyllis said. 'I learned that in college.'

It's what killed Chuck Pierce, Lena wanted to say, but remembered her promise to Lieutenant Lopes.

They spent the next hour and a half researching quails and hemlock on the Internet. At the end of that time Lena had a pretty good idea as to how Janet Pierce had poisoned her brother. Now all she needed was proof.

'Phyllis, do you still have any of those sleeping pills you were taking when you suffered that bout of insomnia? Can I have a couple?'

'Yes to both questions. But are you sure you should take them?'

'Oh, they're not for me. For someone, in fact, I'd like to introduce you to.'

'Male? Nice-looking? Or forget the nice-looking. Male will do.'

'Male. Not your type, though.'

'Let me be the judge of that,' Phyllis said.

'One other thing. Can you get me the phone number for William Jenks?'

'Bill Jenks! That hunk. I've seen him around but never had a chance to actually meet him. Are the sleeping pills for him?'

'No, but maybe I can arrange an introduction.'

When Lena returned home she found Marmalade sulking in the kitchen. 'Feeling neglected? Okay, you can go for a prowl. But if the coyotes get you, don't blame me.' Although she feared for his safety, she couldn't keep the cat cooped up all night. He was, after all, a nocturnal creature.

Bill Jenks? What manner of creature was he? She went to the phone and punched in his number.

'Bill? Lena Lombardi. Do you have a moment?'

He did. He'd fallen asleep in front of the TV and welcomed the interruption.

At home, alone, on a Friday evening. That boded well for Phyllis.

Bill expressed the shock he'd felt when, only that morning, he learned of Chuck's tragic death. 'The police are looking into it,' Lena assured him, then abruptly changed the subject. 'Bill, I'm calling for two reasons. One involves you personally. The second is to seek information. Would you happen to know whether Janet makes deliveries on Saturdays?'

'Yep. She packs the quail in ice and heads out early for Boston or wherever. She doesn't get back until late in the day. She passes right by my house. The only time she stops is if she needs something. The occasional quail she tosses my way hardly makes up for the chores I do around her place. It's not as though she's a warm-hearted woman, if you get my drift.'

'That brings us to my other reason for phoning. I have a good friend who'd very much like to meet you. She works for the Town. Phyllis Baker.'

'The lady who works in the Assessor's office? The one with the ample figure?'

'Yes, that's her.' Ample, and then some. She waited. Now was the moment of truth.

'I'd very much like to meet her. She seems like a nice lady.'

'Yes,' Lena said. 'She is. And warm-hearted.' If you get my drift. 'Do you have pencil and paper? I have her phone number.'

Lena's next call was to Phyllis. 'It's all set with Bill Jenks,' Lena told her. 'I gave him your phone number. Now, I have another favor to ask. Are you free tomorrow morning?'

'The leaves are beginning to fall,' Lena observed as she maneuvered her car around the twists and turns of the winding country road.

'Winter's just a few weeks away,' Phyllis agreed, then added: 'I smell food.'

'I made meatballs last night. They're in a bag on the back seat.'

'For lunch?'

Lena shook her head. 'Breakfast.'

'But we just ate breakfast.'

'They're not for us,' Lena said.

'For who then?'

'Someone I met the other day. A German fellow.'

'You're being very mysterious, Lena,' Phyllis complained. 'You get me out of bed at an ungodly hour, then won't tell me where we're headed, or why.'

'We're going to bring a murderer to justice. I could do it by myself but I enjoy your company. Besides, don't you want to know

31

where Bill Jenks lives?'

'I know where he lives,' Phyllis announced triumphantly, 'He phoned last night. We have a date for later today.'

Both women were in a good mood when Lena turned onto the gravel track that led to Cozy Covey Farm. Phyllis's mood took a turn for the worse when she realized where they were. 'Lena! What kind of harebrained scheme are you hatching?'

'Quail-brained would be more apropos,' Lena said. She got out of the car, checked to make sure Janet was not at home, then opened the rear door on the driver's side. She removed the brown bag and held it up for Phyllis to see. 'It's time to deliver breakfast. Let me introduce you to Bruno.'

Phyllis followed her around to the rear of the house. 'I feel flattered,' Phyllis quipped as the quail became vocal. 'All these males whistling.'

Suddenly Bruno lunged at her.

'A German shepherd!' Phyllis shrieked as, fangs bared, the dog strained at his chain to take a chunk of her leg.

Lena eyed the chain warily. 'Shall you feed him, or shall I?' She held the brown bag just out of reach of the dog's jaws.

'Lena, I don't think a few meatballs are going to pacify this monster,' Phyllis said as she shrank into herself.

'These will.'

'Lena—the sleeping pills. You wouldn't—'

'Here, Bruno. Nice dog.' Lena tossed the German shepherd half a dozen meatballs. He sniffed, gobbled, and slavered for more. When none were forthcoming he licked his chops and resumed growling. Gradually the growls softened until, tongue lolling, he lay on his side snoring.

'Now that Bruno has gone beddy-bye, we can get to work.'

'I'm not getting involved in anything illegal,' Phyllis declared.

'Nothing of the sort,' Lena assured her. 'Would you like a tour of the farm?'

They strolled among the pens. Except for the smallest enclosure, where half a dozen fat hens remained, there were fewer birds in each covey than when Lena viewed them on Wednesday—culled, presumably, for market.

'Very nice, Lena,' Phyllis said as they headed back to the car.

32

'But what's our real reason for being here?'

'To gather a posy.'

'Flowers? This time of year?'

'It won't take a minute,' Lena said.

'I'll wait in the car,' Phyllis declared. 'This wind has a bite to it.'

Lena hastened onto the field, returning minutes later with the paper bag now bulging. She showed its contents to Phyllis. 'How's that for a nosegay?'

'Dead weeds?'

'Deadly weeds,' Lena corrected her.

After dropping Phyllis off, Lena drove to the police station.

Sergeant O'Hara, who had the misfortune to be on desk duty again, mumbled an imprecation when he saw Lena. 'If it's Lieutenant Lopes you're after, she isn't here, Mrs Lombardi.'

'What about Detective Ioanides?'

'You'll find him in the lieutenant's office. Why don't you go right in, Mrs Lombardi? I'm sure Detective Ioanides will be delighted to see you. What is it you have in the bag? If it's donuts, I'll take one.'

Ioanides was in fact delighted to see Lena. He'd taken a liking to the old lady and her cat. 'Have you solved the case yet?' he joked after asking her to sit.

'As a matter of fact, I have,' Lena said, smiling. 'Thanks to you. If you hadn't mentioned hemlock, who knows how long it would've taken me.'

'My boss was none too pleased.'

'She'll get over it once you give her the facts.'

'And what are the facts, Mrs Lombardi?'

'Janet Pierce deliberately poisoned her brother. I never doubted that. She had motive, opportunity, and means. Her motives were twofold: a life-long enmity toward her sibling. And his cranberry bog, which legally became hers upon his demise.'

'You talk like a lawyer,' Ioanides said, smiling.

'I read a lot,' Lena said. 'As for opportunity and means, Janet invited her brother to a party in his honor, where she served him poisoned quail.'

'Interesting theory,' Ioanides said.

'More than theory, Detective.'

'But—'

'Let me explain,' she interrupted. 'We all ate the same foods, served by the guests ourselves from common bowls and platters. The exception: the two hens Janet slid from the platter onto Chuck's plate. Hence, the quail were poisoned.'

'The police have thought of that, Mrs Lombardi. But how were they poisoned? Hemlock leaves contain coniine. You can make a salad with them and kill someone. I suppose you could garnish the quail with it, although I don't know how that would taste. But according to everyone's testimony, there was no garnish. Are you suggesting that Miss Pierce boiled the leaves to make a broth, then injected the two birds she served her brother?'

'Not at all, Detective. She was more devious than that. I've done some research. Quail are known to sometimes eat hemlock berries. It doesn't harm them. They're immune. But eating even one of those birds can be fatal to a human. Chuck ate two. His sister saw to that.'

'But even if you're right, where's the proof?'

'Here.' Lena lifted the paper bag from where it had been resting between her feet. 'Hemlock, otherwise known as poison parsley. I gathered this from the field where she grows herbs and vegetables.'

Ioanides peered into the bag. 'Even if this is hemlock, we can't use it as evidence. It was obtained without a warrant. And even a second-rate lawyer would argue that the stuff grows wild and is just a weed.'

'The patch has all the appearance of being cultivated. As for these plants, I obtained them legally. Janet gave me permission to walk around her property. She never said I couldn't pick a few interesting weeds for a dry arrangement for my mantelpiece.'

Ioanides was still dubious.

'Another thing,' Lena said. 'Janet has one enclosure set apart, smaller than the others. The hens in that pen are fatter than their sisters. I wonder what those little dears have been eating? If my supposition is correct, and those hens are toxic, why—if they were just spares—hasn't she destroyed them? Does she plan to feed them to someone else in the future?' She paused for breath. 'Incidentally, you might want to look into the sudden death a few months back of

Janet's boyfriend. And see if anyone else associated with her has died unexpectedly in the recent past.'

Ioanides stared at her, open-mouthed. Finally he said, 'Maybe I should get a cat. Or is it the water you drink?'

'Not water, Detective. Wine.'

'Whatever it is, it seems to work. I just might be able to convince the lieutenant that what you say makes sense.'

'When you search her place, look for Janet's stash. I'm sure she keeps her hemlock seeds close by.'

As Lena was leaving the station, the lieutenant was coming in. 'It's all wrapped up, Lieutenant,' Lena said. 'I left a bag in your office. Feel free to use it.'

It wasn't until Lena was at home sitting by the fire, with Marmalade on her lap, that the thought occurred to her that her parting words to Lieutenant Lopes might easily be misconstrued. Hopefully the lieutenant understood that the contents of the bag should be used as evidence, not garnish for a baked potato.

Webster's Wallet
Robert Petyo

The body, curled around the trunk of the oak tree at the bottom of the slope behind Steeples Inn, had its arms and legs stretched out to form the letter U. The tree marked the beginning of a short hiking trail that circled the base of the hill along the woods, went through a weeded field where all attempts to start a flower garden had failed, and came up to Main Street and the wooden porch in front of the inn. Residents of the inn and of Mary's Hollow occasionally hiked along the path, though today, due to the morning drizzle, it was unused.

Until now.

As soon as the rain ended, Abigail Trainer, wearing hip-hugging sweat pants and an unzipped vinyl jacket with Philadelphia Fashion's ornate logo on it, went out for a quick power walk to counteract the calories she had piled on at dinner at Pascal's last night.

Instead of exercising, she stared down at the body for several seconds, as if expecting it to move. As she inched closer, she saw the gash on his temple and the side of his face covered with blood that seeped down over his coat. She climbed up the short path to the back entrance, pumping her arms for as much exercise as she could salvage. Once inside, she approached the high counter.

'Tillie, I want to cancel my room for tonight,' she said. 'I'm heading back a day early.'

'Oh, dear. Why is that?'

She told her.

Tillie Kepler hated when police came to the inn. Even when Carl stopped by for his morning coffee in the restaurant before he made

36

his rounds, the guests stiffened up like corpses. Legal authorities were not good for business.

This time Carl skipped the restaurant and met Tillie down at the head of the hiking trail. The morning skies had cleared and brightened, but still he used a flashlight to inspect the corpse from a distance. 'State Medical Examiner is on the way,' he said. 'And Burt should be here any minute.'

Burt Colosso was the State Trooper assigned to the area between Mary's Hollow and Philadelphia. 'What about the Sheriff?' Tillie asked. Other than Sandy Goodfellow who answered phones at the police station, Izzie Brane was the only other member of the local force.

'I called her, but she's out of town. Won't get back for a few hours. I told her not to worry. I could handle it.'

Tillie looked away so he wouldn't see her grin. Carl, who didn't like working for a woman, could barely handle a parking ticket, let alone a dead body. But Izzie wasn't much better. Sheriff was an elected position and Izzie won because she was popular, not because she was qualified.

Carl pointed toward the body. 'Do you recognize the man?'

'Nope.' She hadn't really taken a close look. She didn't particularly like being around corpses. Even at her Aunt Millie's funeral, she had kept her distance.

'He's not staying at the inn?'

'Nope.' The corpse had grey pants that clashed with the dark blue suit coat that was dappled with blood. And white socks! What a disastrous dresser. 'Can I go back inside?'

'Wait until Burt gets here. He'll want to talk to you.'

She backed a step and let Carl prowl about, circling the tree and waving his flashlight like a wand. Once, he pulled out his phone and took a picture like an excited tourist.

The sound of a siren in the small parking lot up the hill made her twirl around. Great. Did he have to use a siren? As she looked up, she noticed people hovering at the back of the inn near the wooden fence at the top of the slope. Great. They're probably taking pictures with their phones. She'll be on the news tonight.

A small man, whose eyes were hidden under the brim of his brown hat, came from the lot, pausing near the top of the path to examine some trampled grass and mud. As he started down, Tillie pointed to the rock about ten feet down the slope. About the size of a basketball, it had a sharp point that was darkened with a few drops of blood. He saluted her with his finger to the brim of his cap as he avoided the rock and continued down to Carl who snapped to attention. 'Good afternoon, Carl,' the small man said. 'What do we have here?'

He told him.

After a few moments, Tillie made a puttering noise to get their attention. 'May I return to my duties?' It was almost eleven o'clock and she had no duties. No more check-ins today and no one would be leaving until this afternoon, so she had nothing to do for a few hours other than relax behind the counter in the lobby and page through one of her fashion magazines. That would be more fun than standing out here.

Burt said, 'Wait five more minutes.'

Tillie folded her long arms across her chest and looked everywhere but at the body. It was at least ten minutes before Burt finally approached her. Another vehicle arrived, though fortunately, no siren this time. It exited the lot and lumbered down the grassy slope on the side of the inn where it wasn't as steep. The car was able to get within ten yards of the body. A woman in a white outfit and carrying a black bag got out and rushed past Tillie and Burt to approach the body. Carl joined her.

'Let's go inside,' Burt said.

'Which is where I wanted to go fifteen minutes ago.'

With a grunt, he adjusted his hat. After they climbed to the inn, he addressed the people who gazed down the slope. 'The show is over, folks. I recommend you get back to your rooms.'

Several young ladies shuffled inside, but Jeremiah, a permanent resident, opened his mouth to protest. Burt nudged up the brim of his cap and hardened his thick eyebrows into a line as he glared at him. He scurried inside.

'This is just the kind of publicity I need,' Tillie whined.

'Oh, don't get in a snit.' He started toward the door. 'Mary's Hollow doesn't get many tourists. In fact, this is the most people I've seen here in months. Maybe the publicity will bring you in a few more. It's good business. You should be excited.' They stepped inside and he hiked up his elbow to lean it on the top of the counter.

'I got plenty of business,' Tillie said, her arms still folded. 'Abby got some of her model friends to stay here.' Abigail was originally from Mary's Hollow and often came back to spend a few days relaxing at Steeples Inn. 'There's some kind of fashion show going on in Philly and they're taking a break for a day. Abby's always helping me out. She brought a few of them here. This is just the kind of peace and quiet they want. Until you showed up.' Because she was taller, she couldn't see his eyes under the broad brim of the hat.

'Think of it as good publicity,' he said. 'Who knows? Maybe you'll even get some reporters to come and stay.'

'Great!'

After a chirping birdlike chuckle that always drove Tillie nuts, he said, 'There was a fight at the top of the hill and the guy fell, or was pushed, down the hill. He hit his head on that rock. That's what did him in.'

'Anybody with half a brain could have figured that out.'

'Thanks for pointing out the rock to me.' He paused. 'I guess you have half a brain, also.' When she unfolded her arms as if to take a fighting stance, he waved a backhand at her. 'Enough. Let's talk business. Do you recognize the body?'

'Like I told Carl, no.'

'He wasn't staying here?'

'Nope.' She shook her head.

'Are you sure he's not staying here? Check your books. His name's Martin Webster.'

'How do you know that?'

'We investigators have our ways,' he said as he tapped the brim of his hat. 'Driver's license in the wallet.'

'Wait. You said Webster?'

'Yes.'

'I was supposed to meet with him this morning.'

'I thought you said you didn't know who he was.'

'I didn't. I mean, I never saw him before. But he had an appointment to meet me this morning. Abby just set it up last night. She met him at the show in Philly and they came here for dinner. She made the appointment, hoping to drum up some business for him. When he didn't show up, I just figured it was because of the short notice.'

'What time was the appointment?'

'Ten.'

He looked at his watch. 'It's eleven o'clock now. That means he arrived here about an hour ago.'

'It was still drizzling then. People stayed inside, had breakfast, and drank coffee.'

'No one would have seen anything in the lot.'

'Nope.'

'What kind of appointment was it?'

'He's a salesman. Trying to get me to sign up for some kind of computer junk.'

He gestured toward the counter. 'You don't use computers.'

'For the customers. Some kind of set-up that lets them use their little computers.'

'You mean wi-fi?'

'Yeah. That's it.' She almost smacked the hat off his head so she could see his eyes. She wanted to see those thick eyebrows that broadcast everything he was thinking, including when he was mocking her.

'You have the name of his company?'

'Sure. Abby gave me his card.' She circled around him and went behind the counter. She stepped up, thankful for the chance to climb onto her chair. Half an hour on her feet was long enough. But unfortunately, now that she was even higher, Burt's face completely disappeared. All she saw was the domed hat. 'Here.' She dug a card out of a pile of papers. 'Webster and Tyler Computer Services.'

He reached up for it, but she yanked it away and grabbed the phone and dialed. A woman answered. 'Can I help you?'

'I'd like to speak to Martin Webster.'

'One moment please.' Tillie expected to be told that he wasn't in the office, but thirty seconds later a man came on the line. 'This is Martin Webster. How can I help you?'

'Um, Martin Webster?'

'Yes. What can I do for you?'

'Do you—did you?'

'Ma'am, what is it that you need?'

'You were supposed to meet me this morning. Tillie Kepler. In

40

Mary's Hollow.'

'Oh.' His voice faded.

'Where were you?'

'I—I'm sorry. Something came up.'

'I'm sure it did. Let me ask you one thing. Do you have your wallet?'

He hung up.

'What was that all about?' Burt asked.

'You better check and see if that corpse has any other identification on him. Because I just spoke to Martin Webster.' She almost grinned when Burt took off his hat to scratch his temple. Finally! She could see those eyebrows, hooked with confusion. 'You have the wallet?'

'Carl bagged it up.'

'Get it.' She dismissed him with a chop of her hand. 'Check on that corpse. He's not Martin Webster. And I wonder how Webster's wallet got there.' Burt ran off. He knew enough to listen to her when she took charge. Because he knew that ninety-nine percent of the time, she was right.

When he returned, he clutched his hat by the brim at his waist and bowed his head like a high school nerd asking a girl to the prom.

'It's not Martin Webster, is it?'

'I didn't really check the picture on the license before.' He held up the wallet and tapped the license. 'He's got glasses and a mustache. Sandy blonde hair.' He closed the wallet, dropping his hat as he did so. 'It's not him.'

'Any other ID on the body?'

'No.'

'And that's definitely Webster's wallet?'

'Yes.' He retrieved his hat and slapped it on his head. 'It's got credit cards and other ID. It's his.'

'Any money in it?'

'Twenty dollars. I told Carl to check if it was reported stolen.'

'Where exactly did you find the wallet?'

'In his pocket.'

'You're sure?'

'Of course, I'm sure.'

'How did it get there?'

41

'Because that's where men carry their wallets, little miss smarty pants.'

She came down from behind the counter and tapped his chest. 'But it's not his wallet, is it? It should be lying on the ground if it fell out of Martin Webster's pocket as they struggled.'

'You think Webster pushed the victim down the hill?'

'That would make sense. We better go see this Martin Webster.'

'We?'

'His office is in Reedsburg.' The city's downtown was about a ten-minute drive on Route 9. 'I just hope he's still there.'

'Now, hold on, Tillie.'

She hustled out the back door of the lobby. 'Hey, Carl.'

He was just lumbering up the slope.

'Did you call Sandy about that wallet?'

'She says some guy named Webster just called to report he lost his wallet.'

Tillie looked at Burt. Right after she spoke to Webster, he called to report his wallet missing.

'He thinks he left it at Pascal's,' Burt continued. Pascal's was the only fancy sit down restaurant in Mary's Hollow. It was on Jackson Street, just off of Main next to the taxi stand and two blocks from the inn. 'The restaurant was closed when he called them. Sandy told him we would check with the owners for him.'

'Did she?'

'Haven't heard from her yet.'

'Let us know when you hear from her,' Burt said, trying to take charge again. 'I'm going into Reedsburg. Please interview the residents staying here. Perhaps somebody saw something this morning.' He shoved the wallet back into his pocket and strutted to the parking lot like he was leading a parade. 'Let's go find Webster.'

'Like I said a few minutes ago,' she said, reminding him who was really in charge.

Webster and Tyler Computer Services was in the basement of a five-story building that had a laundromat on the ground floor. There was a small parking lot between it and another smaller building.

x

42

There were a few cars in the lot, including one in one of two spots that were clearly marked "Webster and Tyler Only" on the pavement, and on the signs behind the spots.

'We'd like to speak to Martin Webster,' Burt said when they reached the cramped office.

The woman hunched behind the cluttered desk stammered. She obviously didn't like being visited by a State Trooper.

Tillie nudged Burt aside, figuring a woman's presence, a civilian woman, might calm her. 'Where is Mr Webster?'

'Uhh.' She still struggled. 'He's not here.'

'Where is he?'

She moved some papers and checked her desk blotter calendar. 'He has a one o'clock appointment.'

'Where?'

'Donny's Donuts. It's in Mary's Hollow.'

'I assume he took the company car?' Tillie asked.

'No. Umm. We don't really have a company car.'

'His own vehicle then?'

'Can I get Mr Tyler to help you? He's the real computer expert.' She stopped and tapped her lips like she had just leaked military secrets. 'I mean, Mr Webster is just a salesman. Mr Tyler is the brains. Mr Webster is just the pretty face.'

'We're not looking for computer services. We're looking for Martin Webster.'

It made sense that Webster would make it all in one trip, meeting Tillie in the morning and Donny Flapp, whose shop was just behind Main Street within walking distance of Steeples Inn, that afternoon. But Webster had missed the first appointment. Tillie believed he fled because he killed the man in the parking lot. He returned to his Reedsburg office before leaving again after Tillie's phone call. She doubted he had gone to Donny's Donuts. But they had to be sure.

Burt used his car radio to call Sandy. She had contacted the owner of Pascal's and he was on his way to his restaurant to check for a missing wallet. 'Also, I asked him if he could confirm that Martin Webster was there last night. You know. A credit card record or something.'

'Did he?'

'He didn't know the man so he couldn't tell if he was there, but he'll check for a credit card payment under the name Webster.'

Tillie knew Webster had been there. He had dinner with Abby. But she didn't want to interrupt.

'Thanks, Sandy. How about Carl? Has he reported anything about the identity of the body?'

'No, sir. The medical team has taken the body to the coroner in Reedsburg. They'll report to us if they get an ID.'

'Fine.' Burt gave Tillie a raised eyebrow and she waved a backhand at him indicating she had no questions or instructions. 'We'll check in later, Sandy.'

It was almost 12:30 when Burt parked on the street in front of Donny's Donuts, a narrow wooden building with a gabled roof. Three customers were in the store, which for Donny's constituted the lunchtime rush.

Burt waved for the gray-haired man in a bright white apron to move to the end of the glass counter that displayed a few dozen doughnuts. 'Belle can handle it for a few minutes,' he said with a wink at the young girl who chatted with a customer who peered through the glass at some chocolate doughnuts.

Tillie asked, 'Do you have an appointment to meet with a computer salesman this afternoon?' She thought it strange that Donny would make an appointment during the lunchtime rush.

'Yeah. A guy by the name of Webster. He called and cancelled though.'

'Oh.' At least Donny got a polite cancellation call. In Tillie's case, he cancelled by leaving a dead body outside her inn.

'He said something came up.'

'Did he say what that something was?'

'I didn't ask. I was happy he cancelled. Rush hour, you know. And what do I need with computers anyway?' He pointed at the oven behind him. 'They don't make doughnuts.'

'Why did you make the appointment for your rush?'

'I didn't. Abby Trainer set the whole thing up last night.'

Abby set up both appointments, Tillie thought. Of course, they would be close together.

'She was kinda high pressure about it,' he said. 'She said he was going to be in town to see you and he could help me out, too.'

Burt pressed against the counter. 'What time did he call you to cancel?'

'I don't know. Half hour ago. Maybe forty-five minutes.'

Burt looked at Tillie. That would be right around the time she staggered him with the phone call mentioning the missing wallet. Burt moved away from the counter and Tillie followed him outside. 'What now?' he asked.

'We check his house.'

'I don't know where he lives.'

As she stood next to his car, she plopped her hands on her hips and struggled to keep the sarcasm out of her voice. 'You have his driver's license, don't you?'

Tillie was surprised to learn that Martin Webster lived in Mary's Hollow. She was familiar with most residents in the town and she couldn't recall the name Webster. Besides, a computer salesman pushing the internet and all that other high-tech garbage should live in the big city, not a quiet computerless village.

14 Dumper Street was a small Cape Cod house with a sagging porch with flaking paint that misted the air when Burt stepped up to the front door and opened the screen door. Tillie stayed back, feeling safer on the scarred sidewalk.

A frumpy woman answered the door and gasped slightly at the sight of a trooper.

Burt asked for Martin Webster.

'What do you want with him? Is he in some kind of trouble?'

'We'd just like to talk to him, ma'am.'

'About what?'

Burt tugged down on his cap and stiffened his shoulders, trying to make himself taller. 'Is he here?'

'He don't live here.'

'He doesn't?'

'Didn't I just say that?'

He took a deep breath. 'Where does he live?'

'Don't matter. You won't find him there. This time of day he's in work. He's some kind of fancy computer salesman.'

'He's not in work, Mrs Webster.'

'The name's Campbell.'

'Oh.'

That name Tillie recognized. Maryellen Campbell. Her husband ran a farm outside of Fleetwood. Dumped her for a farmhand. Maryellen Campbell moved to Mary's Hollow to try to start a new life, but this wasn't really a good place for starting over. It was a place for quiet people who ambled from day to day.

'He's your son, right, Mrs Campbell?' Tillie called.

She looked past Burt as if just noticing Tillie out on the sidewalk. 'You run the inn, don't you?'

'That's right.'

'Nice place,' she said.

'Why, thank you,' she beamed. 'But tell me. Why is his name Webster if your name is Campbell?'

'He's from my first marriage,' she said. 'I dumped his father when I found out he was cheating on me.'

Remembering the compliment she gave her inn, Tillie stopped herself from pointing out that her second marriage didn't work out too well, either.

'Where does he live, Mrs Campbell?' Burt asked

'He has an apartment in Philly. I don't know where, though. He moved out a year ago.'

He handed her a card. 'Will you have him call me if you hear from him? Tell him we found his wallet.'

She snatched the card. 'His wallet?'

Burt pivoted and hopped off the porch, ignoring the woman's questions. Her attitude had obviously miffed him and he was done with her.

But Tillie remained as Burt strode to his car. 'Do you know if he has a girlfriend?' she asked.

She stood on the porch now, staring at the card. 'Lots of them. Martin considers himself a ladies' man. He likes to play the field.'

46

'Did he ever bring a girl here when he visited?'

'Never. He plays the field. He don't get serious.'

'When's the last time he was here?'

'He stopped for dinner about a month ago.' She stuffed the card into the pocket of her dirty apron.

'He works in Reedsburg, but he lives in Philly. Isn't that what you said?'

'Yeah. Some kind of apartment. I've never been there. I told him it was stupid, you know. Rent's high. He has to take the bus every day to work. He shoulda stayed here.'

'He doesn't have a car?'

'Hah.' She started to close the door. 'That's probably part of why he won't settle down. Just plays the field,' she added with a tired voice.

'Thanks, Mrs Webster. I mean, Campbell.'

When she got to the car, Burt asked, 'What was that all about?'

'Contact the Philadelphia police. Ask them to track down Martin Webster. Contact Reedsburg, too. Tell them to check taxi companies.'

'Taxis?'

'They might be missing a cab. And a driver.'

Burt looked at her and flopped his head back so she could see his quivering brows that sought the truth.

'Webster doesn't have a car,' she said. 'He has to take the bus to work. And there's no company car. He took a cab to my inn. The dead man's a cab driver. He brought him to my inn and they got into some kind of fight over the fare.'

Tillie stayed in the state police car when they got back to the station. Burt went inside to talk to Carl and when he returned to the vehicle, Tillie cut him off before he could say anything. 'Can I use your cell phone?'

Burt ignored that request. 'Sally heard from Hernando Pascal. No sign of Webster's wallet.'

'Of course not. Because he didn't really lose it there.'

'We can't even confirm he was there. No credit card.'

'Oh, he was there.'

'How do you know?'

'Don't you remember? He was there with Abby Trainer. That's when she set up the appointment with me. And called Donny. That's why all these appointments were last-second arrangements.'

'Is she in the computer business now?'

'Abby stays here about once a month. She wants that computer hookup stuff you talked about. Says she uses it to stay in touch with photographers and stuff. I think she just wants to play games.' Tillie clamped her mouth shut and grabbed Burt's hat.

'Hey.'

'Give me your cell phone.' She held the hat against the car door.

Burt didn't dare reach across the seat to go for his hat, so he gave her his cell phone and she returned the hat.

When Abby spent a night or two at the quiet inn, away from the Philadelphia madness, she and Tillie often spent an afternoon chatting about the fashion world. Tillie had her cell phone number in her tiny address book that she dug out of her purse.

'Hi, Tillie. The cops still investigating that murder? Or have you figured it all out?'

'Still investigating,' she said with a glance at Burt who pretended to be focused on the road, even though she knew he was listening to every word. 'Did you have dinner with Martin Webster at Pascal's last night?'

'How did you know that?'

'I figured that's where you got his business card that you gave to me. Did he pay, or did you pay?'

'He did, of course.'

'Use a card?'

'No. Cash.'

'He had his wallet with him then.'

'What? Of course, he did. He was pretending to be a big spender. Trying to impress me.'

'Did he?'

'Well, maybe.'

Tillie said nothing. Sometimes that was the best way to gain more information.

'He's a nice guy,' Abby finally said. 'I thought his trying to show off was kind of cute.'

'How did you get to Pascal's?'

'He picked me up.'

'In a car?'

'No. A cab.'

'A cab? Not one of them fancy goober things?'

She chuckled. 'No. A cab.'

'That's not impressive, is it? Business isn't that good for him, huh? I've been to his office. It's not much. Hidden down in a basement.'

'He's ambitious, though,' she said, coming to his defense. 'That's why I was trying to help him out. I set up the appointments.'

'Yes. Very noble of you to help out.'

'I'm trying to get him some work with Philly Fashion, too. That's where I met him.'

'In Philly? At the show?'

'Yeah.'

'He invited you to dinner?'

A pause. 'I invited him.'

'You like him, don't you?'

'What? Yeah. He's cute. And he tries so hard.'

'He spent the night at your room last night, didn't he?'

'Why would you say that?'

'That's why the appointment was such short notice. You knew he was going to be here this morning for my appointment because he spent the night with you.'

'Oh.'

'It's okay, Abby. I don't care. You snuck him in. Don't worry. I'm not going to charge you for a double. But tell me one thing. He had to go back to his office this morning before the appointment with me, right?'

'He told me he needed some brochures and stuff before he met with you and Donny later.'

'Got to go, Abby. Thanks. Make sure you stop by Steeples Inn the next time you need a break from that crazy fashion world. We're always here for you.' She disconnected and waited for Burt to ask her what that was all about. They had stopped in front of Steeples Inn and she watched him struggling, trying not to look like he was begging her for help.

49

'Forget the cabs in Reedsburg,' she said. 'Webster was at the inn last night,' she said. 'Take me to Jack's Cabs.' It was the only cab company in Mary's Hollow. Since everything here was walking distance, most of their business consisted of running people to the shopping mart in Reedsburg, or to the big city. 'He spent the night here with Abby, but he had to get to his office before he met with me. And how does he get there?'

'A cab.'

'It takes him to his Reedsburg office and brings him back for his morning meeting with me. Then they have their little disagreement.'

Burt started the engine.

'Yeah. About that.' Jack Jacobs, Jr. squirmed behind the spotless desk against the brick wall at the back of the two-car garage. 'I haven't reported anything yet. I was giving him some time to get back. Tommy's had some problems.' He kept squirming like a giant spider was crawling up his back. 'But he's a good kid.'

'He might be a dead kid,' Tillie snapped, tired of his squirming. She tapped Burt. 'Shouldn't we take him to Reedsburg to identify the body.'

'Body?' Jacobs rose.

Burt held out two hands, a calming one toward Jacobs and a stern one toward Tillie. 'Let's take a breath here. You are missing one of your cabs, correct?'

'Yes.'

'One that Tommy Jacobs was driving?'

His closed eyes and bowed head answered that one.

'Missing since this morning?'

'Yes.'

He pointed toward a large book on the corner of the desk. 'Check your records. When did a call come in for that cab?'

He ran his bony finger up the page before tapping it. 'There. Eight-thirty this morning. I was out getting coffee. Someone called for a pickup at your inn.'

'You have a name?'

He bent closer to the book. 'M. Webster.'

Elementials and Gypsies combined to fight off that many at once," shoving the vial back at her he said once again. "Now drink."

Izzy looked down at the vial in her hands. "Are you sure this is going to work?" she asked taking the cork out and raising it to her lips.

"No. Not at all – but we don't have any other choice right now. You're the only one with enough power, and we've been saving it until now, but even you need more. This is more concentrated than what you were given last time. It should give your power the boost you need."

She put her lips to the glass and gulped back the tangy yellow liquid – she felt a slight burn as it went down her throat and into her stomach.

Immediately she could feel tingling sensation spreading through her body, right down to her fingertips – she felt her power growing stronger with each passing second.

The dark grey of the cannon smoke and the waning light of dusk grew gloomier as she raised her palms up to the sky – just as she had when her uncle challenged her. Small sparks flew from her fingertips, sizzling and cracking as they arced in the air.

"Are you sure?" she looked up at Aristide.

He looked at her and simply nodded.

With that, Izzy delved deep down inside of herself to the core of her power, reaching down as far as she knew how to. The now bottomless pit of her power beckoning for her to release it. Pulling the power up as she felt herself climbing out of that place deep within her once again, she lifted her head and looked up into the sky.

Black clouds teeming with lightning rolled in above the Emperor's fleet of ships. Soldiers from both sides stopped fighting and gawked at the madness happening overhead – those who'd seen the execution began running for cover.

Looking around, Izzy saw a bow and quiver laying against the stone bricks and after gently laying the old woman down, she quickly picked it up and slung the quiver over her back.

Holding the bow up, an arrow nocked and at the ready, Izzy stalked along the wall towards the steps leading down to the harbour shooting off flaming arrow after flaming arrow at the Emperor's soldiers that dared stand in her path.

At the bottom of the steps and after a short argument about her safety, a failing line of the Lunacian army eventually let her pass. Although Izzy was going to pass them regardless of what they said. She made her way further down the steps and out onto the rocky outcrop below – to her left was the main path that led to the marina.

"They're still out of range," Aristide's voice came from behind her.

She spun on her heels and ran to hug him. "I'm so sorry," she cried into his shoulder.

"Water under the bridge. We have other things to worry about now – like living through today," he said pushing her back and pulling something out of his pocket.

"What's that?" she asked ducking as another canon ball whistled overhead.

"Don't think, just drink," as he shoved the vial into her hands.

"I'm not going to drink this just because you tell me to. I want to know what it is," she pushed the vial back at him.

Aristide let out a groan. "It's the same thing you were drugged with that enhanced your powers. What you did to Christian is what you need to do to the Emperor's ships..." he paused looking out to sea. "But on a much larger scale. They're too far out for any of our powers to reach the ships. We've only just been holding them back because they've been landing in such small numbers. But they're getting set to release a lot more landing boats and we don't have enough

She gave Burt a reassuring shove. 'Everything's falling into place. Webster called for a cab ride to his office, ten, maybe fifteen minutes away. He had Tommy wait for him while he gathered up his papers and whatever, maybe ten minutes. Then ten minutes again back to the hotel. Say forty-five minutes. The call for a cab came in at eight-thirty. Allow up to ten minutes for Tommy to get to the inn. That means, round trip, Webster would be back before ten o'clock.'

'They have their little confrontation over the bill. Webster knocks Tommy down the hill, but then what?'

'He takes the cab back to Reedsburg. The keys were probably still in it.' She slapped her hand on the desk. 'Your missing cab is probably abandoned somewhere in Reedsburg.'

Jacob's head was flopping back and forth as he listened to them.

'But the wallet,' Burt said. 'How did it get there?'

'Yes. That darn wallet.' She spun to Jacobs, again placing her palms on the front edge of the desk. She choked off her first words as she tried to handle this delicately. 'You said Tommy's often in trouble. What kind of trouble?'

'Smokes pot.'

She waved that away. She had heard worse things about Tommy. 'What about theft?'

'No,' he said too quickly, and she leaned closer, waiting for the truth. He looked past her to Burt. 'Twice he got hit for shoplifting. You probably have a record of it.'

'Do you think he's a pickpocket?'

'What?'

She spun to Burt. 'Martin Webster was trying to come across as a rich big shot to impress Abby. Tommy thought he had big bucks and probably picked his pocket when he helped him into the cab. So, they're standing there just outside my inn and Webster doesn't have any money to pay the fare. Next thing you know, Tommy's at the bottom of the hill.'

'My Tommy's hurt?'

'Dead,' Abby said. When Jacobs gasped, she cursed her own tactlessness. 'We think,' she added, hoping that might ease the pain in his eyes.

It didn't.

'I'm heading back to the inn,' she said. 'You better take him in to

Reedsburg to identify the body.' Without giving Burt a chance to say anything, she left the garage. After about fifty yards, she crossed to the Steeples Inn and stepped up onto the wooden porch. Inside, Leah was sitting in a wooden rocker in front of the desk. She usually cleaned the rooms, but whenever Tillie was away, she stayed in the lobby.

'Izzie is here,' she said with a jab of her finger toward the restaurant. 'Wants to talk to you.'

'Great.' Tillie crossed the lobby and pushed open the glass door.

Izzie stood when she entered. 'I got here just as Carl was finishing up with your tenants. Nothing there. Nobody saw anything. Before he left, he caught me up on what's going on. I've been waiting here for y'all.'

'Goody.'

'Do y'all have anything of interest to report on this unfortunate incident?'

She moved toward one of the three circular tables. Her feud with Izzie went back over thirty years to high school where she was caught cheating on a social studies test. Even then, Izzie was obnoxiously law-abiding. 'Nothing for you to worry about. It looks like me and Burt Colosso have already solved things.'

Her red face reddened even more at the mention of Burt, and she took several deep breaths before saying, 'Yep. I talked to that cree— that trooper, too. Where is he now?'

'On his way to Reedsburg with Joseph Jacobs to identify the body. His nephew Tommy.'

'Tommy?' She flashed a smile as she held out a hand. 'That fella's always in trouble.'

'Not any more. I'll give you what I got on Martin Webster.' She handed her the business card. 'He works in Reedsburg but lives in Philly.'

'Who's this one?'

'The one who murdered Tommy.' Figuring it was time to let Izzie in on the investigation in her own town, she said, 'You better contact the various agencies and ask them to be on the lookout for him.'

'Now, you just hold on.'

Tillie was in no mood for arguments. 'If you hadn't been out of town pretending to be a big shot, you could have solved this yourself.' She settled into a chair and lectured her, telling her all that she and Burt had learned.

After some initial sputtering, Izzie sat and listened, her red skin gradually softening and an occasional smirk crinkling her face. It was at least fifteen minutes before she finished, and when she did, Izzie stood slowly, stretching her back muscles for almost a minute before saying, 'What about Webster's wallet?'

'Tommy's a pickpocket. He figured the guy was loaded, so he lifted his wallet. His plan was to make a stink when Webster couldn't pay for the cab ride before cooling down and offering to settle if Webster paid him double, or got him drugs, or women, or who knows what else. I'm familiar with Tommy's tricks.'

'Me, too.'

She stood. 'Unfortunately, things didn't go the way he planned.'

Izzie stood. 'Sounds like you got some of it right. But not all of it.'

She spun to her. 'What's that supposed to mean?'

But before Izzie could speak, Leah appeared in the doorway and called for Tillie.

'What now?'

'The phone for you. It's Trooper Colosso.'

Tillie hurried to the lobby and climbed into her chair behind the counter. 'Yes, Burt?'

'It's not Tommy Jacobs.'

'What?'

'They showed him the body. It's not Tommy.'

The phone slipped away from Tillie's ear as she turned to see Izzie standing next to her. She took the phone from Tillie and said a few words to Burt before re-cradling it. 'Tommy Jacobs is probably back at his uncle's office right now. He's in a heapa trouble. But he's not dead.'

'What happened?'

'Drunk. And high on weed, I figure. I found him in the woods on the other side of town as I was coming back from the Harrisburg meeting I was at this morning.'

'But I don't understand.'

'When I left my meeting, I checked in with Sandy and got an idea of what was going on here. She also told me that Jacobs was missing a cab. That meant the usual. It's not the first time Tommy went off on another drug and booze bender. I knew his favorite hangout is the old campground in the woods just outside of town.'

'What about the dead man behind my inn?'

'Oh, I'd say you got everything pretty well down pat. A struggle at the top of the hill. Dead man takes a tumble.'

'But it wasn't Tommy Jacobs.'

'Don't think so.'

'Another cab driver?'

'Don't think so.'

'But who?'

'Let's go back in the restaurant and sit a spell.' She reached for her elbow.

Tillie leapt back like she was struck by lightning.

Izzie shook her head slightly. 'I know you think you're a detective, Tillie. And I appreciate you trying to help. Really, I do. You figure some things out. Sometimes. Really, you do. But sometimes you come on too strong. You make things more complicated than they need to be. Know what I mean?' She returned to the restaurant.

Tillie followed her and sat at a table, but Izzie remained standing.

'You forget the most important thing, Tillie. The wallet. How in tarnation did Webster's wallet get in the dead guy's pocket?'

'Forget that, Izzie. Who is the dead guy if it's not Tommy Jacobs?'

'Oh, I think that's pretty simple. Sometimes you make things too complicated. It's Martin Webster's wallet. It was found on Martin Webster's body.'

'What? No. Burt said the picture on the license didn't match.'

Izzie shrugged. 'Told me that, too. But you kinda put it in his head that Martin Webster was still alive so that's what he figured. Hair, moustache, and glasses, he said. Not much to go on, huh? The license could be a couple years old. People dye their hair. People get contacts. People shave off moustaches.'

'But I spoke to Martin Webster when I called his office.'

'Did you?'

'Yes.'

'Or did y'all speak to someone who pretended to be him?'

'But I called his office. Who else would be there?'

54

'The guy who killed him. Zach Tyler.'
'What?'
She stood. 'Let's go find him.'
'Where?'
'Let's start at his office.'

'Mr Tyler is out on a repair.'
'Do you know where?'
'Actually, no. He didn't say.'
'He just got up and left?'
She squinted as she thought. 'Yeah, actually.'
'I called here earlier,' Tillie said. 'I asked to speak to Martin Webster.'
'Mr Webster has been out on appointments all day.'
'But you put him on the phone.'
'What?' She leaned back like someone was pushing her. 'Oh. If people ask for Mr Webster and he's not in the office, I'll just give the call to Mr Tyler. He usually can answer any questions they have.' She leaned forward and whispered, 'He really runs this place.'
Tillie wanted to reach across the desk and strangle the woman. 'But he said he was Mr Webster.'
She reeled back. 'Why would he do that?'
Tillie looked helplessly to Izzie.
Izzie said, 'Can I have Mr Tyler's home address, please?'

'Don't worry, Tillie. You done pretty good.'
'Stop that. I'm not a little school girl you have to comfort. Tell me what the heck is going on.' They were in Izzie's car on the way to Zach Tyler's home in Reedsburg.
'It's when you done told me that Webster spent the night here with Abby that I figured it out. He couldn't meet with you without getting to his office, first. Get himself some brochures and flyers and

55

stuff. After all, this wasn't planned to be a business visit. He was having dinner with a pretty girl. But he had no car since he came by cab last night.'

'That's right. So, he tried to call a cab.'

'But Tommy went off on one of his benders. He figured Jacobs would take the fare, and Jacobs figured Tommy took it. After waiting a while for the no-show cab, Webster was running out of time. He needed stuff from his office, so he called his coworker and told him what stuff he needed to bring from the office. Zach Tyler came here and met Webster. They had an argument. I'm not sure yet what it was about. Probably work-related.'

Tillie held up a finger to stop her. 'The secretary said Tyler really runs the place. Webster is just a salesman.'

'Sounds good. Maybe Tyler resented that. Whatever. Their arguments spilled out into the parking lot and the next thing you know, Webster goes down the slope, his wallet in his own pocket. Tyler panics and runs. He drives back to the office where your phone call hits him. He pretends to be Webster. He calls Pascal's to report a missing wallet, even though there isn't one. Figures he'll make people think Webster's still alive. He calls Donny's Donuts.' She parked on a narrow street in front of a two-story brick house. 'This is it.' She opened her door.

Tillie didn't move. 'Abby found the body. She knows Webster. She had dinner with him. Why didn't she identify him?'

She pointed for her to open her door, but Tillie crossed her arms and pouted.

Izzie got out and leaned her head and shoulders back inside. 'How close did Abby get to the body?'

'I don't know.'

'How close would you get to a dead body at the bottom of a hill? One with blood all over the face?'

With a grunt, she got out of the car. 'Oh, you're so darn smart, aren't you?' She planted her fists on her hips. 'You were always such a big show-off.'

At that moment, the door to the house opened, and a dark man wearing thick glasses and carrying a duffel bag, came out.

'Going somewhere, Mr Tyler?'

He leaned forward, his cheeks tensing as he sought to see who

56

was standing outside his door. With a slight gasp, he leaned back, dropped his bag, and held out his hands palms up.

'I don't think we be needing cuffs, Mr Tyler,' Izzie said. 'Care to talk about it?'

'It was that pretty girl.' He leaned against the door frame.

'Excuse me?'

'Marty always got the pretty girls. Even back in school. When I saw him with that girl at the inn, I just lost it. I was sick and tired of him bossing me around. I had enough.'

A Veiled Truth
Karen Keeley

I

'But I state yet again, *madame*. A racing car which idles too fast, too quickly, its engine, it will explode, *voilà*!' François Genest, private inquiry agent, snapped his fingers. 'The medication your physician has prescribed, I beg of you to desist, to throw the little pills forthwith into the trash.'

He fingered his Van Dyke beard, more salt than pepper given his age, tugging at his goatee. 'You flit about like the frantic honeybee. Nay, it is more like the hummingbird. Your heart is racing. Is that not so?'

The woman before him had indeed been flitting about, muttering to herself while inhaling a bushel of air, extremely troubled. She took no notice of Genest's charming office with its magnificent fireplace, his many bookshelves, the bay window with the chintz curtains, the artwork and furniture, all of it laid out with an eye to detail, designed for his personal comfort and wellbeing.

'Come, sit. Calm yourself. The chair, it is most comfortable. I myself have sat on it. Please, articulate your problem.'

The woman heeded Genest's advice and sat perched on the chair, much like a bird ready to take flight, she herself no larger than a starling with her raven locks and stark blue eyes, worry wrinkling her brow. Judging by the look of her expensive tweed suit cut from a good cloth, she was a woman of financial security and social standing.

'How could you possibly know about my medication?' she asked.

'The racing car, *madame*. The engine. It is about to explode, is it not?'

She tittered, for that was exactly how it sounded—a titter. 'I am in a state, aren't I?'

'*Oui, madame*, I have seen such behavior before. Friends, family. I then make the necessary arrangement to unwind, a popular expression amongst you English. A necessary stroll to the seaside. We breathe in the briny air. We walk briskly upon the sandy shore. We listen to the gulls squawking overhead—the birds, the atmosphere, most refreshing.'

The woman fixed her eyes on Genest's resolute expression.

'I beg of you, dispense with the pills,' he repeated. 'They do nothing but cloud your vision. You wander the hallways of your home, deep in thought, perplexed. One pill brings you slumber, another bounces you back to wakefulness, much like Alice when she tumbles down the rabbit hole. But alas, the pills do nothing more than have you flitting about, an engine idling too fast, about to explode.'

The woman before him, most intrigued with Genest's outburst, exploded with laughter.

'Why! You dear little man. I've not laughed in days. I will tell you why I have come,' and she did, laying out the facts. At the conclusion, she replied, 'Why is it you remind me of someone? If only I could put my finger on it.'

Genest offered a most sincere smile. 'I remind many people of a someone—their aging uncle, a grandfather, a church deacon who perhaps makes his living as a shopkeeper, the intrepid baker with his little pork pies. I am no more than a face in the crowd, *madame*. The reason I am successful at my method of employment seeking answers where none exist.'

'That's it!' she cried. 'Method! Are you—'

He abruptly interrupted her. 'No, *madame*. You confuse me with another. I have heard tell of him, known to have discussed the merits of stamp collecting with George V when not cracking the cases involving political intrigue and foreign affairs. I am but a humble inquiry agent. But alas, there are calamities which befall even those of us choosing Worthing as our home—the missing silverware, the missing pet poodle, the poison pen letters. No matter, I find the solution. To live in London, *mon dieu*, the stress would exacerbate my nerves. They too, would explode.'

59

He then took up pen and paper. 'Tell me again of your troubles and I document the notes.'

She did, word for word, as though it were rehearsed, which in its own telling, left Genest to reconsider, who exactly had the problem? Was she being truthful or manipulating the facts? What misfortune could have put her in such dire straits, flitting about like the bumblebee, nay, the hummingbird, intent on finding the sweet nectar, its frantic wings beating.

II

Three days following that remarkable encounter, he accepted an invitation to tea, his delightful godchild professing to have a dilemma of her own. Genest sat in Tilly's drawing room, the velveteen curtains tied back, the lamps lit, the room bright, the silver tea tray before them on the antiquated coffee table. Tilly stated matter-of-fact, 'I asked you here to listen to my little problem, and there you sit, mumbling.'

Genest reclined on the settee, taking comfort in the many cushions designed to ease his lumbago, unable to hide his embarrassment. 'Ah, my dear Tilly. You have me at a disadvantage. My thoughts, they are elsewhere.'

'And why is that?'

'My feet. They hurt.' He wrinkled his nose, fingered his goatee. 'I, myself make the purchase of the new shoes, and now, much to my disliking, they pinch the toes. They do not pinch during the fitting. They do not pinch during the walking about in the little shop. They do not pinch when I pay the exorbitant fee to purchase the shoes. Oh, no, not then. But now! Now, I anticipate a most delightful stroll through Amelia Park, an opportunity to enjoy the cobblestone pathways, the ducks upon the pond, the pigeons chortling near the fountain, all the while looking forward to my tea, only to find my feet, my aching feet, they are, as you would say, killing me.'

'Oh, Uncle! Forget the feet,' exclaimed Tilly. 'Remove the shoes, make yourself at home. What do I care if you tramp about in your stocking feet? You know how fond I am of you.'

She poured the tea, adding cream and sugar, stirring gently with a delicate teaspoon.

'But I mind, my dear Tilly. I do not tramp about in stocking feet, not in my own home, and certainly not in yours. But I digress, what is your little problem?'

He accepted his tea, a subtle blend of lemons and grapefruit, perfectly suited to his palate.

'My friend, Mildred. She and I both volunteer our time at the Women's Institute. She does the books; I do the filing. We sometimes dine together when our husbands are out of town. A meal, followed by the theatre. And now, she has shared a dilemma. Such a dilemma she knows not what to make of it. Which made me think of you.'

'But of course you would think of me,' stated Genest. 'Private inquiries for those in need. A most reputable profession of which I am most proud.'

'As you should be,' Tilly agreed. 'You are very good at what you do.'

Genest's cheeks flared with colour, happy for the recognition. 'If not for my pinched toes, I would be on my toes—as you would say, *chérie*.' He chuckled. 'Yes, I see you too, are chuckling, my attempt at humour. I am not wholly the stuffy little man you think I am.'

'I've never said you are stuffy, Uncle. But you are wont to go woolgathering.'

Tilly raised her eyebrows, burrowed her gaze into her uncle's grey-flecked eyes, her eyes of a similar colour, catlike, ready to pounce. 'The reason I asked you to tea, the reason I am trying to explain my little problem!'

'But explain, *ma petite*. Who am I to stop you? Only your uncle. Such a loving and affectionate godfather, may your dear papa rest in peace.'

'I've heard it before,' bemoaned Tilly, her voice rising. 'Mama's passing shortly after my birth, influenza claiming Papa's dear life when I was but a child of six. If not for you, I'd have been tossed into the street, headed to some orphanage without a farthing to my name—a vagabond, a miscreant, a ne'er-do-well.'

Genest felt as though she'd smacked him. He leaned forward. 'My child, I will take no cheek from you! Do not make light of such an honour. Your papa did me a great service requesting that I, François

61

Genest, be your godfather, a solemn duty I have taken most seriously. Have I not encouraged you to be your own woman? To study! To travel! But no, you marry so young. *Mon dieu*, so young.'

Tilly pooh-poohed Genest's observation. 'I wasn't that young, Uncle. I was twenty, practically an old maid.'

François Genest laughed. He laughed long and loud and hard. He then wiped the tears from his eyes with a handkerchief he'd pulled from a trouser pocket. The little outburst of jovial glee made him forget his sore feet and Tilly's flippancy.

'Twenty! And you believe you would have been an old maid? My dearest, you are but a babe in arms. You had plenty of time to think of marriage and possibly children of your own. But no, you were in a most unbecoming rush.'

'I was not in a rush. I was in love.' It was a statement Tilly made often to her godfather, not understanding his apparent dislike of her husband James, a man some ten years her senior, educated, well-travelled, well-read, a lover of horses and dogs, dedicated to his profession of law, a practicing barrister in their community of Worthing.

Perhaps it was jealousy?

'There will be no children,' she replied. 'Certainly not while James is establishing his career. He's now expressed an interest in politics, most concerned with what is taking place across Europe.'

'As are we all,' Genest stated, thinking of the dark storm rising, democracy threatened.

Tilly brushed a lock of hair from her eyes. 'As for being a babe in arms, I am such a babe with a problem. If you would be so kind as to allow me to continue. James, as you know, is in Northampton, something to do with litigation tied into a court case he's embroiled in. My days are free, and we will now help my friend, Mildred.'

'*We*, you say?' Genest's tone implied skepticism. 'There is no *we*. Genius is but a solo affair and cannot be rushed.'

Tilly pretended she hadn't heard him. She fussed with her wedding ring, turning it round and round. 'When James returns, we are off to Cheltenham for the Gold Cup race. You know how he adores his thoroughbreds.'

'Ah, yes. James and his spirited adversaries. A man much intrigued by the arduous Steeplechase, a most rigorous course with

62

its many pitfalls, that—and his stables. What is the name?'

'The Velvet Priory,' Tilly told him. 'Personally, I've never heard of a stable called a priory but there's no accounting for some people's tastes.'

'Politics and a religious fervor for the horses,' muttered Genest.

'What's that, Uncle?' Tilly drank the last of her tea, lukewarm, the pot empty.

'It is nothing, my dear. Woolgathering just as you have mentioned.' Genest too, returned his cup to its saucer. 'James is part owner of how many horses?'

'Three—along with two of his colleagues. Magnificent animals. But I didn't ask you to tea to discuss James's involvement with horses. Will you listen?'

'But I *am* listening! Am I not listening? James and his horses, and your friend Mildred, and her little dilemma. And my pinched toes. What to do about that?'

'I told you what to do.' Tilly was certainly losing patience.

'Your friend's problem,' declared Genest. '*Oui*, tell me all.'

'Finally,' Tilly sighed, leaning back, relief settling in her bones. 'Mildred's husband, the vicar—he's being blackmailed.'

III

She then explained in detail her friend's dilemma. Genest, most attentive, listened with both ears. He then jumped to his feet, his lumbago and pinched toes forgotten, tugging on his goatee, busily circling the coffee table. 'But my dearest, I know of this woman. Mildred Cooper. She comes to me but three days ago, one day prior to the purchase of the new shoes.'

'Forget the shoes, Uncle.'

'The shoes I forget, but the woman! She flits about like a hummingbird, very much discombobulated. And her tale, it is most fanciful.'

'It is no such thing,' scolded his goddaughter. 'It's the truth.'

'To have read blackmail letters sent to her husband. But the letters, they do not exist! What is more fanciful than that?'

Tilly huffed. 'The letters existed. Mildred saw them. Kenneth must've destroyed them.'

'But why?'

'It's obvious,' said Tilly. 'He didn't—or *doesn't* want his wife upset.'

'But upset she is. She comes to me; she comes to you. What nonsense is that?'

'Oh, Uncle. It is you getting your feathers ruffled. I need you to look into the matter.'

'There is no matter, my dearest. Without the letters I have nothing to go on. No paper from a reputable stationary shop. No envelope, no stamps. There are no facts, no leads. It is nothing more than a fabricated story to cause her husband worry and distress.'

'Mildred is the one distressed. As am I.' Tilly struggled to contain her apparent frustration. 'You must look into it.'

Genest stopped circling, his pinched toes once again causing discomfort. 'If you insist,' he murmured, reneging on his train of thought. 'I am but your humble servant.'

'You're no such thing, and you know it.' Tilly then smiled; the fight gone out of her. 'You're intrigued. Especially since Mildred and I are good friends, and we work together.'

'You know me too well.' Genest now smiled. 'For you, I will look into the matter.'

'Good,' stated Tilly. 'When do we start?'

Tilly wouldn't take no for an answer, telling her godfather, the Women's Institute was closed for the foreseeable future, a forced leave due to the necessary renovations required to bring the building up to code given it was a fire hazard because of its age: plaster workers, plumbers and painters, woodworking crews coming in all hours to liven up the joint.

'Such an expression,' exclaimed Genest. 'You young people, you butcher the English.'

Tilly abruptly stood and gathered the tea tray and its contents. She turned toward the kitchen, remarking over her shoulder, 'We do no such thing. It's called creative expression. How else are we to add new words into the Britannica thesaurus.'

For Genest, there was only one such tome with a formidable pedigree. The Roget's Thesaurus, first published in 1805. With that, he thanked his godchild for the lovely tea, wrapped himself warmly in his topcoat and muffler, and took himself home by taxi-cab, his feet thanking him for that most agreeable decision.

It was nearing eight o'clock when he settled in with his evening apéritif, the sun having long since set, a hearty fire in the fireplace given the time of year—fog, drizzle and rain. He reviewed his notes, Mildred Cooper's telling of her tale. To have had Tilly state those very same facts, why yes, Genest was very much interested, very much indeed.

IV

At eleven o'clock the following morning, the drizzle and fog returned, Tilly arrived at Genest's, her demeanour all bluster and bother, cheeks pink from the cold. She carried a half dozen packages in both arms, setting them on the bench in the foyer. She removed her hat, gloves and coat, and followed her godfather through to his office.

Once settled, Genest informed her, 'I tell you, *chérie*, I was most befuddled. That woman, flitting about, and there I was trying to get on with my tea and biscuits.'

'Good heavens, Uncle. Tell me—do our stories jibe?'

Genest smiled. 'Just as you have stated. She tells me, her husband is being blackmailed, but there is no proof, no letters.'

'Exactly what she told me,' Tilly responded.

Genest took no notice. 'She sees the first of the letters a month ago, there on her husband's desk. She reads it. She cannot understand why anyone would blackmail her dear Kenneth, the vicar at St Andrew the Apostle, such a kind man, busy with his flock, his sermons, his running of the church.'

'Yes, yes, we know all that,' Tilly replied.

'You interrupt, *ma petite*. But alas, that is the way of the young, is it not? To try my patience. To be impetuous. I then look into the building of St Andrew's, its history. During construction, High Church Anglo-Catholics and Low Church Anglicans argued most vehemently, some believing the statue of the Holy Mother was a form of idolatry, a most unfortunate feud which led to the delay in the consecration of the church itself by several years. Such petty nonsense, wouldn't you agree?'

'I wouldn't know, Uncle. Long before my time.'

'And mine,' said Genest. 'But from what I can gather, there were many theological arguments, neither side willing to acquiesce to the other. There then followed the making of the bonfire parades, effigies burned of John Henry Newman, a man of letters, a writer and a poet, along with dozens more, all thought to be traitors to religious doctrine and dogma.'

Tilly's expression was now one of exasperation. 'While all of this is interesting, what's it to do with our problem?'

'I believe the blackmail letters are tied to the Worthing Madonna within the Lady chapel. It is a divine sanctuary made *magnifique* with its stained-glass windows, beautiful artwork and priceless artifacts, all tied to the worship of our Blessed Virgin Mother.'

'And that's led to blackmail?' Tilly inquired.

Genest nodded. 'What if the vicar has been stealing from his church? Holy artifacts, religious relics. The items could be sold on the black market. Perhaps his theft has been discovered.'

Tilly snorted, most unladylike. 'It is now you who fabricates a fanciful tale. Mildred's husband is a respected man of the cloth.'

'Even so, temptation will disguise itself as reward,' mused Genest. 'Perhaps her husband is weighted down with financial burdens. He requires additional funds to keep his wife in the lifestyle she demands. I have seen her shoes, her jewellery, her expensive coiffure. Perhaps he, himself, has committed some terrible deed, a black stain upon his character. If that knowledge is made public, it would be the ruin of him. He is trapped, he cannot wriggle free.'

'Poppycock,' said Tilly. 'I know Mildred. She would not have married a thief.'

Genest appeared lost in thought. 'I have looked through the many newspaper accounts.' He pointed to one of the bookshelves, and there, a month's worth of newsprint rife with stories tied into theft.

'Religious artifacts have been stolen from a number of churches across Worthing, no clues, no suspects. I believe the treasures are then smuggled to the Continent and put up for auction, just as I have stated.'

'And you think Mildred's husband is involved.' Tilly's statement sounded more like an accusation.

'It would give meaning to the blackmail,' Genest observed. 'The reason Mildred's husband plays ignorant as to his having received any such letters. But alas, the hook is set, and he is caught.'

'We must speak with them,' expressed Tilly. 'Mildred and Kenneth.' She bounded out of her chair and hurried to the hallway, the soles of her shoes smacking the parquet floorboards, an intricate design with a mosaic setting most pleasing to Genest's sense of method and order.

While donning hat, coat and gloves, Tilly encouraged her godfather to do the same.

'I do not rush, *ma petite*. First, I must find the comfortable shoes.'

Genest kicked his well-worn slippers from his feet and began searching in the hall closet for comfortable shoes.

'Be quick, Uncle. It's going on for noon. I've had a devil of a time with mice in the pantry, the little critters seeking to get out of the damp and the cold. The reason for my shopping. You've no idea the amount of cornmeal I've had to dispose of.'

'Mice, you say!' Genest acted incredulous. 'We will have the cabbie wait at the curb while you drop your packages, and then, we are off to the races.'

'Oh, Uncle. You make with the jokes when all of this is no laughing matter. Mice, I tell you! What am I to do?'

'You set the trap,' Genest declared. 'Just as we will do.' He flashed his godchild a sly wink while swapping slippers for shoes, an old pair he'd owned for years, finding them hidden behind his galoshes. He then found his topcoat, his hat, and his cane. The pair set off at a brisk clip, Genest happily carrying Tilly's shopping while she flagged a taxi-cab, putting fingers between her pursed lips and giving a sharp whistle.

V

Tilly's terraced home with its wrought iron railings and gabled roof was on Cobden Road not far from the church. Tilly ran in with her parcels, returned, and the cabbie made a second stop at the vicarage where they hoped to find the vicar and Mildred sitting down to their noon meal.

Much to their surprise, members of the local constabulary were rooting through the hedges at the back of the property leaving Genest and Tilly to wonder, what in the world could have happened?

There was no sign of Mildred nor her husband.

Genest greeted Detective Inspector Christopher Scott in the foyer. 'Why Genest, my good man. You've arrived just in time. How the devil did you get wind of this?'

'First, my dear Inspector Scott, I introduce my godchild, Tilly. She is married to the upstanding James Wylder of which you've had the pleasure, no doubt. Despite his love of the horses, he believes indubitably in law and order, a respected barrister.'

If Genest was being facetious, Tilly figured best to ignore. Why get pulled into her godfather's attempt at sarcasm?

'My dearest Tilly and I have come to have a tête-à-tête with Mildred Cooper but instead, we find you and your colleagues about the place. I ask, what has occurred?'

'A body discovered in the back garden,' stated the inspector.

'Oh, dear!' Tilly exclaimed. 'Please don't say it's Kenneth or Mildred.'

'Neither,' said the inspector. 'The missus has identified the deceased as her estranged brother. She hadn't seen him in years.'

'I must go to her,' Tilly responded. 'Is she upstairs?'

Scott nodded. 'With her physician. She fainted upon the grisly discovery; the poor man beaten about the head. She'd been to Greenwich Park in London, visiting a friend, returning but an hour ago. We telephoned the doctor and he is with her now. I believe he's administered a sedative.'

'And what of the vicar?' asked Genest.

'In Brighton,' Scott informed them. 'Attending a church conference according to the missus, but we've been unable to establish those facts. Nothing confirmed as of yet.'

Genest then noticed a dog lying in the corner of the foyer, its snout resting on its paws. A great mastiff, long-legged and barrel-chested with something of a placid disposition, taking no notice of the comings and goings. 'And what of him? This too, is its home?'

Scott turned, noting the dog. 'We've assumed it belongs to the Coopers. It was lying next to the deceased when we arrived. We had a devil of a time enticing him indoors. Didn't want to come at first.

One of the constables familiar with large breeds used a chunk of beefsteak as encouragement, a necessary bribe found in the icebox. The dog then came willingly, as docile as a kitten.'

Ah, thought Genest. Mildred Cooper made no mention of a dog when she arrived at Genest's office earlier in the week. An animal as large as a mastiff would not be a forgotten family member. Curiouser and curiouser, he surmised. Perhaps the dog was meant for protection.

He turned to Tilly. 'Did you know Mildred had a dog?'

Tilly shook her head. 'Perhaps it belonged to the man who was killed.'

'Perhaps,' said Genest.

'But—,' said Tilly.

Genest put a finger to his pursed lips.

'And your arrival?' asked Scott. 'Tied into this nasty business, is it?'

'The *madame*, she came to see me, something of a personal matter. Whether it is tied to this, I do not know. But, as she stated to me, she believed her husband was being blackmailed. The vicar, he repeatedly pooh-poohed the concept, telling his wife, she was imagining things. Without proof, she felt your involvement would be a moot point. You would have viewed it as wasting police time and resources.'

'Possibly,' answered the inspector. He gave his nose a good rub. 'We've a number of active cases on the books, most notable the burgled churches. Six thefts in as many weeks. We're stymied, as you can imagine. Some kind of cat burglar dropping through skylights, using a rope and grappling hooks. No fingerprints, no hairs, no fibers, nothing to go on. And now, the vicar missing, possibly in Brighton. As to murder, we'll certainly have our hands full ferreting out the culprit who committed this dastardly deed. There has been talk it might've been the vicar himself who wielded the weapon, but I soon put a stop to that.'

'You are not a man to jump to conclusions,' Genest stated, having worked with Scott in the past. As to the method of murder, he asked after that fact.

'Hit with a paving stone,' said Scott. 'Taken from the garden path. Never saw it coming. The body had been moved, dragged into a thicket of bushes at the back of the property. The reason for the thorough search. A dog-walker spied the mastiff lying near the bushes, the victim partially exposed. He notified the police, and *voilà*, as you would say, Genest. Here we be.'

'Ah, *voilà*, as you say—as I say. May we see the *madame*?' he inquired.

'Doctor's orders, no visitors at this time,' the inspector told him. 'We haven't spoken to her properly. Perhaps the good physician will offer up a timeline—ah, here he is now—'

A rather tall individual, dark-haired and dark-eyed, was in the process of descending the staircase, coming from the second-floor landing, a medical bag held in his left hand. He shoved his spectacles back up the bridge of his nose, peering down at the three standing in the foyer—Inspector Christopher Scott, François Genest, and his goddaughter, Tilly Wylder.

'My goodness, it can't be!' he exclaimed.

Tilly glanced up, she too, smiling. 'My dearest, Horace! How have you been?'

'Jolly well—and what of you?'

'Happily married. Keeping busy with the Women's Institute, as you know.'

The doctor, having reached the main floor, leaned into Tilly and gave her an affectionate kiss on the cheek. 'Rather capital, my dear. Spot on, that.' He fingered his dark hair, fussed with his spectacles.

'As for our dear Mildred,' he added, 'such a nasty business. And her husband missing. I do hope he too, hasn't fallen victim to foul play.'

'No doubt,' murmured Genest. 'I surmise, my dear Tilly, this is the man who prescribed to your friend Mildred the pills which had her flitting about like a headless chicken, unable to add two and two and deduce four. No, she deduces forty-four times forty-four, most befuddled, unable to land on a coherent thought when I spoke with her.'

'Oh, Uncle,' exclaimed Tilly, turning her attention to the doctor. 'Really, Horace, don't listen to him. Mildred was not muddled. We've worked together these past two years and she's always been calm and level-headed.'

'No offence taken, my dear. I have however, prescribed a mild sedative to help her sleep. Her nerves, rather shaken after the discovery of her brother, the poor man struck down. If she took it upon herself to abuse an earlier prescription, increasing the recommended dose, I have, I *had*, no knowledge of that.'

Genest scrutinized the doctor. 'My godchild, she refers to you as her dear Horace, but *monsieur*, we have yet to be properly introduced. I am François Genest, private inquiry agent.'

The doctor reached out and happily shook Genest's plump fist in a hearty handshake. 'Horace Pritchard, local physician, at your service.'

The inspector, looking on, told the group he had a murder to solve. He then inquired of the good doctor, when could he speak with Mildred Cooper?

'Give it an hour, possibly two,' advised Pritchard. 'Perhaps Tilly could check on her later. It's my understanding their daily help is away, something to do with a sick relative. See if Mildred is up for questions. But go lightly. She's had a great shock. Her brother found dead.'

'Murdered, no less,' said Scott. 'As to her husband, it'll be a right shine on the penny when I finally set eyes on him. Very suspicious, his missing. And the dog. We've still to determine who actually owns the animal.' He then departed to continue with his investigation.

VI

While Mildred slept, the police went about their business knocking on doors, speaking with neighbours and shopkeepers, many simply curious as to what had happened. Tilly set her mind to boiling the kettle and making tea. While she looked through cupboards, Genest sat at the kitchen table. 'You have knowledge of the place,' he said.

'I've been here a few times when Kenneth was out of town on church business.'

'What do you know of the dog?' asked Genest.

'Why, nothing,' noted Tilly, retrieving cups and saucers from one cupboard near the pantry. 'As a breed, they are large animals, protective of their masters.'

'Do you not find it peculiar Mildred never made mention of it?'

'I think the dog belonged to the brother,' said Tilly.

'Possibly,' shared her godfather. 'A death on her property, and she promptly takes to her bed. She does not remain to ask questions as to the whereabouts of her husband. No questions regarding her brother, if indeed he is such a man.'

'She was in shock, upset,' Tilly remarked. 'And why shouldn't the poor fellow be her brother?'

'I am woolgathering,' muttered Genest. 'Something I am good at.' He then added, 'The mastiff is a patient, lovable companion, guardian of the household, if memory serves. They have a natural wariness of strangers which makes me think, whoever killed our victim, the dog knew the attacker. It did not see that person as a threat, believing there was no danger.'

'Meaning the animal didn't belong to the brother?'

'I do nothing more than sift through my theories,' Genest responded.

Tilly replied most forthright, 'I read somewhere that the ancient Romans took the mastiff back to Italy to use for colosseum fighting, impressed with the size of the animal. It was believed it would be a good adversary against the lions.'

She shivered despite the warmth of the room. By then the kettle was boiling. Tilly removed it from the burner. 'If such actions are meant to convey respect for ancient civilizations, I'll forfeit the past and take the present,' she said. 'Anyone who uses animals for blood sport—why, it simply makes my blood boil.'

'Your blood boils for many reasons, *chérie*, just as the kettle. But yes, I can see you are fond of animals. Perhaps when this is all over, you will take the dog, become its mistress.'

'Why in heaven's name would I do that? If the dog has a mistress and a master, it belongs here. If not, the authorities will find it a home.'

'Hmm,' said Genest. 'Perhaps,' and with that, he said no more.

VII

Within the hour, Mildred awoke. Tilly helped her dress and brought her downstairs to the drawing room. The two women sat side by side on the settee, Tilly encouraging her friend to eat a liver pâté sandwich, to drink some tea. Mildred would have none of it.

'It was my brother,' she lamented, dark circles beneath her stark blue eyes, her shock and disbelief causing her much discomfort, her fingers twisted tightly in a knot. 'I had no idea he was in England, no idea he knew where I was. How could he have found me? As wee children, we were sent to Montreal to live with a distant uncle after our parents died. I met Kenneth on the crossing, New Brunswick to Liverpool, both of us passengers on the SS Montcalm. Two weeks on the water and I was never so ill.'

'And what of your brother?' asked Genest. He stood by the window, taking in the garden and the activity unfolding, the coroner having just arrived, an hour late due to other obligations on the far side of town, the police presence still evident in addition to the ambulance parked at the curb.

'We lost touch,' Mildred testified. 'The last I heard of him, he'd left Quebec and moved to Ontario, north of Toronto, Richmond Hill, I think it was. He'd taken up dairy farming. Why would he be here, in Worthing?'

'That we will discover,' said Genest. 'Your brother, had he been to the vicarage prior? Would he have spoken with Kenneth?'

'I have no idea,' Mildred sighed. 'Surely if Kenneth had seen him, spoken to him, he'd have told me.'

'One would think so,' Genest muttered.

Mildred responded, 'The police have questioned my whereabouts. I explained my trip to London, to visit a dear friend, someone I knew from Glossop, our home before Kenneth took up his appointment here as vicar at St Andrew's. Tilly knows something of my history.'

'But not all,' Tilly interjected. 'What of the dog?'

'What dog?' Confusion clouded Mildred's eyes.

'The dog found with your brother, poor man. You must have seen it. I gave it something of a bed in the kitchen, near the backdoor—an old rug from the foyer. It worked splendidly.'

Mildred shivered. 'I'd forgotten about the dog,' she said. 'As children, my brother and I feared dogs. The uncle I spoke of, he raised Irish wolfhounds and rottweilers, all meant for illegal dog fights. He kept them penned most of the time, but sometimes, he threatened us if we hadn't done our chores properly, he'd set them loose, let them have their way with us.'

'How terrible,' Tilly remarked.

Mildred made no comment to Tilly's observation. She simply said, 'Why haven't the police dealt with it?'

Genest spoke up. 'It was believed to have been your family pet.'

'Never,' Mildred told him. 'Perhaps it wandered into the yard having escaped its owner.'

'Perhaps,' mused Genest, busy with his own thoughts.

Shortly thereafter, the coroner, having completed his initial examination, directed the body to be transferred to the ambulance. Genest pulled the curtains shut, wanting to spare Mildred additional sorrow and suffering.

'Have they found Kenneth?' she asked.

Tilly told her, no. The police had sent an inquiry to Brighton, to the conference Kenneth was attending, but still no response.

'I don't understand,' she said. 'He was supposed to be there.'

'Perhaps other duties have called him away,' Genest advised.

Mildred stared at the little man as though he were a stranger. 'Why would you think that?'

'I think many things, *madame*,' Genest remarked with a coy smile.

'It isn't like Kenneth to simply vanish into thin air. Perhaps he's been kidnapped. I have no money. How could I possibly pay for his return?'

'Now, now,' soothed Tilly. 'Put those thoughts out of your mind. You're allowing your imagination to run wild.'

Mildred gasped, as though she'd been smacked. 'But of course my imagination is running wild. Wouldn't yours?'

Tilly knew it would, but she remained quiet.

'What if my brother was involved in some criminal activity,' exclaimed her friend. 'He's part of a gang, and they've kidnapped Kenneth hoping to capitalize on blackmail. Something goes horribly wrong, one killing the other, my brother the victim of murder, and Kenneth has been a witness to the terrible crime. Perhaps his life too, is in danger.'

She was certainly getting herself into a state, Tilly doing her best to calm her.

'The police are searching for your husband,' Genest said. 'I beg of

74

you to eat. To drink. To put your nerves at rest. To do otherwise puts your health at risk.'

Mildred burst into tears, not wanting tea, a sandwich or sympathy. She simply wanted to be left alone.

VIII

Over the course of the next ten days, Genest sent telegrams far and wide, spoke with Detective Inspector Christopher Scott, and Mildred and Kenneth Cooper, the man having returned home from Brighton the day after the murder. Tilly, ignorant of her godfather's inquiries, was left out of Genest's investigation, his focus to play his cards close to his vest.

Late on a Thursday afternoon, he sat in one of two leather chairs before Inspector Scott's desk, Tilly in the other. Genest noted her curt manner, the slight tilt to her chin, her eyes, catlike, looking ready to pounce. She was not at all pleased at having been left out of the equation despite having rung her godfather many times during the preceding days.

'I have come as per your request,' she said, her manner not at all friendly.

Genest smiled. 'So angry, so defiant. Much like your mother when she grappled with a problem, God rest her soul.'

'Leave my mother out of it. Why have you kept me in the dark?'

'But I do not keep you in the dark, *ma petite*. I am busy, as is Inspector Scott, as are you, visiting your friend Mildred, hoping to pull her out of her doldrums.'

Inspector Scott busied himself with the pouring of the tea, handing cups and saucers to Genest and Tilly. He then took his chair and lit a cigarette, tossing the spent match in the ashtray.

'Your Mildred, she led us on a merry chase, having us believe her Kenneth had been kidnapped following the failed attempt at blackmail. But your godfather, he does not fail. And neither do I. We have much to share with you.'

'I am all ears,' Tilly told the inspector. 'I am, however, much displeased with my godfather. And that blasted dog! Mildred has adopted it, thinking she is responsible for its master's death having gotten past her childhood fears, taking pity on the poor creature. She treats it as if it holds more importance than I, a dear friend, or so I believed.'

'And your feelings are bruised,' Genest observed.

'Of course, they are bruised! I believed we were—we are, good friends, and then there's you, shutting me out of the investigation. I am most put out indeed!'

'Ah, *chérie*. You now flail your wings like the hummingbird on a summer's day despite the inclement weather.'

Tilly looked long and hard between her godfather and the inspector, her gaze predatorial. 'Enough with the games, the rhetoric, and the weather! What have you discovered?'

Ah, thought Genest. She now becomes curious like the cat.

The inspector appeared relaxed, almost a man of leisure. He told Genest, 'You did the work, my friend. You begin. I will add details, if and when, necessary.'

Genest gave his friend a slight bow. 'My first order of business,' he told Tilly. 'I make the necessary inquiries into the purchase of large dogs, most notably a mastiff. I find success, one individual who did just that. A tall bony fellow with bushy eyebrows and piercing blue eyes. He speaks with a French accent much like myself.'

'Mildred's brother,' Tilly stated.

Genest smiled. '*Oui, ma petite.* I think that too, at first. Perhaps the brother has overcome his fear of large dogs, no longer the frightened little boy. He seeks a companion while making his travels throughout England, a formidable adversary meant for protection.'

'But why should he have such a need?' asked Tilly. 'The man was after all, Mildred's brother. Surely, he wouldn't have felt threatened at the vicarage.'

'A most reasonable deduction,' Genest told his goddaughter. 'But for the fact, the murdered man was not the brother. He is—he *was*, the husband of Mildred.'

'But that's impossible. Mildred is married to Kenneth.'

Scott then interrupted. 'A deception played upon all who knew them,' he told her. 'Mildred married a fellow called Lester Cox some twelve years ago in Quebec. She and Kenneth Cooper never properly tied the knot, as it were.'

'I don't believe it,' Tilly snorted. 'The both of you have fallen down the rabbit hole.'

'Whether you believe it or not, facts do not lie,' Genest replied, handing Tilly a certified copy of a marriage certificate—Mildred Tidewater and Lester Cox, married at the Église Catholique church in the village of Saint-Sauveur, north of Montreal.

'I don't understand,' exclaimed Tilly, tossing the certificate onto the inspector's desk. 'If this is genuine, why didn't she simply get a divorce?'

Scott interjected, 'She was raised a Catholic, therefore divorce was out of the question.'

Genest nodded in agreement. 'When she married, she was but a child herself, so young. She wishes to escape an unhappy household, the uncle, a cruel and unloving taskmaster.' He left his chair and stepped toward the far window in Scott's office, looking upon a yew tree devoid of leaves, the tree looking oh so sad and forlorn, leaving him to wonder, would spring ever arrive?

He now stood with his back to the window.

'Mildred escapes her harsh life, but sadly, her circumstances do not change. The fellow she marries, he is no better than the uncle, a man who turns to drink when his dark moods descend, failing in his attempt to establish the business of the raising of the pigs. This he does in the village of Saint-Sauveur. The drink, it turns him into a devil, one with a quick temper. A year into her marriage, Mildred is with child. During one foul beating, she loses the baby. She takes herself to the nearest church, seeking solace. It is there she finds Kenneth. He is bewitched by her beauty, her sad tale, her grief. Perhaps in his mind, he turns Mildred's story into one he can relate to, that of the Blessed Lady. Her son crucified on the cross. How does Kenneth's own heart not break? He does the unthinkable. He tells her they will run away together to England.'

'Mildred and Kenneth met onboard the ship,' said Tilly. 'She never knew him prior to coming to England. You've muddled the facts, Uncle.'

'I do not muddle, *ma petite*. Of that fact, I am certain.'

He offered a sincere smile, and continued, 'Mildred's husband, he toils with the pigs, but alas, any small profit in his pocket, he drinks it away. Some years later, he ferrets out the brother living north of

Toronto, they would have met when Mildred and Lester married. He believes the brother will provide employment, but much to his surprise, the brother's business too, has failed. Over a shared pint, Lester learns his wife and Kenneth fled to England.'

Tilly sat there dumbfounded. 'You're certain Kenneth and Mildred were acquainted prior to the voyage?'

'They were,' confirmed her godfather. 'They travel by ship, New Brunswick to Liverpool, just as Mildred has stated. Kenneth finds work in Glossop on the Sheffield Road before taking up his posting here in Worthing. As a couple, they believe they have found sanctuary far from the wicked husband, their exile has been successful. Then woe and mishap strike with the force of a hammer blow, the husband and the brother, they arrive on the doorstep of the vicarage.'

Scott then spoke up, his cigarette half smoked. He leaned back in his chair, sharing what he had discovered. Cox and Mildred's brother joined forces, turning to a life of crime. When things became difficult, with the law closing in, they fled to England, intent on plundering the many churches scattered hither and yon. The dog was meant as a weapon to intimidate those they frightened, making them potential allies: parishioners, elders, parish priests, all embroiled in the thefts, their very lives threatened. When Cox and the brother stumbled upon Kenneth at St Andrew's, imagine their surprise. The perfect victim with which to tighten the screws.

'It's horrid,' said Tilly. 'Using the dog as a weapon. All of it, horrid.'

Genest nodded. 'It is that, *chérie*. But such behaviour is found within those who believe their salvation lies in the almighty dollar. As for Mildred, she knew nothing of Cox nor her brother having arrived in Worthing. Kenneth gave her no details as to the blackmail, wanting to spare her the worry and concern.'

He returned to his chair, straightened the crease in his trousers. 'The initial meeting, it took place four weeks ago. Mildred, she is not at home. She is at the Women's Institute, volunteering her time, with you, my dearest Tilly. They threaten Kenneth with exposure, his reputation ruined, having committed the sin of adultery. What is he to do? He agrees to steal money from his church, saying nothing to Mildred. The blackmail, it has begun. Kenneth feigns ignorance, stating there have been no letters. He knows Lester Cox to be playing a game of cat and mouse, upping the game, instructing Kenneth to now steal precious artifacts from the Lady chapel. He tells Mildred he has a conference in Brighton, but alas, he does not. She herself has gone to London to visit her friend from Glossop. The daily help, she too, is away, a sick relative in Newhaven. The vicarage, it is empty. Kenneth uses this time to embezzle additional funds from the business accounts, upwards of three hundred pounds, but to commit theft upon the sacred Mother? *Mon dieu*, he cannot do such a thing!'

'Something then went horribly wrong,' sighed Tilly, no longer annoyed at her godfather, very much intrigued with the story.

'That it did,' Genest told her. 'When his blackmailers arrive, he gives them the currency he has taken but tells them there are no sacred treasures. He implores them to leave, to never return. He will remain silent, to do otherwise, he would implicate himself in the sordid affair, but his days as a thief have ended. A terrible argument ensues and it is then the dog takes centre stage.'

'How so?' asked Tilly.

'The animal, it is much agitated by the yelling—the pushing and the shoving. It lunges at Kenneth with its ferocious growls, sending him scurrying toward the vicarage, fleeing to safety. The great beast then lunges at the brother, snapping and biting. The brother has taken up a paving stone to use as a weapon. Lester Cox, his partner in crime, sees the brother about to attack the dog. He lunges at the man. The brother brings the weapon down upon Lester Cox's head, killing him. In horror, he tosses the paving stone and races off, down the footpath, the dog in pursuit. Kenneth witnesses all from his vantage point. He tries to hide the body in the bushes after retrieving the stolen money from the dead man's pockets. The dog returns and takes up its vigil beside its fallen master, whining and whimpering, no longer the adversary but the grieving companion. Kenneth hurries to St Andrew's, to make amends, to pray for his sins. Mildred arrives home from her overnight trip, sees the dog and the murdered man, believing Kenneth has struck the fatal blow. Now what to do?'

'My heavens,' said Tilly. 'You leave me quite breathless.'

'He is good, isn't he?' observed Scott, having finished his smoke, butting out the remains in the ashtray.

'It's like something out of a Verdi opera,' Tilly told him. 'But what of Kenneth? Did he remain in the church, Mildred still thinking him guilty of murder?'

'Eventually, he returns to the vicarage,' Genest observed. 'He confesses all to Mildred. She then devises her plan. She encourages Kenneth to remain silent, to say nothing of his involvement, to stay hidden in the church—he is, after all, supposedly in Brighton. She then tells the authorities the murdered man is her brother, making no mention of Lester Cox. A day later, Kenneth returns home, a most unfortunate muddle the police was not able to locate him.'

'Just so,' said Scott. 'Mildred has accomplished two things—she has given her brother the opportunity to forge a new identity, never suspected of murder, the authorities believing him to be the deceased. As for Lester Cox, he is well out of the picture, never more a threat to her or Kenneth. Those of us investigating, she believes we will put it down to a random attack. A vagabond passing by on the footpath who notices the vicarage is empty, temptation calling. While skulking about, looking to gain entry, he comes upon the brother in the back garden, a fight ensues followed by death.'

'To think Mildred was capable of such deception,' Tilly remarked. 'I was so certain I knew the woman.'

'She is quick to think on her feet,' observed the inspector. 'It was her belief, once the waters calmed, Kenneth would resign his posting at St Andrew's, stating ill health. They would then depart to the Continent, as if running away ever accomplished anything.'

'Indeed,' said Genest. 'Why is it, we think we can run from trouble?'

Tilly bounced onto her feet and gave her godfather a kiss on his plump cheek. 'But not you, Uncle. You're as solid as a rock.'

'A rock you say?' Genest laughed. '*Mais oui*, I am immovable. Headstrong like a dog with a bone. Not quite a paving stone, but a good weapon, nonetheless.'

Tilly's smile beamed down at him. 'If not for your inquiries, the inspector would still be running about like a headless chicken, searching for answers.'

Genest chuckled at the metaphor, so like his darling godchild to throw headless chickens into the mix. 'Yes, yes, we have covered all that. The inspector, he agrees, do you not, *mon ami*?'

The inspector readily agreed.

'And what of Mildred's actual brother?' asked Tilly, perched on the armrest of Genest's chair, her grey-flecked eyes focused on the inspector. 'Has he surfaced?'

'It is possible the dog inflicted an injury upon the brother. If he sought medical assistance, we will find him. We've alerted our sister constabularies and the port authorities should he try to flee the country having stolen a new identity. For now, we drink the Earl Grey. We bask in the glow of your godfather having cracked the case.'

Genest took Tilly's hand in his. 'And what of you, *ma petite*. You are satisfied I did not leave you out of it, as you so solemnly stated. Oh, the anger in your eyes.'

'I am satisfied,' she told her godfather. 'I'm just sorry I wasn't brought in sooner. I feel like an afterthought.'

'You are never an afterthought, *chérie*. You are my Tilly. If not for you, I would not have sought out answers to your friend Mildred's dilemma which led me to the dog, that most formidable creature which remained loyal to its master, even in death.'

Tilly laughed. 'My word, Uncle. All of it makes my head spin.'

'Mine as well,' observed Scott. He'd been listening intently, much taken with Genest's method. 'You've made good work of it, my friend. Solved a murder and discovered those involved in the theft of the religious artifacts.'

Genest happily accepted the compliment while fingering his Van Dyke beard and smoothing his mustache with his fingertips. What he had yet to share with Tilly, that her friends, Mildred and Kenneth, would be held as material witnesses in the coming days, charged with the crimes of having perverted the course of justice, lying to police, and theft. He would disclose those facts at a later date.

'Now, tell me, James and his thoroughbreds. Of which you too, are a spirited adversary. If I had shared my findings sooner, you'd have forfeited your attendance at the Cheltenham Gold Cup, neither of us forgiven. I understand his Artemis did well, staying well ahead of the pack.'

'He did,' Tilly exclaimed. 'He ran like a trooper, despite the mud.'

'Ah, the mud,' Genest said. 'Always we must deal with the mud at this dubious time of year—the mud, the drizzle, the fog. Such is England, such is Worthing. We now leave the inspector to his work. You and I, we partake of an early supper at a fine restaurant, my treat. If your James is not drowning in legal briefs, he too, will come.'

'James has taken himself to London, to parliament. There is a debate for and against the sale and trade of armaments to Germany. James fears there is a veiled truth, much like Mildred and Kenneth, not all as it appears.'

'So true, *ma petite.*' Genest's tone spoke to his concern. Perhaps it wasn't jealousy, it was Tilly's welfare which troubled him. He added with solemn aplomb, 'An ill wind blows for which many, including the monarchy and Britain, will be made to pay a terrible price.'

'Do not fret, Uncle. James is an absolute brick, he too, like a dog with a bone when it comes to political accountability. You and he have more in common than you think.'

'Perhaps, *ma petite.* But before we make the pleasantries, I do the buying of the supper.'

'Supper is my treat,' she insisted while linking arms with her godfather. 'Your method, your madness, most extraordinary.'

Genest stood smartly with thumbs tucked in the pockets of his waistcoat, happily accepting the compliment. He rocked back on his heels, smiling.

Tilly added, 'As for your shoes, we will return them. Capitalism at its finest, your money reimbursed. Why suffer added insult to injury?'

'Ah, my dear Tilly. I wear the shoes; do you not witness them upon my feet? I give them the breaking in. It takes time, of which I've had plenty these past ten days. My pinched toes and the shoes, we are now reconciled.'

Tilly laughed most gaily. 'As are we, Uncle. As are we.'

Gunning for a Promotion
Jon Matthew Farber

Dr Patrice Picard, full-time professor of astronomy and part-time host, gazed up at the darkening sky he loved so well, unaware that this would be his last night for delighting in its beauty. At the same time, across the campus, Dr Leonard Simon, full-time professor of mathematics and logic, and part-time solver of murders, was grading the last of the midterms, before arranging them lowest score to highest, and stacking them on his uncluttered desk. Middle-aged, he was a few inches taller than average and of slight build; he would have preferred to think of himself as wiry, as he had been in his youth, but he was nothing if not objective. A lean face with expressive eyebrows was topped with short-cropped hair. His most distinguishing feature was his pointed Stahl ears, sometimes referred to as "Spock ears".

The evening being brisk but pleasant, he put on a light coat, left his office, and crossed the quadrangle as he headed towards the outskirts of the university. Approaching his destination, Simon strode up the hill, with the observatory looming above him. The dome was closed. A terrace, reachable by an outside staircase, wrapped around the circumference of the dome. A figure on it waved hello. Simon waved back, and continued walking along the path to the door. His knock was answered by a rotund young man, in blue jeans, blue shirt, and an ill-fitting red sweater, who took his coat and hung it up next to a bright yellow windbreaker. He then led Simon to the center of the room where the other guests were gathered, after which he promptly fled, leaving Simon to make his introductions himself.

Shortly thereafter, an energetic man, grey hair at the temples fringing a bald dome of his own, entered the room; Simon recognized him as the person he had seen on the terrace coming up.

'*Bienvenue, mesdames et messieurs,*' he said. 'I am Patrice Picard, and I welcome you to our newly opened observatory. My countryman, Jules Verne, wrote De la Terre à la Lune, From the Earth to the Moon, but with this new telescope, our vision can roam farther than he ever conceived possible. I'll let you all see what I mean for yourselves, but first let me give you a guided tour.' He walked over to the ultrasleek telescope, gleaming from the light in the room, mounted on a platform taller than himself, and which reached to within a few feet of the ceiling. 'This telescope is 25 feet long with an aperture of 22 inches, making it one of the largest privately owned telescopes in the world. *C'est magnifique, non?* You'll all get a chance to view through it later.' Continuing around the room, he went over to the wall opposite the door, where three framed pictures were lined up horizontally at eye level. Two feet above them was a clock, with a figure in the middle of Mr Spock from Star Trek, his arms functioning as minute and hour hands.

'*Bien sûr*, I've taken the liberty of adding a personal touch. Like many astronomers, I grew up with Star Trek first catalyzing my interest in space, and have placed these three pictures from my private collection. They're all signed by the original cast members themselves.' The first showed Captain Kirk, communicator open, and was inscribed 'Beam me up, Scotty' with William Shatner's signature.

In the second, of Leonard Nimoy as Spock, he was seen executing the classic Vulcan Salute, a V formed by fourth and fifth fingers together, separated from the second and third fingers, which were also touching each other. Nimoy had written the Vulcan greeting "Live Long and Prosper" on it. The last picture was that of an exasperated Dr "Bones" McCoy; DeForest Kelly had autographed "I'm a doctor, not a bricklayer" on this one.

Picard continued to show the guests around, before finally arriving at a large control panel. '*Et maintenant*, for what I trust will be the highlight of the evening. Although this telescope can go well beyond our own solar system, the planets are properly aligned tonight so that I can treat everyone to a spectacular view of both Jupiter and Saturn.' So saying, he pressed a button on the panel, and the roof slowly began to retract. When it finished after a few minutes, a beautifully bright night sky, lit by nature and not artificial lighting, glowed above. 'I have set the telescope to Jupiter first. You'll be able to get an excellent view of the giant red spot, an atmospheric storm which still has secrets for us to uncover.' After everyone had a chance to look through the lens, he went back to the control panel, and adjusted a dial; the telescope rotated to a new position, then stopped. 'And now, you should see Saturn in all its glory; the rings are especially vivid this evening.' As before, the guests took their turns at the eyepiece, this time with some oohing and aahing.

When they were all done, he said, 'Once again, I want to thank you all for coming. Au revoir, and have a pleasant night.' As the roof was closing and the guests shuffled out past him towards the only door, he added, 'Liv, Al, and Victor, please stay behind for a bit. We have something to discuss.' Simon saw three people turn. The first was the uncommunicative man who had showed him in when he had first arrived. The second was someone who could only have been his twin, with the same body build, dressed similarly except that his sweater was charcoal. The third was a woman, athletic-appearing, wearing black jeans and a black turtleneck. Simon shook Picard's hand, thanked him for the evening, and headed out.

Early the following afternoon found Simon sitting at his desk in his office. The room reflected the man. Escher and Magritte reproductions hung from the walls. If one looked closely as his book collection, in addition to scholarly material, one could also find more playful works such as Hofstadter's Godel, Escher, Bach: An Eternal Golden Braid, Seife's Proofiness, and a first edition of John Dickson Carr's The Hollow Man. The shelves were also stocked with various puzzle items including a Rubik's Cube, tangram, and wrought-iron entanglement puzzles; a table by the window was graced with a Staunton chess set flanked by a chess clock.

Detective Tasha Crosby sat across from him. Tall and fit, with short blond hair and blue eyes, she and Simon had been friends for many years, starting out as bridge partners in college. She had married, moved to New York, and returned to her roots after her husband, also a police officer, had been killed while on duty. 'Sorry I had to cancel our morning walk on such short notice,' she began. 'I

85

assume you heard about Professor Picard?'

'Yes, new travels rapidly in a closed community such as a university. A tragedy. I assume there's no doubt it was murder?'

'None indeed, but there are several curious features, and I could benefit from your input. I know how much you like puzzles, and how valuable you were on the last case, so this should be right up your alley. Did you know him well?'

'I'd seen him about, but yesterday was the first time we'd actually met. The observatory had just opened last week, and he'd been conducting multiple tours. The one last night was for the heads of the science and related departments.'

'Why don't you fill me in on how it went while we head over.' Simon narrated the events of the evening, and when they arrived at the observatory, Crosby punched in a key code and the door unlocked. Even with the bustle of the crime-scene technicians, the pristine telescope still dominated, as if it were watching over the activity. After they were inside, she asked Simon to look around and see if he saw anything different since last night. Simon immediately pointed to a window which was taped over. 'That's clearly new, and no doubt relevant. Can you tell me about it?'

'The cleaner, Thea Butler, came over early this morning. She entered the passcode, but couldn't open the door. She walked around to the side, looked in the window, and saw the professor lying on the floor, blood congealed around him, and a gun by the body. That's when she called us. Mrs Butler didn't see anything suspicious, or pass anyone, on her way to the observatory. We had to break in the window to gain access, so that's on us. The door had been bolted from the inside. As you can see, the windows are all fixed in place, like large portholes; they don't open or close. I assume that's to minimize the amount of dust that enters. The other windows haven't been tampered with, nor was this one, except by us. The roof was sealed shut. The door itself fits snugly in its frame, practically air-tight. We couldn't find a way to monkey with the bolt; we even tried manipulating it from outside with a magnet, but that didn't work either. And, of course, there aren't any hidden openings into the observatory.'

'You said this was definitely a murder. How did you rule out a suicide?'

'He was shot from around three feet away, and there was no gunshot residue on his hands. So, we have a locked-room puzzle for you to solve. But that's not all. We also have not one, but two, dying messages.'

'That is most fascinating. What are they?'

'I can show you pictures of his hands, which is where he left his clues. The ME has confirmed they weren't due to death spasms.' She brought out the pictures. The left hand was splayed in a V with a cleft between the third and fourth fingers, while on the right, the third finger was overlapping the second. 'Any thoughts?'

'I'll need some context. I assume you have some suspects in view already. May I have some background?'

'We know from interviews that the professor continued to work late last night, after the event was over. He was killed around one in the morning, and someone accessed the passcode at 12:47 a.m. Presumably the murderer. Besides Picard and the cleaner, the only other people who knew the passcode, which had been set by the professor himself, were his four research assistants.'

'That presumes nobody has shared the passcode with anyone else.'

'True, but that's unlikely given how short a time the observatory has been open, plus it would make for a royal headache if we had to expand the pool of suspects, so we'll keep it simple for now.'

'Please tell me about his assistants, including any unusual features.'

'There's Victoria Trexler. She's a junior, who was in the infirmary overnight with food poisoning; her alibi checks out so far. The other three are all seniors, and, like Miss Trexler, all brilliant students. Olivia Dix is a varsity gymnast, Alvin Fox is head of the robotics team, and his twin, Victor, has apparently been making some breakthroughs in 3D printing. Does that help any?'

'Do you have any reason to suspect one more than the others, or what a motive might be?'

'Apart from Miss Trexler, none of the other three have alibis, and they all have motive. Miss Trexler informed us that she'd been chosen to be his second-in-command, leaving the other three to scramble for graduate training and jobs for next year. The others confirmed that the professor had told them his decision last night, when he asked them all to stay behind. They also knew that he had planned on working late in the observatory, as he often did, to go over his research and write papers.'

'I see. Give me a minute to cogitate.' When Simon spoke again, it was to make an announcement. 'I know who the murderer is, and believe I know how it was done.'

'Fantastic! But will you be able to prove it?'

'I have a thought along those lines as well. Here's what I suggest we do…'

The three suspects, having been asked to arrive at times which were five minutes apart, had all been prompt, no surprise in view of the circumstances, and were now standing in the observatory, facing Simon. Detective Crosby stood off to one side. Miss Dix was again wearing black jeans, with a red turtleneck this time. Alvin had also changed, this time with a white shirt and yellow sweater, while Victor appeared to be wearing the same clothes as on the previous evening.

'I am here to inform you that I am prepared to name the murderer of Professor Picard. I do admit to a slight weakness for the theatrical, and I do enjoy elucidating my reasoning, so I will start by introducing you to the clues I used in my deductions. Please feel free to interrupt with any questions.

'I will commence by showing you pictures of the deceased's hands; do not be alarmed, they are not graphic. What do you make of them?'

'That one's a V, 'said Miss Dix. 'And that other looks like an X,' offered Alvin. 'I suppose they could also both represent Roman numerals,' added Victor.

'Excellent suggestions all,' replied Simon. 'However, allow me to cut to the chase. They unambiguously identify the killer—and that's you, Miss Dix.'

'That's preposterous.' she said with a smirk. 'A V and an X? That's all you've got? We all have those letters in our name, even Miss V for Victory, Victoria Trexler.'

'You are misreading the symbols. That is not a V, which would be

88

made with the second and third digits, as exemplified by Winston Churchill. What you are looking at is a Vulcan salute. That in turn conjures up the phrase "live long and prosper". Now, focusing on the first word, we have "live", which is your first name. I heard Professor Picard call you Liv last night.'

'This is just a fantasy from someone who's read way too many mysteries. I suppose you have some fanciful way to tie me to the X as well?'

'Indeed, I do. Before I get to that, I will take a moment to comment on the entire concept of dying messages, and the coincidence of the one used here. The first instance of a dying message was perhaps in The Tragedy of X, written by Ellery Queen under the pen name Barnaby Ross. In that work, as with us, the victim also left an X behind with his fingers, which in that instance. represented a mark. The authors (Ellery Queen being two people) did not use this theme of dying messages often in their novels, finding it more adaptable to their short stories and radio plays, but the next two times they did were in The Siamese Twin Mystery and The Scarlet Letters. In both of these, an X was again featured, as a letter in the former, and a symbol in the latter.

'With Professor Picard, we come across still another interpretation of X. That's because here, as was already suggested, the X represents the Roman numeral for ten. And what would the late professor, a Frenchman, use for ten? The word in French is pronounced to rhyme with geese, thus deese, but is spelled D-I-X, so you see it points yet again directly to you.'

'Your imagination is running amok. Even if all this nonsense were true, do you think any jury will buy it? Especially since there was no way anyone could have killed him. The grapevine says that the room was sealed up.' She turned to the other two students, who murmured their assent. 'The windows don't open, and the door was locked. I'd put my money on suicide, and that the forensics are wrong.'

'The forensics are correct, Miss Dix,' said Simon. 'I agree you did not use the door or windows, but instead egressed by way of the roof.'

'You're kidding me. The roof has to be at least forty feet high, and is locked up more tightly than even the door, to keep rain out.'

'While I agree the roof is sturdily closed, by no means is it locked.

I will tell you precisely how it was done. Let me enlighten everyone. You would not have been able to find a rope ladder of sufficient length on such short notice, but any late-hour hardware store would have a heavy-duty rope long enough for your purposes. After killing Professor Picard. you went to the control panel and opened the roof. You next exited the observatory, leaving the door open, and climbed up the stairs to the terrace. From there, you fastened the rope you had brought with you to the railing, and tossed the other end into the room. Heading back inside, you closed the door and shot the bolt. The next step was to press the button to close the roof, a process which, as we know, takes several minutes. After that, all you needed to do was to clamber up approximately 12 meters of rope. The world record for 14 meters is around 14 seconds. There was thus ample time for a trained gymnast such as yourself to reach the roof and haul the rope up after you. By way of corroboration, we found some rope fibers by the staircase outside.

'Bolting the door was overly clever, and a miscalculation on your part. I realize you wanted to pose an impossible conundrum for us. However, had you not set up the proverbial locked room, then the pool of potential suspects would have expanded to include anyone the professor might have invited in. As you left it, though, you whittled this number down to essentially one.'

'I admit you're spinning a marvelous tale, and might be able to convince a yokel of it,' she said, her voice with a slight catch, less confident than before. 'However, it would take twelve yokels, and I don't think you can do this on what you've got. Can you prove it? A few strands of string aren't going to cut it.'

'Now that the police know what to look for, I anticipate they will be able to show that you purchased such a rope last night.' Some of the colour drained from Miss Dix's face. 'However, I expect to do better any minute now. Do you see the clock on the wall?' Simon said, pointing to the one above the Star Trek pictures. 'You have probably heard of the infamous Elf on the Shelf nanny cam, where parents insert a camera in the Elf to spy on babysitters. It transpires that the late professor had what I have dubbed a 'Spock in the Clock.' This clock contained a small wireless camera trained on the door; it appears the good professor wished to keep track of who entered and left the observatory. The police are unloading the footage from last night as we speak.' At that moment, a knock was heard. Detective Crosby went to open the door, and a policeman handed her a flash drive.

'Thank you, Officer Hagstrom. Here it is,' she said, turning to the group. 'I had them set it up to the time in question.'

'Very good.' Simon opened up his laptop and inserted the drive. 'When the passcode—1701, as you all are aware—is activated, the electronic lock records the time. What we are going to see is the last person to enter this room before the murder, after accessing the passcode last night.' A slightly grainy narrow-field image, looking down toward the mid-level of the door, showed it opening, and a distinctive yellow windbreaker with a flash of red at the neck appeared. One of the twins gasped. As the figure advanced further into the room, the face came into view. 'That is quite clearly you, Miss Dix.'

What happened next was unexpected. As Simon turned off the computer, Dix launched herself at him, throwing him to the ground, while screaming about how he had ruined a perfect murder, how Picard was an absolute ingrate who deserved what he got, and so on, degenerating into incoherency. Eventually, the others were able to pry her off of Simon. Crosby handcuffed her, and, after making sure that Simon was unharmed, she and the other policeman led Dix away, still ranting.

'Are you sure you're okay?' asked Alvin, after they had gone.

'Yes, there may perhaps be some minor bruises, but overall, I expect I am none the worse for wear.'

'I want to thank you for solving the case,' said Victor. 'Without that, we could've been under a cloud of suspicion the rest of our lives. It was lucky there was a camera, and that you figured out to look for it.'

Le hasard ne favorise que les esprits préparés—Chance favors only the prepared mind, as the good doctor Louis Pasteur observed. But in this instance, there was no chance involved. You may have noticed that the camera took a narrowly focused picture when it would normally be much more practical to have a wider view. Furthermore, you no doubt observed some red peeking out from the top of her jacket. She wore a black turtleneck yesterday, and only today was it red. We installed the camera this afternoon, using a tight shot to prevent unwanted extraneous material from coming into view, and what we saw was her arriving this evening.

'After seeing herself on the video, as often happens in a high-pressure situation, she lost the ability to think rationally, or she would have been able to deduce the trickery, instead of which she started blaming me and the good professor himself for her downfall. However, as an astronomer and a scientist, she should have realized,' Simon concluded, 'that the fault, dear Brutus, is not in our stars, but in ourselves.'

Take Care of Zozo for Me
Christina Hoag

No sign of Isla. Simona squinted into the harsh slant of the desert's early morning sun and surveyed the prison parking lot again. Maybe she'd fallen asleep in the car. It was only 7 a.m. She would've had to get up at dawn to make it to Chino from LA, and Isla wasn't a morning person. Nope. She hadn't come. A snake of unease coiled in Simona's stomach. Isla hadn't answered the phone last night. Something had happened. Something bad.

Simona hefted her duffle bag on her shoulder and set off down the access road. She'd get a local bus into town and find her way to LA from there. She heard a vehicle pull up alongside her and turned. Frankston, one of the decent COs, looked down at her from the cab of a pickup.

'Hey, Borondy. Need a ride?' he said. The white kernels of his teeth showed bright against the dark hue of his skin.

'I need to get to a bus station.'

'Hop in.'

She slung her duffle in the back and climbed aboard. 'How d'ya like my new truck?' he said once she was belted in.

Paid for with the profits from smuggling cell phones inside, no doubt. 'Nice.' Simona told him what he wanted to hear. What did she care?

They turned onto the main road. He glanced at her a couple of times, then spoke. 'You in a hurry? Wanna stop at my house, relax a while first?'

She slid him the side-eye. Seriously?

He raised his eyebrows at her. It seemed an honest proposition, no hard edge. She'd never taken him for the aggressive type. You never knew, though. He still pissed standing up.

'I mean, you been in a long while, right?' he said.

Like he'd be doing her the favor.

'Four years, seven months and thirteen days. Bus station's good.' She remembered to add, 'Thanks.'

Thirty minutes later, Frankston had wished her luck, and she was in a window seat on a bus to Union Station Los Angeles, pressing her forehead to the grimy glass, trying to summon the rhythms of normal life from the recesses of her memory. Counting bills from a wallet. Grabbing a burrito from a food truck. Curving a lipstick around the fleshy swell of her mouth. It was like riding a bicycle, she told herself, and tried to relax.

When she got off the bus in downtown LA, she debated whether to go find Isla or Antonio first. Antonio, she decided. Everything depended on picking up the stash he'd been holding since the Bel-Air job that got her arrested. Isla, well, if she'd abandoned their plan to live on the beach in Zanzibar in favor of some dude or crank or both, that was on her.

Simona took the Metro to West Hollywood and strolled down Santa Monica Boulevard. Trendy restaurants, weed shops, a pet hospital. There seemed to be more people and cars than she remembered, but maybe it was because she wasn't used to the bustle anymore. She spotted the bright blue roof of the IHOP and then the sign, Hollyway Motel. Paint still peeling. That much hadn't changed. She sped up then stopped cold. A chain link fence surrounded the place. It was closed. What the hell? Antonio's beat up Subaru was still parked in the courtyard though. He must be there. She approached the fence. A notice of impending demolition was attached to it. The owner must've finally sold the property. Shit.

'Hey, Antonio!' She rattled the fence. 'Toneee!' A faint barking sounded in response. Antonio's dog.

The coil in her stomach tightened. She walked around to the rear entrance off the less trafficked Holloway Street, clambered over the fence and beelined for the office. The door was ajar, so was the interior door that led to the manager's apartment. She pushed it open, calling Antonio's name. She was greeted by an overpowering foul smell and Tony's normally placid beagle mix bounded out of the dimness and jumped onto her legs, beside herself with excitement. Simona bent down to pet her.

'Zozo! How ya doin', girl? You remember me? Where's Antonio?

94

Let's find Tony.'

She stepped into the living room and gasped as her vision adjusted to the dark. The place had been ransacked. Coffee table upended, legs broken. Lamps smashed. The large screen TV, playing ceaseless soccer games from Antonio's native Argentina, gone. Sofa cushions slashed. Zozo disappeared behind the tattered couch and whimpered. Simona followed her. Lying in a pond of blood was Antonio, sightless eyes locked into a stare. He was missing fingers on his right hand, his shirt drenched with blood. Stabbed numerous times, it looked like.

She raced into the bedroom. The bed was pushed to the side. The trapdoor in the floor lay open. Shit, shit, shit. She got down on all fours and stuck her hand in the square hollow. Felt every corner. Just in case the black velvet packet had blended into the shadow, but she knew it would be in vain. Whoever it was knew what they were looking for. She sank back on her heels.

Isla. Isla was the only one who knew about El Flautista, the little man of solid gold. She'd sold Simona out. Never trust a crankhead, no matter how long she'd been clean. How had she been so stupid? Well, she knew how. Loneliness. It got to everyone inside. She was constantly surrounded by people yet had never felt so alone.

She returned to the living room and spotted a blood-spattered piece of paper on the bar amid smithereens of glasses, bottles and a mirror. Writing on it. She picked it up. It was a shaky scrawl, almost like a child learning to form letters. 'Take care of Zo for me.' It was for her. She'd told Tony when she was getting out. They'd tortured him to reveal the whereabouts of the safe then left him to bleed out. The note had been his last act, written with his left hand.

She scooped up the dog.

Isla lived in an illegal garage conversion in East Hollywood. Half a garage, actually. The owners had squeezed two apartments out of the space for one car. It was tiny, but importantly for an ex-con, lacked the requirements of a background check, credit score, security deposit or employment. Cash only, month-to-month.

Simona put down the bag of dog food she'd bought on the way

over with her gate money and knocked on the door. She tried the knob without waiting for a response. It was unlocked. She was about to enter when a voice landed on the nape of her neck. Simona pivoted. A small-boned Asian woman stood on the back stoop of the main house.

'She's in Hollywood Hospital,' she said in robotic English. Isla had said she was Thai.

That took Simona aback. 'What happened?'

'Beat up real bad. Cops were here asking questions. You the friend she say was coming?'

'Yeah, that's me. When did this happen?'

'Day before yesterday.' Probably about the same time Tony was hit.

'She paid for the rest of the month, right?' The woman nodded. 'I'll stay til she gets back.'

The woman shrugged. 'I get you the key.'

Simona walked into the tiny apartment. The place was gagging hot and smelled of unwashed bedclothes. She found plastic bowls in the sink, rinsed them off and poured kibble in one, water in another. The dog wolfed it down. She refilled the bowls.

'Stay here and guard the place, Zozo. I'll be back soon.'

If Isla's name weren't on the door outside her hospital room, Simona would never have recognized her. Her face was a mushy pulp of reds and purples.

'Oh, Isla,' she breathed.

Isla's eyes glossed with tears. Simona crossed to the bed and held her hand between her palms.

'It was Declan,' Isla said in a voice muddled by sobs and swelling. 'He's back. He knew you were getting out, that you'd be coming for El Flautista.'

Declan! Simona had figured her former lover would be long on the other side of the world by now, or maybe back in his native Ireland. She hadn't heard from him since his arrest. She knew he'd cut a deal for himself, given her up for a lighter sentence, which was rich, considering the robbery was his brainchild. He'd been in charge

96

of slicing a Monet and a Picasso out of their frames while Simona grabbed the collection of Mesoamerican pre-Columbian figurines, all solid gold. She'd handed him the bag, but she kept a piece as insurance: a two and a half-inch tall man playing a flute. He had an oversized head for his body, slits for eyes and mouth on a flat face, nude except for an elaborate headdress of coils and bands around his upper arms, waist and ankles. Something about that little man spoke to her. She'd stuffed it down her pants without thinking twice. She'd envisioned that little figure many times over the past four years.

The LAPD's art theft detail collared Declan when they received a tip out of London about the Monet appearing on the black market. They managed to recover all the gold pieces, except one, which happened to be the most valuable, dating to 200 B.C.E. When she was arrested, she stuck to her story that she'd given everything to Declan.

'How did he know I was getting out? And how did he find you?' Simona said.

Isla shook her head. 'I don't know. He thought Antonio had given me the gold man.'

So Declan had gone to Antonio first, didn't find the gold, then tortured Antonio further, but Antonio didn't even know Isla's name, let alone where she lived. He just knew Simona would be living with another ex-con. How would Declan have found Isla?

'What're you going to do?' Isla said.

'I'm going to find Declan. I'm staying in your place in the meantime. I have Antonio's dog.'

'Be careful, Mona.'

'Rest up. We need you bikini-ready for where we're going.'

'The place you showed me in the magazine, right? Zanzibar?'

Simona smiled and nodded. Zanzibar.

Simona bought some groceries and returned to the garage apartment. She had to think, but her head was cloudy, overwhelmed with getting out of prison and then finding her best friend murdered and her lover almost murdered. She wondered why Declan hadn't killed Isla. Maybe he'd just had enough after Tony. She lay down on the sagging mattress. It felt luxurious after years of metal racks. Zozo curled up beside her like an embryo. Simona stroked her. The dog had a small bone-shaped doohickey attached to her collar. She drifted to sleep.

She woke the next morning to a hammering noise and Zozo barking. What the hell? She staggered to the door and opened it. A woman stood there, white, forties, complexion like mashed potatoes.

'Hey, Simona. How was your first day of freedom?'

That gravel voice. She blinked, trying to get her brain in gear. Then recognition flooded her. Holy shit. It was that cop, the LAPD's art theft detective.

'What do you want?'

'I think you know. But let's talk about it inside.'

'No, let's talk about it right here.'

The cop shrugged. Spinelli. That was her name. 'Where's the gold?' she said.

'What gold?'

Spinelli twisted her mouth into a sardonic smile. 'Don't play dumb with me.'

'Declan Mulroney killed my friend. Why aren't you arresting him for murder?'

Spinelli didn't look the least surprised. Realization crashed into Simona's brain. Spinelli knew about the murder, which meant this wasn't an official visit. She and Declan were in on it together. That's how Declan knew she was getting out. 'You got my parole notification.'

'Declan didn't need much convincing to come back to LA for the gold. He's a greedy son of a bitch. He figured Antonio would either be holding the gold or know where it was.'

'You could've leaned on me without involving Antonio.'

'That shithole motel is going to be torn down any day. We couldn't wait.'

'He didn't have to kill Antonio.'

'Agreed. Declan went overboard, and now he's in the wind with the gold piece. I don't care about the murder. I get the gold and he can get lost.'

She didn't care about Antonio's murder? Simona felt a surge of anger. 'I don't know where the gold is. This is on you. It has nothing

98

to do with me anymore.'

Spinelli scrunched her face. 'Not that easy. You're going to find Declan for me and get the gold.'

Simona snorted. 'He wouldn't tell me. Why would he? Besides, he's long gone by now.'

'I don't think so. He's waiting for you. His torch is still burning bright for his dear Simona.'

'Not interested,' Simona said.

'Would another stint in prison be enough interest for you? Let's see, possession with intent to distribute is always a good felony charge. You and Isla would both be second strikers.'

The mention of Isla's name jolted Simona. It must have shown on her face. Spinelli broke into a smug smile. 'I got the address you registered with parole and discovered another parolee was registered at this same address—got out just a month ago.'

Simona knew she had no choice.

Spinelli reached into her pocket and took out a burner phone. 'My number's on here. You got twenty-four hours.'

Declan loved being by the beach. 'Why else come to California?' he'd say. He always stayed in a shabby motel in Santa Monica or Venice within walking distance of the Pacific Ocean. He'd go for daily therapeutic dips in the sea for his psoriasis. Spinelli should've known that—then again, maybe not. Declan had no love for cops. He had probably planned to rip her off from the get-go. He would've laid a false trail.

The thing was, Simona didn't think Declan had the gold piece at all. If it had been in Tony's safe, he wouldn't have gone after Isla. And if Declan didn't have the little gold man, he would indeed still be in LA because he'd be waiting for Simona to lead him to it, not because he was still sweet on her. Spinelli was right about one thing. Declan was a greedy son of a bitch. But where would Tony have hidden the little gold man? And why? Maybe because he was going to be thrown out when the motel was demolished. He didn't have any friends. She knew he'd have tried to hang on at the motel until the last moment possible.

She'd get to that in due course. First, Declan.

Simona finished the last bite of the sausage McMuffin and feeling fortified, crumpled up the bag, tossing it in a garbage can at a bus stop as she powerwalked to the third motel on her list, the Sunny Shores in Santa Monica. A housekeeper emerged from a room with an armful of dirty sheets, which she deposited outside the door and returned inside. Perfect. Simona stuck her head inside the room. It smelled of stale beer from the crowd of empties on the table.

'*Buenos días,*' she sang out.

The housekeeper emerged from the bathroom. '*¿Sí, señora?*'

In Spanish, Simona asked the woman if there was a male guest with red, scaly blotches on his neck and chin and a lot of skin lotions in his room. Blue eyes, brown hair. '*Un irlandés.*' The housekeeper said that description sounded familiar, but she wasn't sure. When Simona produced a twenty-dollar bill, the maid plucked the money out of her fingers and pointed to room six.

Simona walked over. A do-not-disturb sign hung on the doorknob. Too bad, wakey-wakey time, Declan. She knocked. 'Housekeeping.'

'Go away.' The voice was muffled, but it was Declan's.

Simona felt her knees weaken. There was a time when she did anything this guy asked. She couldn't let herself slide into his smile again. She steeled herself, knocked again. 'Housekeeping.'

'I said, get lost!'

Now she pounded with the heel of a fist. 'Housekeeping, sir.'

The door flung open. Declan, clad in just his boxers. He'd been scratching. His torso looked like raw meat over bone. How on earth had she ever fallen for him?

'Top o' the morning to you.' Simona pushed past him into the room.

It took him a moment to get over his surprise, then he closed the door. 'Well, well. Simona Borondy. You saved me the trouble of looking for you. You're looking good, I must say.'

'Can't say the same about you, Declan.'

'I've had a few health issues.'

Simona sat in a chair by the window. 'I hear you're looking for El Flautista.'

Declan smiled. 'Glad to see your hearing is still acute. Made you a good lookout.'

100

'I don't have it,' she said.

'But you know where it is.'

Simona shrugged. She hoped she could carry out the bluff.

Declan scratched the blotches on his neck. He was nervous. Simona wondered what Spinelli had on him.

'How much do you want?' he said.

Now he was talking. 'Two hundred grand. Cash.'

Declan guffawed. 'You always were a climber.' His lips thinned. 'Be reasonable, girl. I can't come up with that amount of cash on short order.'

'That piece is worth a few million, and if I know you, Declan Mulroney, you have a buyer lined up. There's probably an escrow account in the Caymans with your name on it already. You can borrow against it, use your connections to get the cash.'

Amusement played in his eyes. 'You don't miss much, Simona. I'd forgotten what a good team we made. We can do it again.'

'It didn't work out so good the first time, so I'll skip it. Listen, I don't have time to play around. You get the cash, we'll do the exchange, say goodbye and good luck. By tonight.'

Declan nodded slowly as if he was reflecting, then he perked. 'Deal. You got a phone yet?'

'No.'

He rummaged in a gym bag and tossed her a burner. 'I'll ring you with the time and place.'

The lulling rhythm of the train back to Hollywood cleared a path in Simona's mind, allowed her to think. She'd have to give up on finding El Flautista. For now, at any rate. Declan would know she knew about Tony's murder and the assault on Isla. He wasn't going to leave a loose end like that swaying in the ocean breeze. He wouldn't show up with cash. He'd show up with a gun, knife or baseball bat, kill her, and snatch the gold man, or so he presumed. He always thought he was smarter than everybody else. But he didn't know that she was in contact with Spinelli.

Trouble was, Spinelli could easily pin Antonio's murder on Simona. She'd always have that threat hanging over her. There was only one way out of this mess. She'd have to get out of town, forget about the gold man, at least until things cooled off. Then she could come back to LA, nose around who Tony was hanging with before he died. For now, though, she had to get rid of her competition. And to do that, she'd have to do what she vowed never to do. Snitch, set them up. She'd call the cops, and get to the border with Isla, pronto. She owed Declan nothing, Spinelli even less.

Simona got off the train and walked to Hollywood Hospital. Before she entered, she ducked into the doorway of a shuttered pupusería and phoned the detective.

'I found him,' she said.

'I knew you would.'

'It wasn't that hard.'

'It was easier to get you to do the work for me.' Yeah, Simona thought, and cover your tracks, implicate me if the plan went south. Spinelli continued. 'Does he have it?'

'He's stashed it somewhere. He'll call me later to meet him. You were right. He still has a thing for me. He thinks we're going away together.' Everybody loved being told they were right. The play to Spinelli's ego worked. The cop gave a smug chuckle. Simona went on. 'As soon as I hear from him, I'll call you with the deets and you can take it from there.'

She hung up and strode into the hospital.

Isla was sitting up, looking brighter, an empty lunch tray in front of her. 'I was hoping you'd come,' she said.

'We gotta get you out of here,' Simona said. 'I have a plan.'

'Zanzibar?'

'More like Mexico.' She noted Isla's crestfallen face. 'For now. Where's your clothes at?'

They returned to the East Hollywood garage apartment stopping on the way at a small hardware store to buy a pair of wirecutters. They packed a bag of Isla's belongings, collected Simona's duffle and the dog. Then Isla called a taxi to take them to West Hollywood. Simona had the driver drop them on Sunset, about five blocks away from the Hollyway. By the time they reached the motel, Isla was flagging and in pain. Simona sat her on a bench at a pocket park on the other side of the IHOP.

'Wait here with Zozo,' she said.

She darted to the rear of the IHOP and pushed through a hedge to the cement wall separating the property from the motel. The tall chain-link fence was on the other side of the wall. She hauled herself up on top of the cement blocks, cut a hole through the fence with the wirecutters, then fetched Isla and Zozo and helped them through.

'We'll be safe here until tonight,' Simona said.

The place looked like it hadn't been disturbed since her visit the previous day. She glanced at the office, where Antonio probably still lay as she found him. His body might not be discovered until the demo crew came. She tried the room doors and found one open. They piled inside.

'Now what?' Isla said.

'Now we wait.'

They fashioned a bed on the floor by spreading out jackets and patting the bags into pillows. They huddled against each other. Isla slid into an uneasy doze as Simona used Isla's phone to check the timetable for buses to Tijuana. The last one left just before midnight.

When Declan hadn't called by early evening, Simona slipped out and got omelettes to go from the IHOP. She was crossing the motel parking lot, bag in hand, when the burner finally rang. Declan.

'You got the gold?' he said.

'You got the money?'

'I'm going to collect it right now,' Declan said.

'What a coincidence. I'm going to pick up the gold right now.'

'You're funny, Simona, a right comedian. Eleven o'clock, the alley behind El Gato Tuerto.'

'You couldn't pick a better place?'

'Be there.' He hung up.

His choice of location confirmed Simona's suspicions that he was setting her up. It was a bad part of town where no one ever saw or heard anything. She called Spinelli. 'We're on. The alley behind El Gato Tuerto. It's a strip club by Macarthur Park. Eleven o'clock tonight,' she said.

'Got it.'

'This is it, Spinelli. I kept my end of the deal. You stay away from me and my girl from now on.'

'As long as you're being straight with me, you got nothing to worry about.'

Simona ended the call and hurried back to the room.

At 9:30, it was time to make her last call. 'I'll be right back,' she told Isla, holding up the burner Spinelli had given her.

'We're taking Zozo with us, right?'

'Absolutely,' Simona said.

Simona stepped outside the building, took a deep breath and dialled 911. She felt like a traitor, squealing to the cops. It went against every grain of her being, but Declan had had no compunction about doing it to her. The operator came on the line.

'A man's been murdered at the Hollyway Motel on Santa Monica Boulevard in West Hollywood. His name is Antonio Raimundo. A woman named Spinelli and a man named Declan Mulroney killed him. You'll find them tonight at 11 o'clock in the alley behind El Gato Tuerto strip bar down by Macarthur Park.'

She hung up, threw the phone onto the tarmac and ground her heel into it. Then she did the same with the burner Declan had given her. She picked up the pieces and chucked them into a dumpster. Hopefully, the cops would do their job.

She re-entered the room. Isla was holding the dog's collar. 'Something's inside this little container, but I can't open it.'

'It's probably the empty spool for doggy bags.'

'Maybe?' She shook it. Something rattled inside it. Something hard, bigger than what Simona had supposed.

Realization crashed in her brain. In a stride, she was bent over the dog's neck, pulling at the plastic container.

'I think he's glued it.' She looked around, grabbed the wirecutter and snipped the container free of the dog's collar. Using the point of the blades to gouge a hole in the plastic, she gained purchase with the wirecutter and managed to make a jagged slice.

Something inside glinted. She wrestled to cut a bigger hole. It fell out. A tiny gold figurine of a man playing a flute. Simona let loose a burst of hysterical laughter.

'Tony, oh my god. You did it.'

Isla's eyes came alive. 'Zanzibar?'

'Zanzibar,' Simona said. 'Let's get the hell outta here.'

A Study of Death
A Doctor John Watson Mystery
Teel James Glenn

It was only a few months after the horrible incident at the Reichenbach Falls where I lost my dear friend Sherlock Holmes when I received a most unusual summons from his brother Mycroft to meet him for luncheon. I was not to meet him at his habitual residence or offices at Whitehall nor the Demosthenes Club, but at a nearby restaurant across the street in Pall Mall.

'Took a slow rug uptown, John?' Mycroft Holmes said with a slight smile. He was seven years older than his brother—whom he resembled—and though almost my height was considerably stouter. He had alert steel-grey eyes with which he regarded me with almost scientific precision.

'Mycroft,' I said, as I extended my hand. I had not seen him since Sherlock's funeral and had concentrated on my private practice to distract me from grief. He, I suppose, had returned to his routine working in a shadowy department of the Foreign Office. I had never seen him express much emotion, much like his brother, but I think, much like Sherlock, he simply masked powerful emotions with a screen of reason.

We were in the stylish, quiet restaurant, the gaslamps casting golden light on us. The corpulent Holmes ordered a plate of beef stroganoff and ale. I had only soup and some wine. We sat quietly until the food came, at which point my curiosity was at a peak.

'Talk to me, Mycroft,' I said between sips. 'Your note was mysterious—you implied this was important.'

'Patience, John,' he said with an enigmatic smile. 'Better if you hear the details from—ah, here she is.' Just then we were joined by a third for lunch, and you could have knocked me over with a feather.

The figure that swept into the restaurant was the loveliest woman

I had ever seen. She had fire-red hair, and the kind of perfect facial features that Renaissance artists aspired to.

The fact that she was followed by gentlemen who, though in civilian clothes, had the bearing of military men on guard duty made her more interesting.

Mycroft rose and I followed suit.

'Doctor John Watson,' Mycroft said formally, 'may I introduce Princess Flavia of R-----'

I was at a loss for a moment whether to bow or offer my hand.

'Forgive me, Doctor Watson, for such mystery and urgency,' the princess said, 'I asked Mister Holmes to ask you here.' She offered me her hand, palm down, and I took her fingers lightly.

The four bodyguards took up positions around us and were not shy about being visible. The princess called the waiter over and ordered an ale for herself. Not my idea of a royal diet.

'I imagine you are wondering why Mister Holmes arranged this meeting, Doctor Watson?' the royal said.

'Your Highness, I am a bit confused.'

'But first, I offer you my condolences on your friend Sherlock's death.'

'Thank you, Your Highness,' I said.

'I have, of course, read your accounts of the cases with Mister Holmes's brother and Mycroft has also spoken highly of your integrity and skill when he said you could help me.'

I glanced to Mycroft wondering just what he had promised me for. 'I am flattered, Your Highness, but how can I be of use?'

Mycroft had a stony expression which was all but unreadable—deliberately so, I thought, and I had a sinking feeling in my stomach.

'My brother Rudolf was murdered last night, Doctor Watson,' she said, her voice choking. 'A violent death in a most impossible of circumstance.'

'I am so very sorry for your loss, Your Highness…but how can—'

'I suspect someone is intent on destroying treaty negotiations with R-----'s neighbors,' she said quietly.

'But how can I help? That seems a matter for the authorities.'

'It is, Doctor,' Mycroft said, 'but there are jurisdictional issues as the Prince died in the R----- embassy—it is sovereign territory. And Princess Flavia has reasons to want outside eyes on this, but that can not be seen to be biased for The Empire.'

'Are there no investigators in your realm, Your Highness?' I asked.

The princess shook her head. 'We have never had such…such a violent and vile act before, and by the time we could have a police official come here from our home…' Her voice trailed off and I could sense hopelessness in her tone.

'I still do not see where this concerns me,' I said. 'I am a simple doctor—'

'Far from it, Doctor Watson,' Mycroft said. 'Your association with my brother, and the publication of your adventures with him, has more than established your good reputation. You are seen by the public, I think, as one devoted to fairness and honesty.' He gave a rare smile. 'I trust you and so does by default, Princess Flavia.'

'Your comments are flattering, Mycroft,' I said, 'And I mean no disrespect, Your Highness, but murder especially at so high a level is a serious matter.'

'Indeed,' he said, 'and of a most diplomatic sensitivity as R----- is in a very key position in European relations—a small country but vitally placed. Your Queen needs you to do this, John,' he continued sincerely. 'My brother had utmost confidence in your abilities and I trust that judgment, Doctor.'

Mycroft had really put me in the middle of it. Were I to turn her down, I would seem ungrateful—and offend a royal at that—but if I accepted and failed to meet the expectations, it could have grave consequences.

'We only ask a fair and impartial investigation, Doctor Watson,' the princess said, coming to my rescue to overcome my indecision. 'No blame will come to you, but I do want to know how my brother was killed. How and why and by whom; none of that can happen if you will not help us.'

My mind went to my dead friend, who, while he had little regard for the intricacies of politics or the intrigues connected to it was steadfast against injustice and would have been touched by both the nobility and sincerity of Flavia. I could do no less than try to undertake the venture in his memory.

'Well, Your Highness,' I said, 'please tell me in detail what happened; I know it will be painful but—'

'Yes,' she said, sitting up a little straighter. 'You should know all, it is only fair.' Mycroft looked at me with a slight nod of reassurance that I thought was a good sign.

'It was last night,' the princess began, her tone flat. 'I was with my councillor, the Colonel Sapt, my scribe, Gustave, and a visiting royal from the Duchy of M-----, Balor. Rudolf, my brother, had taken the treaty to his private study some time before to look it over prior to signing. We all went to our rooms to rest but he did not return for the meal. We went to his study. The heavy door was locked. I pounded on it but he did not answer. I cried out to him but there was no response.'

I exchanged a look with Mycroft who was stoically taking it all in.

'Gustave knelt and saw that the key was still in the lock from the inside,' the princess continued. 'My scribe is a clever fellow and used the stylus he uses to affix seals to push through the keyhole to knock the key out so that it fell to the floor.'

'How did that help?' I thought about how Sherlock would say, 'I can not make bricks without straw—I must have all the facts,' and the thought made me smile.

'Oh, yes,' she continued. 'I did not mention that he first slid a parchment beneath the door, so the key fell onto it. Then he slipped it out and we opened the door and—' Her voice cracked and Mycroft reached for her, but she offered a wan smile. 'Inside, my brother was dead on the floor, his chair overturned, his…his head bloody. Yet, somehow his face was in an expression of peace.'

'There was no one else in the room?' I asked.

'No,' she said.

'So, your brother was slain in a locked room, with no known exit?' My stomach churned.

'That would seem to be the circumstance,' she whispered weakly.

Once more I remembered Sherlock's saying, 'When you have eliminated the impossible, whatever remains, however improbable, must be the truth.' Here I seemed faced with the impossible for certain.

'There are no hidden passages that we know of in the mansion,' the princess said.

'Sherlock has said, 'It was a capital mistake to theorize without data.' I said, 'So it is clear I must visit the scene in person—as an unofficial guest—if I am to offer any real assistance to you, Your Highness.'

'Capital,' Mycroft said. I could see relief in the royal's posture immediately.

'I will look, I will think, and I will make a report, Mycroft.'

'Good,' the princess said. 'You will come with me now?'

I looked to Mycroft, who nodded. 'We cannot stand on ceremony,' he said. 'You will not, of course be an official representative of Her Majesty—'

'Of course,' I said.

'I have the faith in you, Doctor, that my brother had. I know you will do all that can be done.'

'Time matters, for there will be much suspicion in many quarters,' she added, 'which is why I asked Mister Holmes for his aid. His brother had helped my country previously—'

When I looked at her curiously, Mycroft added, 'Before his association with you, Doctor, and he was sworn to secrecy.'

We stood, took our leave. 'Take care, John,' Mycroft called as we left. 'Godspeed.' I thought it a heartening and heartfelt send off and was touched.

I accompanied the princess and her entourage out to the front of the restaurant, where a carriage-and-four was waiting to transport us to her country's embassy in Mayfair on Portman Square. Two of her guards entered the carriage with us but were silent and stoic for the short trip.

We made good time in the afternoon London traffic but exchanged no conversation. I am sure the princess was consumed with thoughts of her brother, as I was with thinking of similar rides I had taken with Sherlock.

How often had we taken such a ride to enter a mystery? Baskerville Hall? The Priory? Puzzles and killers. I felt the familiar excitement at being on the hunt but tempered by a deep sense of loss that I was embarking on this adventure without my friend.

Before I realized it, we were pulling before the R----- Embassy building, a townhouse with some minor grounds. As the carriage rolled to a stop, we were met by a delegation from the embassy, consisting of several men in colorful uniforms.

'Your Highness.' A white-haired, mustached older gentleman

inclined his head to her and kicked his heels in salute. 'We have been anxious for your return.'

'Be at ease, Colonel Sapt,' she said. 'This is Doctor Watson who is well qualified to investigate Rudolf's death.'

He regarded me through a monocle, clearly not so sure his royal's words were true. I returned his look with a genial smile.

'We have left the room as it was, Your Highness,' a second of her countrymen said. He had red hair like Flavia's and was in civilian dress. He was some thirty years old. Looking at his hands, I saw some calluses and a small smudge of ink that told me he had to be her scribe. His features were slightly wolfish with sharp cheekbones and an easy smile. I was put in mind of Caesar's admonition, *'Beware lean and hungry men.'*

'Good, Gustave,' she said to him, confirming my deduction.

'I would like to see the location as soon as possible,' I said.

The princess introduced the third member of the greeting committee—also a lean fellow with a close beard—as, 'Balor, of the M-----, here to sign for his people on certain documents.'

We passed those occupying the entrance hall of the stone townhouse, and they all bowed to the princess and looked at me with hooded eyes. We We went down a corridor to a thick plank door with an old-fashioned handle and keyhole that was being guarded by two uniformed officers, who came to attention when we showed up.

'This is the room,' Flavia said, working to keep her voice tone even. 'Where my brother was—'

'I understand, Your Highness,' I said quietly. 'I will have to ask you some questions as I progress but will try to be gentle about it.' I tried to keep myself in the rational detective mind I had learned from Holmes and not be affected by my desire to help this noble lady. I knew the best way I could comfort her was to give her closure and answers.

'So, these three were with you when you discovered your brother?'

'Yes,' she said. 'We had all agreed to meet in the great hall, but when my brother did not join us, we all came here together.'

'And this door was locked?' I knelt to examine the lock, an old style, wrought iron with a large keyhole. I could see through the hole to a darkened room within.

'Yes,' she said, pulling a key from a hidden pocket. It was the oldest type of barrel key, with a long stem and a key ward—at the ends that turned the tumblers. The loop at one end, the bow, was elongated into an oval. I knew all this from my association with Holmes and smiled at the thought of all the unusual skills and subjects he had exposed me to.

'It was locked when you arrived?' I could see a gap above and below the door. The lock itself looked standard with a cylinder, a bolt and a strike plate on the doorjamb.

'Yes, Herr Docktor,' Balor said. 'We all tried it.'

'And the key was in it on the inside?' I examined the key that looked perfectly normal.

'Gustave was able to push the key out and recover it,' the princess said.

When I looked at him, he gave a wan grin and held up a slim stylus used to affix seals to documents. It was wooden with dark ink smudges on it and a slight hook at the end, like a crochet hook. 'My father's study had a similar lock and when I was smaller. He would lock himself in, overindulge on wine and sleep heavily. I learned to get in and my brothers and I would steal sips.' He grinned. 'He never discovered we had done it.'

I slipped the key in the lock of the dead prince's study. It turned easily. I stepped into the room and turned up the gaslamp on the wall by the door to allow me to survey the scene.

The room was a good-sized and comfortable study with tapestry-hung stone walls and bookcases all about. There was a table used as a desk in the center of the room with a high-backed chair tilted over on the stone floor. At the head of the chair on the floor was a dark splotch that could only be a pool of dried blood.

Up to the right was a slot window, barely four inches high and perhaps a foot long. Not big enough for anyone to get in. There appeared to be no other entrance or exit from the room and no other windows.

I stood in the doorway for a long moment to take the whole space in, taking in every little detail, feeling the enormity of the task ahead of me. Then I remembered another of my friend's sayings, '*To a great mind, nothing is little.*'

I could hear Flavia inhale hard behind me.

'You do not need to come in here, Your Highness.'

'No, it is something I must do, Doctor Watson.' She was every inch the royal.

'I take it he was there,' he said, pointing at the fallen chair.

'Yes,' she said. 'The chair is exactly as it had been.'

'We raced in and knelt by Prince Rudolf,' Sapt said. He had stepped forward to look down at the stain on the floor. 'His head had been crushed with a blow from behind.'

'With what?' I asked.

'With that stone.' Gustave said as he stepped up and pointed to a fist-sized stone. It looked to be part of the type that made up the walls and was off to the right of the door where I assumed the killer had thrown it.

I knelt by the rock to study it a moment; one side had gore and dried blood on it.

I took it all in, stood up and took another deep breath.

'Is this exactly how the room was found?' I asked them all. They agreed. 'Then, if you would all head outside, I will lock the door and do my investigation. And you, Gustave, I will ask you to open it the way you did before but wait till I ask you.'

They all filed out.

'I will figure this out, Your Highness,' I said at the door. 'Take heart.'

Then I closed the portal and put the key in the lock. I turned it again noting how easy the action was. I jiggled the key to get the feel of the lock. That gave me an idea, but I wanted to explore some more before forming any conclusion.

'Please stand by, all,' I called out, then turned back to the room.

My next action was to walk the entire room, feeling my way along the walls, sounding it out with my knuckles.

I could detect no hollow spots, trap doors nor stones on pivots. And when I pulled myself up on the windowsill, it was indeed narrow and even had two bars in it. Anyone entering would have had to be no bigger than a cat.

So anyone coming into the room, short of magic, had to do it through the door.

Yet a man had been killed in that room. A reasoning, caring being, deliberately killed.

I put myself in his place and tried to reconstruct the circumstance of his death much as Sherlock might have.

He was sitting at his desk, back to the door—the window giving light off from his right and a candle on the left side of the desk. Paperwork spread out before him.

So, the door—closed, but unlocked?

Certainly, why lock it in your own home. Reading the papers concerning the treaty. Intense. The door opens, you say 'who is it' and they answer?

I stepped to where the chair was and tipped it back up to sit in it. There was blood on the upper right part of the chair and a slight splinter where the rock had caught an edge.

My back was directly to the door and with the high back of the chair I could not turn to look at the entrance without rising. *So, he did not turn because he knew who came in?*

In front of me there were a few drops of blood on the table and a clear space where the blood stopped in a hard line. The treaty papers he was reviewing must have been there—which the killer removed.

I leaned back a little and before I realized it the chair fell over with a thud.

'Doctor Watson!' the princess yelled. 'Are you all right?'

'Yes,' I replied, rubbing the spot where my head struck the floor, 'Nothing amiss, Your Highness.' I saw stars and looked to the right to see that I was in exactly the same spot that the murdered prince had been. That blood spot sobered me and only reinforced the gravity of my mission.

I had an inkling of an idea what might have happened to the murdered prince, though there was still much fog in the horizon of that idea. I went to stand in the very center of the room.

'Okay,' I said out loud. 'You can open the door, Gustave.'

A slip of parchment slid under the door and then the key in the lock was pushed out to fall on the paper. It was pulled out of the room and in a moment the door was unlocked from the outside and opened.

'That is how it was done, sirrah,' Gustave said. He beamed with his achievement as he entered the room.

'Yes,' Flavia said, with less enthusiasm. 'Have you learned anything, Doctor?'

I said, 'I have some theories, Your Highness. If I may see the body to confirm them?'

I saw her blanch but she bucked up and said, 'Of course, Doctor Watson, he is in the chapel.'

She addressed Colonel Sapt. 'Please conduct Lord Balor to the audience room. Gustave, if you would redraft the treaty as it was, I shall sign it with you all as witnesses when I join you.'

'As you wish, Your Highness,' the scribe said. 'I shall prepare two copies.'

The princess led me to what was clearly an older section of the townhouse. We closed the double bronze doors hung with black bunting behind us.

'My brother will lie here until we can arrange for his—his remains—to be returned home to a state funeral and burial,' she said reverently. We entered a room lit by gas sconces spaced between the tapestries hung on the stone walls. There were no windows.

On an altar in the center of the room was the body, draped in a golden cloth, of Prince Rudolf.

He had been a handsome fellow with a more masculine version of his sister's jawline, though his hair was blond. From where we stood, he looked as if he were just asleep, his expression almost serene. He had a ceremonial sword clasped in his crossed arms, looking much like so many sarcophagi of knights from ages gone.

The princess stood planted just inside the door and I was afraid for a moment it might be too much for her.

'You can stay there, Your Highness,' I said quietly. 'I just need to confirm one thing and then we can leave.'

I think she appreciated that and just nodded as I walked across the floor, my footfalls sounding loud in the sacred chamber. I went around to the other side of the body, where I could see the effects of the attack on him.

On the right side of his head, high up, the skull was crushed in, a gory hole that looked to match the size of the stone that was in the study. There it was then. It was what I had expected, but it still affected me.

The light was beginning to dawn on a solution to the mystery just as the gaslamps went out and we were standing in darkness!

'Doctor Watson!' the princess exclaimed with sudden terror in her voice.

'Be at ease, Your Highness.' The room was in pitch darkness with the sconces off, so I pulled a match from my waistcoat, struck it and made my way to her. 'We can just open the door.'

When I tried the door, it would not budge. Worse still, I heard the hiss of gas. Someone had cut off the gas flow to extinguish the flames then turned it back on.

My match went out.

The hiss was like a dozen snakes in the room, a fact that was not lost on the princess.

'I think we should be fine if we can open the door,' I said to be reassuring, though I did not believe it myself.

While I talked, I knelt down to peer through the slight space between the doors. I could see the bar holding them shut.

'We are indeed locked in, Your Highness.'

'What can we do?' She stood near me, her hand on my shoulder, as I knelt. I could hear fear in her voice, but not so much—she was indeed stern stuff. She knew that in the confined room we would eventually suffocate, though we would pass out from the gas before that occurred.

There was the thinnest of space between the two doors with light from the hall seeping through, the black shape of the bar that had been thrown across clearly visible.

'I think I can slip the bar up.' I stood up. 'Wait here a moment.'

I stood and made my way by memory to the altar where the murdered prince was resting. I said a silent prayer and by touch found the sword that had been slipped in his crossed arms. 'Thank you, Your Highness,' I said, then made my way back to his sister.

I took the sword and slipped it though the space in the door. After a couple of tries I was able to get it under the bar and lift it out of place.

I pushed the door open and stepped out.

'By Minerva!' she exclaimed as we gasped for air in the hallway. 'What a terrible accident at this time.'

'It was no accident, Your Highness, it was a deliberate attempt on our lives—either to silence me or as a continuation of the assault on your line.'

'This is horrible!' she sobbed. 'But why?' she asked, shaken by all the death but working to stay royal.

'Your brother was killed by someone he knew, someone who was afraid when you went to seek help in this. And I think they have the idea that I know who they are. This was intended to finish me and possibly make it look like you were the target.' We were moving down the hall now.

'You know how my brother was killed?' she asked.

'I think so—yes,' I said as we rounded the corner to the great hall to find Colonel Sapt, Balor and Gustave seated at a small table looking over parchments. When they saw us run in, they all rose and stared with questions in their eyes, but one man's expression revealed a truth to me. 'And now I know who.'

I had the final confirmation of the killer's identity. He also saw my gaze zero in on him and turned to run, grabbing a sword off the wall.

'Stop him!' I yelled as I raced at him. I got the dead prince's sword up just in time to parry a panicked attack at my head.

The colonel yelled for the guards.

Balor was stunned and cursed as Gustave attacked me over and over with the sword.

Even with his comparative youth, the scribe was no match for my university-learned sword skills. I was soon able to beat the blade from his hand and put him on point.

'This Englishman is mad!' Gustave screamed as he tried to pull free of the two guards who seized his arms.

'No,' Flavia yelled, 'Doctor Watson has solved the murder of my brother—and the attempted murder of himself and our person!'

This brought the colonel up short.

'I tell you he is mad,' Gustave insisted. 'I did no such thing.'

The colonel asked. 'What do you mean, Your Highness?'

She told him the events that had occurred in the chapel while the guards held the scribe fast.

I moved to the scribe and I pulled the stylus and a loop of silk string from his waistcoat pocket. 'This is the final proof I need.' I saw some fear in his eyes then and indicated to the others to follow me as I walked back down the hall toward the murder room.

'I may not be able to prove directly that you slipped the bar on the door—by the way, you had best dispatch someone to deal with the gas feeds to the chapel for safety's sake. You, Gustave, had so little regard for your own princess that you didn't care if you killed her along with me.'

I led the group to the study, where I went in and slipped the key into the lock on the inside. 'Prince Rudolf left his door unlocked and when you walked in, Gustave. He didn't even look up, knowing it was you. He simply kept reading the treaty. You had the rock with you and smashed him on the head like the coward you are.'

'You are daft, sirah,' Gustave insisted. 'The door was locked from the inside. I am not a magician.'

'Neither am I,' I said, looking to the princess, who was watching me like a hawk. 'But you didn't need to be. You told me yourself how you did it when you said you used to sneak into your father's study.'

'But that was how he knew to open the door,' Colonel Sapt said.

'But it is also how you knew to close the door to leave no trace,' I said. 'You boasted yourself your father never discovered you sneaked in. That was because you did this—'

I used the string looping onto the stylus that I passed through the bow then ran the string up over the top of the door. I pulled the door closed.

'The lock has a very easy tumbler,' I said. 'So all he had to do was slowly reel this in, it pulls on the stylus—see the little hook on the end, and it turns the key, just a little before the stylus slips out and he pulled it up. Like this.'

I pulled the stylus up over the crack in the door and it dropped into my hand.

The others stood in stunned silence. 'You just had to look like a hero and tell us how you did it,' I said to the scribe. 'Why did you do it?'

He looked like a captured animal, wide-eyed looking from one of us to the other.

'I will make him tell,' Sapt said. 'I learned many things in the wars.'

'No,' the captive pleaded with sudden fear, 'It was the treaty; I accidentally put one of the versions where I had hidden a codicil within it to give myself certain concessions. I had planned to have him look at the undoctored version and then switch them when you all signed. It was a foolish mistake.'

'A mistake,' the princess screamed. The pain in her voice was palpable.

'I will have him held until trial,' Sapt said. 'I think the verdict is a forgone conclusion.'

'Thank you, Doctor Watson,' Flavia said to me as the murderer was escorted away. 'You have done my country and yours an invaluable service.' She stood tall, every inch the royal and I felt proud for her country and to have helped her. She would miss her brother but she had answers now and that mattered.

'Remarkable deductions, Doctor,' Balor said to me as the guards led the scribe away. 'How is it you came to your conclusions?'

Once more I quoted my absent friend, *'There is nothing more deceptive than the obvious fact in dealing with the strange enigma that is man.'*

I hoped he would have been proud.

Storm in a Teapot
Chris Hook

George had pulled the door knocker back but froze when we heard the scream from inside. Now he stood holding it idiotically in the silence, as though to release it at this moment would be gauche.

I felt a chill despite the warm afternoon, and Millie, George's fiancée, shuddered.

George finally dropped the knocker and the sound of brass hitting the heavy cedar door announced our arrival.

'What was that sound?' Millie's voice quavered.

'A scream, Millie,' I said. Poor girl, she's not the brightest. Little wonder she seemed to do her utmost to avoid our company.

Hooves clattered on cobble and we three turned to see a hansom cab depositing a tall, dark-haired, broad-shouldered man in a cream suit with matching boater and sky-blue tie.

He stepped through the gate as the cab departed and smiled in our direction.

'Joseph Kailis is my name. Why do I feel I'm late to something?'

I'd been desperate to meet Walter's solicitor friend, given the splash he'd made in Sydney society, not to mention in criminal circles. He had secured stunning acquittals for a number of working-class clients, providing glorious copy for newspapers like mine and annoying the police and the establishment alike.

'You must be Francine Ross, and Millie Pierce and George Farley.'

As we swapped hasty greetings, the gate squeaked again and we were joined by our chums James Yeadon, Will Claxton, and Dolly Keddie. The whole gang was here for what should have been a relaxed late-summer soirée at our friend's Glebe home.

We'd met Walter while at university a few years ago. He was a dashing young archaeology tutor and convener of the university

119

branch of the Socialist Society, a philosophy that intrigued our young bourgeois minds. Much bonding was done in deep discussions over red wine and cheese late into the evening. We'd all moved on a little since then. Walter had become a scholar of some stature in his discipline, achieving tenure at a very young age, while I was writing gossip for the Sydney Sunday Gazette ladies' pages and James and Will were at the Bank of NSW. George had taken over his father's business. Somewhere along the way he'd collected Millie, daughter of the wealthy industrialist, philanthropist, and arch-conservative member of the NSW Upper House Sir Bartholomew Pierce. Dolly, well, I was never quite sure how she spent her days. Though our politics had softened, our friendship with Walter remained. He'd invited us over to celebrate "momentous" personal news and I had begged him to invite Kailis.

Before we could launch into a fresh round of salutations, the door was flung open to reveal Walter's maid Margie in a state of distress.

'Mr Melville is dead,' she cried.

'What the devil is she on about?' asked James.

'I think we'd best find out,' Kailis said, stepping forward. 'Margie, why don't you show me.'

She led us to Walter's study, a large room with wall-to-ceiling bookcases, a reading area with two armchairs and a small settee and French doors opening out to the garden, with a mahogany desk to one side.

Splayed face down on the Persian rug between desk and door was our dear friend, Professor Walter Melville. His left hand clutched the carpet while his right lay underneath him. Beside the desk, upon which sat a teapot and teacup, lay a little pool of vomit.

We all gasped except George, who wailed, and Kailis, who dropped to his knees and placed his index and middle finger on Walter's neck.

'Margie is correct.'

He stood, staring down at Walter for a few moments before turning to us, his expression unreadable.

'Some kind of heart failure?' I asked.

Kailis shook his head. 'I think not, Miss Ross.'

'What's going on?'

We turned to the door of the study, in which stood a tall man with an impressive mane of grey hair swept back off his brow and a thin moustache, wearing a grey herringbone suit, white gloves and a stern expression.

We all knew him. Professor Alan Cotter had once run the schools of classics and archaeology—had been Walter's mentor—and was now university vice chancellor.

'Ah, Professor Cotter, I believe. I'm Joseph Kailis. And I'm sad to say your friend is dead.'

Cotter put his gloved hands to his mouth then drew them away. 'How? His heart?'

Kailis shook his head and tutted.

'No; it's curious you think this of such a young man.'

'How then?' George cried, his voice cracking. I feared for a moment he was about to cry like a girl. I didn't think I could bear it.

'Perhaps he died of shame,' Millie muttered, so softly I could barely hear.

'Of course it was his heart, man, you're being absurd,' Cotter declared.

'What do you think?' I asked Kailis.

He looked at me for a moment then at the faces watching him: Cotter, who looked irritated; Millie, who seemed excited; dear sweet George, who was all grief; and the others, who simply looked baffled.

'I shall explain,' Kailis said, crouching again. 'But first, look.'

He rolled Walter over and everyone shrank at the sight of his bulging eyes and open mouth.

'You see, Walter's tie is loosened, his top buttons have been torn off and his right hand is underneath him as if grasping at his clothing, clutching at his throat in an attempt to take in some air.'

Kailis lifted Walter's hand. 'Here you can see abrasions on his fingers, as though he has bitten them while probing his throat. It seems to me he suffocated, which is not a symptom of a heart attack. So, could it have been some kind of fit? No, he has arisen from his chair, turned and collapsed on to the rug, but he was still trying to propel himself forward, hence the rug still clenched in his left hand, and the gather of the material under his legs.

'A stroke? Again the choking and sudden struggle do not fit.'

He pointed. 'And what are we to make of this vomit? Not the

symptom of a man having a fit, a stroke or indeed a heart attack. Our friend was poisoned.'

'Oh that's absolute piffle, Kailis,' said Cotter. 'Let's do the decent thing and fetch a doctor to declare it then get the mortuary to take him out of here before the heat does its work.'

Kailis spoke past him to Margie who lingered in the doorway.

'Margie, might there be somebody to send to the Glebe Police Station?'

'There's a stable boy two doors down who often runs messages for us, I'll tell him to go immediately.'

'Thank you, then return to this room, please.'

'You're wasting their time,' Cotter huffed.

'He's right,' Millie spluttered. 'This is absurd and morbid, do let us get a doctor and we can all go home.'

Kailis shrugged. 'We can let the detectives decide. He may need a post-mortem.' He gestured to the settee and armchairs near the bookcase.

'Please all make yourselves comfortable in this room as best you can. I appreciate this may seem strange but we must be sure there is no opportunity to remove or change anything. Meanwhile I wish to examine the kitchen and talk to the cook, and Margie when she returns. Miss Ross, I could use your reporter's keen eye for details, and in order that I too have a witness, you may be my chaperone.'

The rest mumbled their assent and sat, Dolly, Millie and George on the settee, James and Will in the armchairs, while Cotter took the study chair and moved it into the corner away from Walter.

'Can we at least cover him with a sheet?' I asked.

Kailis nodded.

George leapt from his chair. 'I'll fetch one from upstairs,' he said.

Millie snorted. 'You seem to know your way around.'

George ignored her and vanished into the hall.

Kailis turned back to the desk, took out a handkerchief, lifted the lid of the teapot and peered inside it, then sniffed. He replaced the lid, and used the same cloth to lift the pipe sitting in the ash tray and study it, then he inspected Walter's leather tobacco pouch.

'Hmm,' he said, somewhat unhelpfully, as he put the handkerchief away and turned his attention to the book in which Walter had presumably been writing, then on to some open letters on the desk.

As he rifled through the correspondence I saw his eyes narrow and he gasped, although it was so subtle I could not be sure.

George returned, spread the sheet across Walter then shuffled to his place beside Millie.

Cotter, who'd been grumbling all the while, now got up to leave, but was nimbly blocked by Kailis.

'Professor, I'd have thought the mystery of our friend's death would be more than enough to compel you to stay, but if not, then I will. Please return to your seat.'

Cotter obeyed, folding his arms with a sigh.

'This is absurd, ghoulish and grotesquely fantastical.'

'It is murder.' Kailis' face was dark. 'Given Walter's standing as a prominent Socialist, unmarried, with a complicated private life, this may be our one opportunity to ensure justice before it is dismissed as natural causes and swept under the rug.'

He addressed Millie. 'I believe your father has used parliamentary privilege to make insinuations about Walter's character and call for his removal, as part of his campaign for moral renewal.' Millie glared at him but said nothing.

Kailis looked around the room, shaking the sheets of paper in his hand.

'He had also received correspondence accusing him of degeneracy and threatening to make public his private life should he not remove himself from the university and leave NSW. Did anyone know?'

Heads shook. I'd certainly not heard of any poison-pen letters, but then Walter was not one to share his burdens.

Kailis replaced the papers, about three sheets as best I could tell, and turned his gaze to the maid, who was standing quietly near the door.

'Margie, when did you find him?'

'Just as you arrived, sir. I heard voices out front and came to let him know before I answered the door.'

'When was the last time you saw him in good health?'

'When I brought in his special tea, sir.'

Kailis pointed at the teapot and cup on the desk.

'Yes, Walter habitually drank a brew made out of tea tree leaves, in the fashion of the native people. It was, he told me, a habit adopted by Captain Cook himself in the interests of good health.'

Margie nodded. 'He had it in his study just after his lunch, sir. Didn't hold with it myself but I made it for him most days.'

'Did Walter receive any visitors today?'

'No sir, he spent the day writing, but was very much looking forward to receiving you all. Poor Mrs O'Reilly's been in and out all day fetching bits and bobs, she'd only just come back with the last of it when, well, this happened.'

'O'Reilly?' Kailis asked.

'Kate O'Reilly the cook sir.'

'Take me to the kitchen, please.'

We proceeded, the maid, the lawyer and I, to the kitchen, where Mrs O'Reilly was sitting on the steps gazing out to the back yard. She stood, smoothing her pinafore. The kitchen was a still life of half-prepared food. I watched as Kailis took it all in.

'Mrs O'Reilly, what time did you leave after making Walter's lunch?'

'Almost immediately, sir. He don't eat much during the day, so there weren't much cleaning up and then I had to run to collect a few things before preparing tonight's meal,' she said, faintly.

'He preferred a working man's lunch—cold ham, cheddar and pickle sandwich for instance?'

She nodded and opened the ice chest. 'Here's the leg sir, and the cheese, there's nothin' wrong with them, me and Margie had the same ourselves.'

I looked around. The kitchen was clean, so the object on the tiles stood out—a small green frond with a white flower, dried. As I picked it up I saw another, just like it, on the floor at the top of the few stairs down to the garden path.

'Mr Kailis, is this a tea tree leaf?'

He turned from the ice chest and I held the frond out for his inspection. He took a sharp breath.

'It is not,' he said, tearing a scrap of brown paper from one of the packages on the bench. 'I recognise that plant. Please place it here, then wash your hands very thoroughly with soap in the sink.'

I did as I was told. 'What is it?'

'That, Miss Ross, is what I was looking for, although I did not yet know it. You see, I did need your keen eye!'

I blushed as he continued questioning the servants.

'So, no visitors. Was anyone else here today?'

Margie shook her head. 'No sir, there was only the gardeners, to tidy up before tonight.'

'Did anyone you did not recognise make their way into the house?'

Margie shook her head, but then seemed to remember something.

'There was one fella, Mr Kailis, but he said he were with the gardeners.'

Kailis's eyebrows shot up toward his dark, shining hair.

'Oh,' he said gently. 'What time did this fellow appear?'

'It was as I was making Mr Neville's tea, so about two o'clock. He came in wanting a glass of water, so I ran him one and he drank it then he was gone.'

'Did you see him with the other men?'

'No sir. See, they'd gone to the Friend in Hand for a pint and a ploughman's, as they do. When I asked this fella why he weren't with them, he said he'd taken the pledge and brought his lunch along with him, but didn't have any water to wash it down.'

'And what did he look like, this fellow?'

'Tall sir, with a big scraggly black beard.'

'And his face?'

'Well, between his beard and the big, wide-brimmed floppy hat he had on I couldn't see much at all, but I were busy and weren't really looking.'

Kailis nodded gravely.

'And did you see him again?'

'No, Mr Kailis. While we were in the kitchen we heard Mick, the gardener, and his lad Liam come back, and he left real quick like, but I didn't see where he went after that.'

'Thank you Mrs O'Reilly, and my thanks to you, too, Margie.'

He raced back to the study, me scurrying along behind him.

We burst in to see George standing at the desk, studying the correspondence Kailis had been waving about. He turned as we entered, his face red and his eyes damp, dropped the papers on the desk and stood staring at Millie, his brow furrowed. Meanwhile, Kailis began poking about in the teapot with the pen once more, before whipping around to face an expectant crowd.

'It is my belief Walter was poisoned with the addition of deadly hemlock to his tea.'

There was silence, until Cotter broke it with, "Poppycock."

'It is true, Professor Cotter. Miss Ross found leaves on the kitchen floor, and I can see similar fronds among the tea tree leaves in Walter's pot. It takes a careful eye, as the dried flowers of both are quite similar in appearance.'

'Then it must have been the maid, or the cook,' Cotter declared, as James, Dolly and, of course, Millie nodded along.

'Why would they do such a thing? They've been here many years and Walter is a good employer and a friend of the working class. And what would they know of hemlock? It is a rare plant in this country, but not in Greece. All the children of my village knew not to touch it for fear of a painful rash, or even worse.'

'I know who it was,' George said, his voice now clear and unwavering.

He turned to address Millie, seeming more like himself than he had for a long time.

'Those awful letters are in your handwriting. No doubt about it: the loops, the backward slant; you sent those horrid missives to Walter.'

I felt as though the rage would burst out of me as I marched to the settee and stood in front of Millie. 'So it was you,' I hissed. 'Your family's estate has a greenhouse with all manner of exotic plants. And you hated Walter because of his friendship with George. You hated Walter because he was corrupting your fiancé.'

'That's absurd,' Millie spluttered.

'George, we've known about your close friendship for years. Millie is the first romance you've ever had but clearly she's worked out where your heart really lies and taken radical action. She must agree with her father's moral crusade, so she's found this plant and somehow snuck it into Walter's tea.'

Millie leapt to her feet. 'Walter was a pervert, a disgusting pervert who took advantage of George. Yes, I sent him those threats, but I didn't kill him! Even if I wanted to, when could I have done it? We had lunch together today, George, don't you remember?'

Kailis cleared his throat.

'She did have the motive, that is true. But as she asks, when and how? No. I believe the person responsible for placing the hemlock in

126

the tea is our mysterious gardener, who came into the kitchen looking for water, then disappeared. But I believe he is now in this room.'

He turned and stood with his arms folded staring at Cotter.

'Look at this rash on your chin, and the red blemish above your top lip. They are fresh, a reaction to the adhesive you used to fix the fake beard to your face.'

The rest of Cotter's face flushed the same shade as the irritated areas and he shrank into his chair.

'And although hemlock is not a plant native to these shores, there is some growing in the university greenhouse, is there not? Part of a foolhardy plan to release it into the wild in a bid to curb the rabbit problem.'

He pointed to Cotter's hands, which were balled into fists.

'Would you remove your gloves, Professor? They are an odd accoutrement for such a casual occasion on a very warm day.'

Slowly he did so. Both hands were covered in a bright red rash.

'You need to be careful when harvesting and drying hemlock, Professor. As a classics professor you couldn't resist the symbolism of this particular poison, the deadly brew Socrates drank when he was sentenced to death by the pompous Athenian elders for corrupting the youth. Walter was "corrupting the youth" with his Socialism. Then there were the other rumours.

'Once Millie had voiced her suspicions about Walter and George to her father, Sir Bartholomew, he threatened to withdraw his very generous annual gift to the university, an act that would have grave consequences for the university's coffers and might well have provoked similar actions from other donors.

'Walter told me of your request that he tender his resignation for the good of the university. He, of course was tenured, and had no intention of leaving, which put you in the position of being forced to move publicly to remove him from his position—and attract much attention from our ferocious free press.'

Cotter, clearly seething, moved towards the door but Kailis blocked him again while James and Will circled, ready to grab him if necessary.

'No, Professor, I think we need to have you in our keep until the detectives have time to inspect your lodgings, whereupon they will find evidence of your raid upon the university glasshouse and your perfunctory disguise.'

'You killed him to save your job?' I asked Cotter, my voice trembling.

Kailis shook his head. 'Not just the job. Walter had invited you all here to celebrate his invitation to speak at the Royal Archaeological Society, an honour his mentor never received. Walter was inadvertently set to outshine not only Cotter's current standing but his past achievements too.'

'He was shaming us all, with his careless indiscretions and his radical politics,' Cotter shouted. 'He was corrupting young minds, he was a menace.'

Millie leapt to her feet and strode to stand by Cotter's side. 'He's right. But Mr Kailis, we needn't tell any of this to the police. Walter shamed my beloved, shamed me and disgraced his position. The scandal will cast a shadow over us all.'

Kailis sighed. 'No, Miss Pierce, the shame is elsewhere. We are free people living in a supposedly free society and yet so many of us must conceal who we are.'

The silence broke with the echo of the heavy brass door knocker landing on cedar once more and a few moments later Margie entered the room.

'The detectives are here, sir.'

The Roman in the Fountain
Ron Fein

Joshua the Seer, a slight young man with a disappointing beard, crossed the vineyards of an estate overlooking the ruins of Jerusalem and the fires of the Roman army camp below. When he reached a portly Roman officer waiting outside the villa, he dropped a heavy cedar box, exhaled in relief, and sneezed.

'Sorry,' he said in Greek, the empire's common language. 'A spring cold—all this pollen. Otherwise, a fine morning to you!'

The Roman scowled down at Joshua. 'It's bloody well not fine. Last night, the master of the house drowned in his own fountain.'

'Yes, of course, that's why I'm here.' Joshua bowed with a flourish. 'Joshua the Seer, at your service.'

'Marcus Scandilius Rufus. The governor's law officer dispatched me to investigate the death.' He scrutinized Joshua with distaste. 'I must confess, I expected someone more senior.'

'And I must confess I've never divined for Romans.'-

'Not my choice. I've never hired a Jewish seer before. An Egyptian, once. Greeks, from time to time. But we can't get the bloody Pythia out here in Judaea, so you'll have to do.' He pivoted and swept toward the villa's entrance.

With some difficulty, Joshua lifted his box and followed. 'Do you suspect foul play?'

Rufus shrugged. 'The simplest explanation is usually correct. Decimus Junius Silanus wasn't the first gentleman to drink to excess, stumble, and fall. However, I'm obliged to conduct an inquiry.'

'I assure you, I am versed in not only the Jewish arts of sight, but also the Greek and Egyptian sciences. Whatever—or whoever—caused the gentleman's untimely death, the Holy One will reveal in time.'

'I hope so. If you prove to be a charlatan, I'll recommend your

129

execution.'

Joshua swallowed.

Cypress branches, signifying a Roman house of mourning, surrounded the villa's double oaken doors. 'You're entering the estate of a patrician Roman family,' Rufus warned. 'Silanus and his wife were supposed to host an engagement for their daughter tonight. Instead, the family members and their guests are preparing for a funeral. Tread carefully.' He opened the doors.

An atrium conveyed them to a lush garden. On three sides, a walkway framed with peristyle columns enclosed the garden; a graceful fountain provided a cooling mist. Near the fountain stood a rough wooden bier, and atop it, a man's body.

Joshua cocked his head toward the bier. 'May I?'

'Respectfully.'

Joshua eased his box down and gently examined the deceased, a male in his late forties. He'd been cleaned and dressed in his toga, but he looked terrible—even for a corpse. Consistent with drowning, the body was bloated. Other insults included a purplish bruise besmirching his forehead, red welts on his skin, a swollen tongue, and stiff rigor mortis. Joshua murmured a quiet blessing.

'Was he facing up or down in the fountain?' Joshua asked.

'Ask the prefect.'

'The who?'

'The legionary camp prefect. A distinguished officer—he received silver armillae for valiant service in the battle of Jerusalem. Retired, naturally, with extensive holdings in Galilee. He's here for the engagement—and he found the body last night.'

Joshua knelt and traced his hands across the marble tile beside the fountain. 'I just thought,' he said, 'these scuff marks—'

'Let's get on with it,' urged Rufus. 'What do you need? Dice? Candles?'

'No. But the divination process can be unsettling. So first, I should pay my respects to the family.'

Rufus sighed. 'They're finishing up their prandium. After me.'

They crossed the garden to a doorway curtained by a light wool tapestry. Rufus coughed, waited a moment, and drew the curtain aside.

Inside, three women in black mourning dress lounged on couches surrounding a central table. A platter bore the remains of their lunch: white bread, herb cheese, and salted fish.

Rufus exchanged a few words in Latin with the ladies, then switched to Greek and made introductions: Claudia, the widow, in her late thirties, with a sharp nose and almond eyes; Junia, her daughter, a pale girl of about eighteen with tearful dark eyes and honey-colored hair; and Livinia, Claudia's mother, an elegant woman well into her fifties wearing green eyeshadow.

Joshua bowed to each in turn. 'May you be comforted, my ladies.'

Claudia nodded. 'We've been told you're some sort of oracle.'

'Not precisely, my lady. I'm a seer, trained in the art of divination.'

'I'm completely confident,' said Livinia, deadpan. 'Undoubtedly with your magic ball or whatever you will gain mystical insights into Silanus that have been denied to those of us who knew him best.'

'Mother,' interjected Claudia.

Livinia shook her off. 'Before we came to this accursed place'—Livinia drew her hand in a wide arc, as if to encompass all Judaea—'my late husband Claudius—that's Claudia's father, you understand, a difficult man, but distinguished—Silanus was just a few years behind Claudius in the course of honors, and he often dined at our house. A picky eater, but chatty, and I came to know him well, long before you were even born. So I'll listen extremely skeptically to anything you might claim to hear Silanus convey from the land of the dead.'

'Madam, you mistake me,' said Joshua. 'I do not speak to the dead, which our holy law forbids. Rather, I have brought with me'—Joshua gestured to his box—'assorted tools for permitted methods of divination, some unique to the Jews, others learned from Babylon or Egypt. First, though, I should tour the villa, to evaluate the, er, light.'

'The light?' asked Junia, the daughter, sitting up.

'For, ah, reading patterns in . . . liquids of various . . . descriptions.'

'I'll escort you,' said Rufus.

Junia leapt to her feet. 'No need; I'll take him.'

Joshua started to hoist his box, but hesitated. 'Might I leave my items here?'

Claudia shrugged.

Joshua followed Junia out into the peristyle walkway. 'I'm sorry to bother you while you're mourning.'

'No, I could use some fresh air—and a break from my mother.'

Joshua smiled. 'I understand that, before this tragedy, your family was preparing for your engagement party.'

Junia's face darkened. 'Yes.' She looked away for a long moment, then returned Joshua's gaze. 'Let's start the tour.' She opened both arms to encompass the arch-shaped villa. 'We've just been in the triclinium, our dining room, at the northwest corner. Our guest Pictor has been staying there at night—I wouldn't find it comfortable, but he's a military man and he says he's slept in far worse places.' She led him east along the corridor. 'Now, here are the four bedrooms, one after the other: the guest room, where the prefect has been staying; my grandmother's; mine; and finally, this one here is my parents'. It's the largest, naturally. If you look right, the slave girls' quarters are in the east wing.'

'How many slave girls?'

'Only two: the cook and the maid.'

'They're both in today?'

'The cook, but not the maid. My mother gave her the day off.' Junia averted her eyes. 'Mother hoped not to have people rustling around the villa while we're mourning.'

Joshua ignored the remark. 'Where do the male slaves sleep?'

'Out at the farm quarters. Father would never allow male slaves in the villa at night with his daughter and wife.'

'Why not?'

'Imagine one of us got peckish late at night, so we visited the kitchen for a snack, and a male slave was feeling a bit rowdy.'

Joshua tripped and sprawled onto the floor. 'Excuse me,' he mumbled.

'Are you okay?'

'Fine, thanks.' He studied the marble by his right hand for a moment before standing. 'It's hard to keep tile floors in tip-top shape, isn't it?'

'I beg your pardon?'

'Nothing.' He wiped his hands on his tunic and nodded toward her room. 'It must have been so distressing for you last night. You'd just settled into bed when you learned of your father's accident.'

'Actually, I hadn't gone to bed yet—I'd just returned from the bathhouse. Now let's see how the light falls in the other wing.' They walked back toward the dining room at the northwest corner, then Junia pointed southward toward the west wing. 'There's the kitchen, and beyond that the larder.'

Joshua craned his neck toward a colonnade leading westward, beyond the villa's main arch. 'Where does that breezeway go?'

'A few minutes' walk west to the bathhouse and an adjacent shed. The light by the bathhouse is magnificent. Say, here's the prefect—and Pictor.'

Two men in white linen tunics approached from the breezeway. One was tall, young, and muscular, with a mop of tousled brown hair. The other was old, bent, and limping, with a short haircut several emperors out of style.

Junia gave a shy smile. 'Good morning, gentlemen. This is Joshua the Jew. He'll—well, I'm not sure how he'll do it, but he'll discern how father died.'

The older man nodded to Joshua. 'Brilliant. I found Silanus last night. Tragic.'

'Tragic,' agreed Joshua. 'When did you find him?'

'About nine. I was in my room reading when I heard a loud splash.'

'So you ran out instantly.'

'Well, not quite instantly,' the prefect confessed. 'It took me some minutes to arise from bed. Straighten my tunic and so forth. I don't get around as quickly as I once did. Miss Junia and I had gone for a long walk in the vineyards yesterday before dinner, and I must admit, my legs were beyond weary—not to mention the ruined knee.'

'A war injury,' added the younger man. 'By the way, I'm Titus Fabius Pictor.'

Joshua bowed. 'Such misfortune to encounter as a guest, when you've only been here for—?'

'Two nights,' finished Pictor. 'I'm a military tribune with the Tenth Legion, but I visit often. Well, not often enough.' His cheeks flushed, then he composed himself. 'I'll return to the camp once arrangements have been made.'

'Of course. I assume you were with the prefect when he heard the splash.'

'No.' Pictor furrowed his brow. 'After dinner, everyone but me left the dining room. I stayed—I've been sleeping there on my visit. I heard the splash, but I assumed some innocent explanation. When I heard the prefect shout, I came running.'

'Ah.' Joshua turned to the prefect. 'You called immediately after you came outside.'

The prefect blinked. 'Not immediately. I stepped into the corridor, and Miss Junia called to me.'

Joshua turned to Junia. 'You were coming from the bathhouse?'

She hesitated, then nodded. 'I was about where we're standing now. I'd passed my grandmother a few moments before—she was heading toward the bathhouse as I was leaving it. I saw the prefect over there'—she pointed vaguely toward the prefect's room—'and called out to greet him. We chatted for a few minutes about this and that.'

'But,' said Joshua, 'this was before the prefect shouted for help.'

'Right before,' confirmed the prefect. 'After speaking with Miss Junia, I returned to the garden—and saw Silanus, may the gods have mercy, lying in the fountain, staring blankly at the stars.'

'Why are you asking all these questions?' asked Junia. 'Are they necessary for the divination?'

'Oh, no.' Joshua smiled. 'The Holy One supplies the answers to the important questions. I'm simply curious.'

A brief silence passed.

'Pictor,' said Joshua, 'would you show me the kitchen?'

'The kitchen?'

Joshua's index finger traced an uncertain figure in the air. 'One of my spells will require the use of certain, ah, birds.'

'Birds?' repeated the prefect.

'Yes, birds. An Egyptian technique.'

Pictor clapped him hard on the shoulder. 'Afraid I can't help you, old man. I've never been in the kitchen. Not a military man's domain, if you gather my drift.'

'My apologies. Lady Junia, would you be so kind?'

Junia and Joshua entered the kitchen, where the cook slave stood working with her back to the door. Junia clapped twice.

The slave spun around and bowed. She was around Junia's age, with slender eyebrows, caramel skin, and dark curly hair struggling

134

to escape a clasp at the nape of her neck. 'Yes, milady?'

'This man needs birds.'

'Birds, milord?'

'Pigeons would be ideal,' Joshua clarified.

'I'm afraid we haven't any, milord.'

He sighed. 'Let's see what else you've got. Have you any fowl?'

'Not anymore, milord. They ate it last night at dinner.'

'You didn't save any?'

'Sorry, milord. The family don't eat a heavy breakfast.'

'What about vinegar?'

'We've a bit, milord, but not much. I need it for tonight's dinner.'

'Honey, then?'

'Pardons, milord, the gods ain't smiled on your timing. We're fresh out.'

Joshua's shoulders slumped. 'You're out of honey?'

The slave nodded sadly. 'Milord, that is, milord of the house—the one what's as deceased'—Joshua encouraged her with vigorous nodding—'he loves him some honey. Milady the grandmother came last night as I was bringing out the tarts platter, right where you're standing, and she asked me to fetch more honey. I gave it to her, and she poured all what was left onto the tarts.'

'Where was the honey?'

She turned around and pointed to an empty glass jar behind her.

'Completely out of honey,' repeated Joshua. 'I don't suppose you have any cloves?'

'I do, milord, if you likes 'em whole. I can't find my mortar and pestle.'

'Not ideal,' said Joshua, 'not ideal. Well, there's a Persian mixture I can use instead. I'll need cardamom, almonds, pistachios, and rose petals.'

'Sounds delicious,' Junia said.

Joshua leveled his eyes at her. 'It's for a divination potion, not a pastry.'

'Forgive me, milord,' said the slave girl, 'but we never buy cardamom. Too precious. And milord of the house didn't never want no almonds or pistachios, so we don't got them neither. But I could fetch some rose petals from the garden if you like?'

'No, the rose petals are pointless without the rest. One last try—

saffron?'

The girl giggled. 'Milord is jesting, I'm sure.'

'Why would I be jesting?'

She lowered her eyes. 'Begging your pardon, milord. I ain't used to men asking so many questions. Usually they give orders, or that army man . . .' She darkened. 'I'm just a little put aside.'

'Never mind, I'll develop an alternative. My lady Junia, would you conduct me back to the dining room?'

'Of course.'

In the hallway he asked, 'Is your family accustomed to eating at home seven nights a week?'

Junia sighed. 'Not my choice. Father prefers—preferred—not to eat anywhere else. We're stuck here, surrounded by Jews and poverty. So when we're invited to another Roman estate for a banquet, I'd love to go. But Father always refused.'

They'd returned to the dining room; Claudia picked listlessly at a bowl of grapes. Joshua addressed Livinia. 'My lady, a word?'

She frowned, but followed Joshua out into the garden.

'Thank you, my lady. I know this must be difficult for you, losing your son-in-law.'

Livinia nodded. 'Such a fine husband and father. But there'll be time enough for eulogies at the funeral. What's this about?'

Joshua cast his eyes downward. 'My lady, I could not help but notice you're blessed with dark, lustrous hair.'

Livinia stifled a smile. 'Go on.'

'I was just in the kitchen, seeking some ingredients I might require for the divination. Unfortunately, the slave girl told me she's quite low on vinegar.'

'I don't follow.'

Joshua reddened and stared at the floor. 'I am told, my lady, that certain Roman ladies—your contemporaries—youthful, that is, at the height of their beauty, yet having been blessed with grandchildren—'

'Let me stop you there, young man. Are you asking if I darken my hair?'

Joshua swallowed and nodded.

'Your question is impertinent.'

He closed his eyes. 'Forgive me.'

'I'm not in the mood to discuss beauty secrets, with my son-in-law lying on a bier, unless you can tell me why you're asking.'

Joshua rubbed the back of his neck. 'I've heard that a popular Roman method of dyeing the hair involves a lead comb dipped in vinegar. Since the kitchen is out, I hoped you might have some extra vinegar.'

Livinia softened. 'In that case, you're out of luck.' She leaned toward him and lowered her voice. 'I do color my hair, of course; I'm not ready to go gray. But my dye doesn't contain vinegar. I use a mixture of ashes, boiled walnut shells, and earthworms, once a week. I don't suppose that helps you?'

He gave a heavy sigh. 'I'm afraid not.'

She winked. 'Not a word about this to any of the men in the household.'

They returned to the dining room, where Junia and Claudia still reclined on their couches. Once Livinia was settled, Joshua turned to Claudia. 'My lady, I must now ask a delicate question regarding an item I'll need for the Seeing.'

Claudia narrowed her eyes. 'Proceed.'

'There is a certain, ah, Persian methodology that may be appropriate here. If your ladyship permits, I'd like to try a technique called dactylomancy.'

'I'm not familiar.'

Joshua cracked his knuckles. 'I'll borrow some locks of your hair, suspend your wedding ring from them, and make some inquiries.'

'Absolutely not!' Claudia exploded. 'This is ridiculous. My beloved husband has drowned, we haven't even completed funeral arrangements, and you want to interrogate my hair?'

Joshua flinched. 'Technically,' he said in a small voice, 'I'd be interrogating your ring.'

She glowered.

'Yes, and, ah, regrettably, the hair must be collected in a specific manner. I must remove the locks myself—in the very room you shared with your noble husband.'

'How dare you,' she seethed.

'A thousand apologies, my lady. I'll see if I can find a different method.'

'Maybe we should cancel this whole thing,' suggested Junia.

'I agree,' said Claudia. 'We don't need any fancy divination techniques. We know exactly what happened.'

Joshua frowned. 'We do?'

'My poor beloved Silanus, may the gods protect him, left dinner early, saying he felt unwell. He must have been dizzy and lightheaded. Evidently, he stumbled, fell into the fountain, and drowned.'

Junia nodded in assent. 'We'd just started the sweet course when Father left. We'd eaten the tarts—in fact, they were so delicious that Pictor ate one of Father's. But we hadn't gotten to the cheesecake, and Father loves cheesecake.' She paused. 'Rather, he loved cheesecake. So he must have felt quite ill to skip that course.'

'That makes sense,' Joshua acknowledged.

'The cheesecake?'

'No, stumbling into the fountain. That would explain the scuff marks on the tile.'

'So it's settled,' said Claudia, indicating, as a wealthy Roman lady does, that it was.

'Not quite,' said Joshua. 'Why would your lord husband cross the garden to get from the dining room to your room? The peristyle walkway is more direct.'

'He must have been disoriented.'

'What about the prominent bruise on his forehead?'

'I assume he hit his head as he fell into the fountain.'

'But the prefect found him lying face up.'

The ladies considered this in silence.

'Which suggests,' Joshua continued, 'that someone struck him in the face. A hard punch, or a blunt object.' A long pause followed. 'This casts an unfortunate pall on the household and its guests.'

Junia and Claudia exchanged an uneasy glance.

Claudia rose and removed a purple fillet of wool from her hair to loosen her bun. 'Let's get this over with. Rufus! Come with us, if you would.'

Joshua, Claudia, and Rufus started down the corridor toward the master bedroom in the villa's northeast corner. 'I apologize, my lady,' said Joshua, 'for my blunt manner. It must have been so shocking for you to hear the prefect's news when you hadn't even finished your dinners.'

'Oh, we'd finished,' said Claudia. 'Roman dinners are long, but we finished about an hour after Silanus left. I accompanied Junia to the bathhouse.'

'That's where you heard the prefect's cry of distress?'

'Not quite. I'd left the bathhouse a few minutes before Junia, and I was chatting with my mother beside the shed. Afterwards, I returned to my room. I'd just changed tunics when I heard the prefect cry out. And here we are.'

The spacious and well-appointed master bedroom centered on a bed. Joshua approached it and lightly brushed the cover with his hand. 'It appears you slept poorly last night, with your lord husband passed.'

'Actually, I didn't sleep here, or anywhere,' said Claudia. She sighed and sat on the bed. 'After the prefect found poor Silanus, none of us could sleep. So Junia and I fetched some snacks from the kitchen and we all passed the night together in the dining room.' Claudia unwrapped the last fillet and shook her hair loose. 'Let's get on with it.'

Under Rufus's watchful eye, Joshua carefully plucked three locks of Claudia's hair, while mumbling incantations.

'Do you need my wedding ring too?'

'Not yet. First, I'll assemble the apparatus. But it's rather heavy, and I'll need some help.'

'I'll send for some slaves from the fields.'

'This work is too delicate to entrust to slaves, my lady. I need someone strong, but of nobler station. Perhaps the prefect?'

Claudia chuckled. 'That old fool can barely walk. Rufus!' she commanded. 'Take the Jew to Pictor and ask him to help build his magic contraption.'

As Rufus and Joshua left the master bedroom, Joshua murmured, 'I hope Pictor isn't too distraught by the interrupted engagement.'

'Pictor?' said Rufus. 'Why would he be upset?'

'As Junia's betrothed, of course.'

Rufus chuckled. 'Don't be daft. Pictor's a solid chap, but his family sided with Domitian at the wrong time, and they're barely clinging to senatorial rank now. He simply hasn't the funds to support Junia in comfort. She's marrying the prefect, of course.'

'I see.'

139

'Now hurry it up. You've been here nearly an hour but all you've done is pluck the widow's hair and upset the family. I haven't seen one bloody entrail yet.'

They arrived at the dining room, but Pictor wasn't there—just Livinia, Junia, and the prefect. 'Wait here while I fetch Pictor,' ordered Rufus.

'With pleasure. The villa is so big—merely walking back and forth between the rooms takes so much time!' He plopped on a couch and whistled tunelessly.

'Must you do that?' snapped Livinia.

'Sorry, my lady. I'm all nerves.'

'What in Hades have you got to be nervous about?'

'My lady,' said Joshua in a hushed voice, 'certain topics are better left unspoken in such refined company.' He arched an eyebrow toward Junia.

'I don't catch your meaning.'

'Nor do I,' said the prefect.

Joshua turned to him. 'Sir—or my lord as the case may be—may I have a word?'

'If you must,' huffed the older man. He rose with difficulty and hobbled after Joshua into the corridor.

Once outside, the prefect waved his hand. 'Speak.'

'I couldn't help notice that the kitchen slave is rather attractive.'

'So?'

'Do you think his lordship—that is, the deceased, Silanus—do you think—'

'Get on it with it, boy!' reprimanded the prefect. He drew himself up to military bearing as much as his broken body allowed.

'Do you think he was, ah, taking liberties with the slave girl?'

The prefect's nostrils flared and he let out a noisy breath. 'I suggest,' he growled, 'that you avoid such despicable insinuations, if you value your life.'

'Forgive me, I'm unfamiliar with Roman customs. But—'

'What?' demanded the prefect.

'That would provide a motive.'

'You think the kitchen girl killed him to stop his advances? Come on. Too obvious.'

'You're right,' said Joshua. 'I shouldn't be making hypotheses at

140

all. My mind must be clear for the Seeing to work.'

The prefect snorted. 'I don't know about all that.'

'Not to worry, here's Pictor.' Joshua lifted his box, and they walked to the garden. Once there, Joshua began unpacking various metal bars, beams, and joints.

'What's all this?' asked Pictor.

'A divination method I learned from an Egyptian.' He tossed an iron bar to Pictor, who caught it expertly with one hand.

'Interesting,' Joshua murmured.

Pictor pointed to the bars. 'How do we put this thing together?'

Joshua straightened himself. 'I need to, ah, consult the manual, so to speak.' He rummaged in the box for a few minutes and flipped through some arcane manuscripts. Eventually, with Pictor's help, he assembled a four-foot metal tripod topped by a small hoop.

'It's ready,' said Joshua. 'Let's gather everyone for the Seeing.'

The six Romans crowded around Joshua and his strange apparatus. Joshua requested Claudia's wedding ring. He tied the strands of her hair to the ring and hung it from the hoop.

'We now begin a venerable Babylonian truth-seeking ritual,' he announced. 'Gird yourselves, for the Holy One will soon reveal all. Is everyone ready?'

After uneasy nods of assent, Joshua recited a lengthy Aramaic formula, focusing in turn on each Roman. When he finished, he translated the incantation's final line into formal Greek. 'Enlighten us, Lord, upon the truth we seek—who killed Decimus Junius Silanus!'

He gave Claudia's ring a gentle push. It revolved in a small circle, which resolved into a tight ellipse—nearly a line. Silanus's relatives and guests leaned forward in their seats as the ring continued to sway.

It came to a stop and hung dead plumb.

'What—what does it mean?' asked Junia in a hushed voice.

Joshua frowned. 'Hold on.' From the wooden box, he retrieved an oversized book of cracked yellow parchment running with tiny red and black script. He flipped through a few pages and mumbled to

141

himself.

'I don't think it's working,' said Pictor.

'You shouldn't have hired a Jew,' complained Livinia to Rufus. 'You need a proper Chaldean for this kind of job.'

Joshua squinted at a page. After a full minute, he blinked and flipped the book upside down. Claudia let out a loud sigh.

'Eastern Aramaic,' Joshua apologized, 'you know how it is.'

Rufus cleared his throat. 'Young man, are you stalling? Recall the penalty for charlatanry.'

'Oh, all right,' said Joshua. 'Look, it's obvious. I can't get the apparatus to work. It's not telling me anything.'

'I knew it!' the prefect bellowed.

Livinia snorted. 'He's a fraud!'

'However,' added Joshua, 'you don't need divination to understand what happened here. It's perfectly obvious.'

'It is?' asked Rufus.

'Perfectly!' repeated Joshua. 'In the case of the murder of his lordship Decimus Junius Silanus, the obvious suspect is—Pictor!'

Pictor's eyes widened. 'What?'

'You had motive. Silanus betrothed the lady Junia to the prefect.'

'What of it?' grumbled the prefect.

'Pictor,' said Joshua, 'is in love with Junia.' They both blushed. 'Furthermore, Silanus had a fist-sized bruise on his forehead, suggesting he was struck with a heavy object. No woman could have hit so hard. No male slaves were in the villa last night. The prefect, with all due respect'—he inclined his head—'does not have the physical strength or, frankly, adequate posture to deliver such a blow. Finally'—Joshua paused for dramatic effect and stared straight at Pictor—'you're handy with an iron bar. When I tossed it, you caught it one-handed, without hesitating.'

Pictor shook his head. 'There's been some mistake. I didn't touch Silanus.'

'You struck him in the forehead.'

'No, he was dead in the fountain when I saw him! I panicked and left.'

'A-ha!' cried Joshua. 'So you saw the body before the prefect's hue and cry.'

'Yes. I'd gone to the shed just after dinner. When I returned, I saw

142

Silanus in the fountain.'

'Earlier you said you stayed in the dining room after dinner.'

Pictor sighed. 'That wasn't true.'

Joshua folded his arms and smiled. 'So you admit you lied!'

'Bloody good work,' Rufus muttered.

Pictor nodded. 'Yes, I lied. The others—well, except Silanus, he'd left an hour earlier—they all left the dining room together at about eight-thirty. I said I was going to lie down after eating a few too many tarts for dessert. But I sneaked over to the shed, where I hoped to meet Junia. I was standing there in the shadows when I heard a loud splash.'

'You were with Junia?'

'No. She was in the bathhouse with her mother. They quarreled, and Claudia left. I saw her pass, but she didn't see me.'

Claudia swore under her breath, but Joshua proceeded. 'Did you see anyone else near the shed?'

'No. I waited for Junia to come out of the bathhouse. But a few minutes after Claudia left, I heard the splash coming from the garden. So I went to the fountain to see.'

'You lied about all this earlier,' Joshua chided.

Pictor exhaled. 'I may be a military man, but when it comes to this weird family drama, I'm as nervous as anyone else.'

Joshua smiled and put his hand on Pictor's shoulder. 'Poor Pictor. So tall, so handsome, and yet so—well, did you see anyone else in the garden?'

'Not at first. Then I heard Junia call for the prefect, and I saw him. I realized he might soon see me, so I dashed back inside the dining room for a few minutes. When the prefect called for help, I came back out.'

Joshua nodded. 'Thank you, Pictor, for being truthful. Of course, I knew it wasn't you.'

'Now wait,' said Rufus. 'You said Pictor was the murderer.'

'No, I said he was the obvious suspect. Obvious, however, does not mean guilty.'

'So why accuse me?' asked Pictor.

'It pleased the Holy One for you to admit your whereabouts. Because they incriminate the prefect.'

'Rubbish!' swore the prefect.

143

'Too often,' said Joshua, 'the person who "finds" the body is the murderer. It's a classic misdirection tactic: kill the victim, then cry for help.'

'Bollocks! I stepped into the garden when I heard the splash. After Junia and I finished speaking, I reached the fountain and found Silanus.'

'Your story, sir, contains unexplained gaps. The only evidence is that Pictor saw the dead body—and Junia saw you. Most likely, you were already in the garden when Pictor arrived, because you'd just killed Silanus. Perhaps, afterwards, you hid behind a column, because Pictor didn't see you. But Junia did.'

'Shame on you,' said Claudia to the prefect.

'What's the motive?' wondered Rufus.

Joshua cracked his knuckles. 'The family's kitchen slave is quite comely. I believe the prefect is besotted with her.' The prefect turned crimson; Junia raised a hand to her mouth. 'The slave seemed weary of an "army man," which could mean either the prefect or Pictor. When I spoke to the prefect, I deceptively implied Silanus had been imposing himself upon the girl. The prefect denied it—too fiercely, in my opinion. I don't know all your customs, but I know that no Roman would blink at a wealthy citizen conducting himself in that manner.'

Livinia sighed. 'Sad, but true. My own husband was given to such indulgences.'

'Mother!' interjected Claudia.

'For present purposes,' said Joshua, 'your late husbands' mistreatment of their slaves is immaterial, except insofar as they render the prefect's unusually hostile reaction suspect. Perhaps he sought to buy the slave, but Silanus rebuffed him; perhaps, he hoped, with Silanus gone, his bride Junia would inherit the girl, and thus she would join their new home.'

Claudia scowled at the prefect. 'I don't care about the girl. But did you kill my husband?'

'Never!' swore the prefect. He faced Joshua. 'Your own words prove my innocence. A few minutes ago, you admitted I lack the strength to deliver the strike that killed Silanus.'

'True. However, Silanus was not killed by a blow to the head.'

'He wasn't?' asked Pictor.

'His skin had welts, and his tongue was swollen. A blunt object cannot explain these.'

'Then what killed him?' demanded Rufus.

'Poison.'

A murmur spread amongst those assembled.

'But what about the bruise?' asked Junia.

'Excellent question. When I first examined the body, it appeared that his lordship had died from too many causes—drowning, a blunt strike, and poisoning.'

'Oh gracious,' said Rufus. 'Don't tell me you're going to suggest that three different people killed him in three different ways.'

'Not at all. As I've said, Silanus was poisoned. At dinner, he felt ill, and left for his room. Along the way, he became disoriented. He stumbled or shuffled toward the garden. I saw the marble tile scuffed in two different places—near his bedroom and near the fountain. Silanus made those scuff marks as he staggered, tottered, teetered—and fell into the fountain.'

'You still haven't explained the bruise,' noted Junia.

'From the fall.'

'The pieces all fit,' Rufus observed.

'No, they don't,' protested Claudia. 'When I earlier suggested that precise account—'

'Minus the poison,' interrupted Joshua.

'—you observed that Silanus was found face up, yet with a bruise on his forehead.'

'That's not the least of it!' roared the prefect. 'You claim I poisoned Silanus. But no Roman man would be caught dead anywhere near the kitchen.'

'Correct,' said Joshua. 'Pictor and the kitchen slave confirmed that.'

Rufus tilted his head. 'So you don't think the prefect did it?'

'Of course not. I just wanted to see the old man squirm. My grandparents died in the battle of Jerusalem.'

Livinia leaned toward Rufus and stage-whispered, 'I told you not to hire a Jew.'

'Now see here,' said Rufus to Joshua, 'you will give the prefect due respect and refrain from baseless accusations, or I'll have you brought up for charlatanry.'

'I'm confused,' said Pictor.

'There, there,' said Joshua. 'All will soon be clear. Only a woman could access the food, and the three noble ladies may enter the kitchen at any hour. Thus, one of them delivered the poison.'

'But which one?' asked Rufus.

'Recall,' said Joshua, 'that as soon as the prefect entered the garden, his attention was immediately diverted by—'

Pictor gasped. 'Junia?'

'Her motive is clear,' said Joshua. 'Silanus betrothed Junia to the prefect. With all proper respect to you, sir'—he bowed to the prefect but arched his eyebrows toward Rufus—'you are a gentleman of advanced years and, ah, uncertain vigors. The lady Junia is young, fine-spirited, and pretty'—Junia blushed—'and anyone with sense can see she's got eyes for someone tall, muscular, and handsome—I mean, of course, Pictor.'

Pictor blushed.

'Junia may have begged her father,' Joshua continued, 'not to force her to marry a gentleman so, er, distinguished as the prefect. Silanus, however, insisted. Rather than bewailing her virginity, her youth, and her fate, Miss Junia took matters into her own hands— with help from her lover, Pictor!'

Pictor rubbed his temples. 'I thought you cleared me.'

'You alone,' corrected Joshua. 'But working with the lady Junia—what young love will do! You and Junia together pulled it off.'

'How?' asked Rufus.

'Pictor admits he was in the garden. He conspired with his lover, the charming Miss Junia, who has free access to the kitchen and its poisons. Strong Pictor dragged the body to the fountain.' He turned to the prefect. 'After you came outside, Junia engaged you for several minutes in pointless conversation before you reached the fountain. Since you are presently of somewhat reduced mobility compared to your more rapacious days of combat service, that was all Pictor needed. He raced back to the dining room. By the time you reached the fountain, he was long gone from the garden.'

'The previous theories contained defects,' Rufus said, 'but this one seems airtight.'

'It's true,' admitted Junia, 'I deliberately distracted the prefect.'

'Aha!' said Joshua.

'And I did this precisely so he wouldn't see Pictor.'

'Precisely,' confirmed Joshua. He smiled and folded his arms.

'And we're in love.'

'Go on, go on.'

'And I'm not a virgin.' (Pictor blushed.)

'I didn't mean that,' hastened Joshua. 'I meant the murder.'

'But I did not kill Father. I loved him. And I remained in the bathhouse after Mother left. I couldn't even hear the splash from inside the bathhouse. But as I returned from the breezeway, I saw Pictor and the prefect, from a distance, before either saw the other. So I called out to the prefect, and spoke with him for a few minutes so Pictor could slip away.'

'Why?'

'I didn't want the prefect to think Pictor was meeting me for an illicit rendezvous.'

'Dear girl,' said the prefect with a pained expression, 'why did you not simply tell me that you didn't wish to marry me?'

Livinia scoffed. 'A question only a Roman man would ask.'

'Furthermore,' Junia added, 'I spent all day with the prefect in the vineyards right up until dinner.'

'Which proves,' said Joshua, 'that you lacked opportunity. Therefore, all eyes must turn to—the lady Claudia!'

'How dare you!' Claudia shouted.

Joshua chuckled. 'The wife poisoning the husband—it's the oldest story in Rome.' He gave Claudia an appraising nod. 'She did it to prevent Junia's forced marriage to the prefect.'

'How do you know?' asked Rufus.

'In the master bedroom, the bed sheets were disturbed. However, Claudia told me she didn't sleep there at all last night. But someone did.'

The assembled guests leaned forward in their seats.

Joshua clenched his teeth. 'Silanus, obviously.'

'Obviously,' agreed Rufus.

'Silanus excused himself early, stating he was ill. He made it all the way to bed, but died there from the poisoning. Claudia had been in the baths with Junia. On some pretext of an argument, she left early, hurried back to the bedroom, and confirmed her husband's death.'

'Lies!' cried Claudia.

'She dragged his body to the fountain, scuffing the tile. Then she heaved him in.'

'Mother!' moaned Junia.

'To cover this up, Claudia created a false alibi. She claimed that after leaving the bathhouse, she conversed with Livinia at the shed. But Pictor has confirmed that he was at the shed. He watched Claudia leave minutes before the splash—and no one else was there!'

'This theory makes more sense,' said Rufus.

Claudia leveled an icy gaze upon Joshua. 'It does nothing of the sort. Your timeline proves you wrong. It takes quite some time to walk across the villa; the shed is even further.'

'So?'

'Pictor saw me leave just minutes before the splash. There wasn't time for me to go all the way to the bedroom, pull a full-grown man from bed, drag him as dead weight across the garden, and heave him into the fountain.'

'Which is why,' announced Joshua, 'it is plainly obvious that Silanus was murdered by—the lady Livinia!'

'You're just using process of elimination!' accused Livinia.

'Not at all, madam,' said Joshua. 'All the pieces fit together. You were, begging your forgiveness, yourself married to a difficult man. I would hazard your own father arranged your marriage against your will.'

Livinia darkened.

'You pitied your granddaughter,' Joshua continued. 'You didn't want Junia forced into marrying the doddering old prefect.'

'I say!' the prefect objected.

Joshua kept his eyes on Livinia. 'So you poisoned Silanus. His death meant no one would force Junia to marry the prefect. Later, you dragged Silanus's body into the fountain.'

Livinia laughed. 'But that's absurd! You conceded that my daughter Claudia couldn't drag her husband's lifeless body to the fountain. I'm spry, but I'm not stronger than my daughter.'

'Maybe Pictor helped,' offered Rufus.

'No,' said Joshua. 'Claudia did.'

148

'Impossible!' said Claudia. 'You yourself said so!'

Joshua smiled. 'After arguing with Junia, Claudia left the bathhouse. She was returning to her bedroom when she saw Livinia struggling with a dead body. Realizing what had happened, and that nothing more was to be done but hide the crime, Claudia helped Livinia drag Silanus to the fountain. The dragging made the scuff marks I saw on the tile. They dumped the body into the fountain around nine o'clock. Most of you heard a loud splash.'

'Lies!' said Livinia. 'After Claudia left the bathhouse, she and I chatted near the shed.'

'You two concocted that alibi to explain your whereabouts between eight-thirty and nine. But you didn't know Pictor was at the shed. He contradicted your story.'

Claudia scoffed. 'You have nothing to place my mother or me at the garden. Not one person claims to have seen us there before the prefect's call for help.'

'You each left quickly and went your separate ways—Livinia toward the bathhouse, where Junia passed her, and you, my lady Claudia, to your room to change. I suspect you'd both gotten wet from tossing his lordship's body into the pool. Junia couldn't hear the splash from inside the bathhouse, and the prefect took several minutes getting outside. Meanwhile, Pictor arrived first, but you'd already left. So when the prefect shouted for help and you two returned to the fountain, no one knew you'd been there just minutes earlier.'

Livinia smirked. 'This entire fanciful tale makes no sense. If I'd poisoned my son-in-law, why would I take the elaborate effort to drag his body from his bed to the fountain?'

'That's the flaw in your theory,' said Rufus. 'If Silanus died in bed, a poisoner would leave him there until he was discovered—not move the body.'

'The particular poison led to a distinctive appearance of the victim. The poisoner Livinia and her accomplice Claudia moved the body to the pool to create confusion about how Silanus died—to imply he'd fallen and drowned.'

'Then what, pray tell, caused the bruise on his forehead?'

'Their ladyships dragged him to the fountain face down—and inadvertently dropped his face on the marble tile.'

Livinia forced a dry laugh. 'Your story is quite persuasive, but for one key fact: my daughter Claudia ate the exact same dinner as Silanus, from the very same plate.'

The assembled relatives and guests murmured quiet assent; Junia spoke up to explain. 'You've seen the dining room, with its three couches. Mother and Father shared the central couch—and shared a plate.'

'In other words,' said the prefect, 'your entire theory is absurd. Silanus cannot have been poisoned at all. Claudia ate from his plate, and she's alive and well.'

'So she is,' agreed Joshua. 'That's because the poison—wasn't a poison!'

Joshua let that sink in before continuing. 'Livinia was in the kitchen last night before Silanus died. The cook slave told us that Livinia came and poured honey on the tarts.'

'Father did love his honey,' said Junia.

'But honey obviously did not kill Silanus; he repeatedly consumed it without ill effects.'

'Thus proving,' said Livinia, 'that my sweetening the tarts had nothing to do with my son-in-law's tragic death.'

Joshua met Junia's eyes. 'The slave kept the honey in a jar at the rear of the kitchen. To reach it, she had to turn her back on Livinia.' Junia nodded. 'That gave Livinia the opportunity to add the poison.'

'But I still don't understand,' said Pictor. 'Claudia ate Silanus's food, and she's fine.' His eyes widened. 'Great Jupiter, I myself ate a tart from Silanus's plate.'

'In fact, you all ate it—Livinia added it to all the tarts. As I said, the poison wasn't exactly a poison. To the contrary, it's perfectly safe for most people. Yet it was toxic to Silanus.'

'You're speaking in riddles,' said Claudia.

Joshua addressed Junia. 'Do you recall when I asked the slave girl about cloves, and she reported her mortar and pestle were missing?'

Junia nodded.

'Well, there it is.' He folded his arms in triumph.

'Er—what is?' asked the prefect.

'Oh, come now. It's plain to anyone with half a brain.'

'Now see here, young man,' chided the prefect, 'I've endured much abuse through your little speech, and I won't be condescended to. What in Hades are you driving at?'

'Forget the old codger's dignity,' said Livinia. 'You've accused a Roman matron of a crime; you'd better make yourself clear.'

Joshua threw his hands up in exasperation. 'Fine. I'll lay it for you like a bunch of R—er, respectable gentlepeople.'

They all leaned forward with anticipation. Pictor crossed and uncrossed his legs; Junia covered her face and peeked through her fingers.

'I grew suspicious when I learned the kitchen's mortar and pestle were missing. I realized that the lady Livinia must have "borrowed" them to grind something into fine dust. She asked the kitchen slave for honey. While the girl's back was turned, Livinia sprinkled the poison-that-is-not-a-poison onto everyone's tarts. Once the girl gave her the honey, Livinia added it to the tarts as well. The honey misdirected the girl, created an alibi for Livinia's presence in the kitchen, and probably overpowered the taste.'

'The taste of what?' asked Rufus.

Joshua sighed. 'Look, this is elementary. When I examined his lordship's body, I noticed red welts and a swollen tongue. These are signs of—I'm not sure how to say it in Greek. It's well described in Jewish medical scrolls, but perhaps it hasn't yet made its way into Western medicine. You are familiar, I trust, with how a wasp killed the Egyptian Pharaoh Menes?'

The Romans all nodded.

'For most people, a wasp sting hurts, but doesn't kill. But the Pharaoh had a different reaction. So it was with Silanus. He had a different and dangerous reaction to an ordinary foodstuff.'

'A reaction to what?' demanded Rufus.

'An item that Silanus would have never allowed into his kitchen, but which was present in the house for other purposes.'

Rufus jumped to his feet and shook his hands. 'Spit it out!'

Joshua smiled. 'Livinia poisoned Silanus with—walnuts!'

'Walnuts?' repeated Rufus.

'Harmless to most, but deadly to Silanus. He must have realized his susceptibility years ago, but he guarded the secret carefully. He could control the ingredients in his own kitchen, and to Junia's distress, he rarely ate outside home. But when he was younger, and his career and ambitions required that he dine elsewhere, he often ate

151

at his future in-laws' house in Rome. Livinia noted he was a picky eater; she must have learned his vulnerability then.'

'Just as the poet Lucretius wrote,' said Claudia. '"What is food to one, is to others bitter poison."'

'How did you determine it?' asked Junia.

'When I arrived, you were finishing lunch. From your remainders, I learned that wheat, dairy, and fish are served here. However, when I asked the kitchen girl about almonds or pistachios, she said the kitchen doesn't stock them—his lordship never wanted them.'

'I thought he just didn't like them,' said Junia.

'Wait,' said Pictor, 'I thought you said walnuts.'

'They have similar properties,' explained Joshua. 'What puzzled me was how tree nuts would enter the household at all. Then I learned that Livinia enjoys a regular and ample supply of walnuts. She uses a mixture containing boiled walnut shells to—'

'Stop right there,' interrupted Livinia. 'Some matters are better left undisclosed.'

Junia gave Livinia a watery gaze. 'Is all this true, Grandmother?'

Livinia smoothed her tunic. 'Your mother and I implored your father to let you marry Pictor. But he insisted that marrying the prefect was best for your future.'

Junia turned to Claudia. 'Last night, in the bathhouse, I begged you to call it off.'

'The pater familias had made his decision,' said Claudia. 'Evidently, however, your grandmother had other designs.'

Livinia started to respond, but Rufus interrupted. 'I am impelled to admit, the Jew's theory has some merit. Obviously, none of this would stand up in a Roman court of law. But I'd be obligated to report these suggestions to the law officer, who would launch a more comprehensive investigation on the governor's behalf.'

'Forget all that,' Livinia said. 'Just torture the kitchen slave until she confesses she added ground walnuts to the tarts.'

'No,' said Junia in a sharp tone. Everyone turned to her in surprise. 'I won't have that poor girl tortured.'

Livinia narrowed her eyes. 'I did it for you, my dear—so you should not suffer, as I suffered, in an unhappy marriage.'

'I appreciate your care, but I can't forgive you for murdering Father.'

'Also,' Joshua suggested to Livinia in a low voice, 'it might have been smarter to poison the groom.'

The prefect sputtered, 'In my day—'

Rufus cleared his throat. 'Further investigation would necessarily include both the alleged murderer and her alleged accomplice after the fact'—he bowed toward Claudia—'which could cause some discomfort to the family from the negative publicity, and with a young woman of marriageable age and a pristine reputation—'

Livinia sighed and raised her hand. 'Say no more, Rufus. My time is over; I see that now. But I request one last day. In the morning, we'll bury Silanus; in the evening, we'll celebrate my granddaughter's wedding to Pictor. Before the night is done, I'll greet Charon on the banks of the River Styx. Assuming, that is, you can delay your report another day?'

Rufus bowed.

Livinia granted Joshua a bitter smile. 'Congratulations on your cleverness.'

'Indeed,' said Rufus, 'your powers of observation, inference, and deduction have proven quite impressive.'

'That's kind of you,' Joshua replied, 'but I'm still upset the divination didn't work!'

The Lunt
S. B. Watson

The first to arrive at the scene was Police Constable Hector Mackenzie. PC Mackenzie telegraphed Detective Sergeant Alex Chisholm, at Inverness HQ. Chisholm, in turn, phoned Glasgow for backup detectives, and then called local to Invergarry Station, where he spoke to PC Roderick Kennedy, and told him to fetch Dougal Grieve.

And so it happened that one wet, January afternoon, PC Kennedy drove his battered police Wolsey down the mucky country roads to Achnadarag Manor, on the banks of Loch Arkaig, with Grieve in the passenger seat.

Grieve fought at Mons and the Aisne. He saw the great Race to the Sea, the week-long bombardment of the Somme, and the abyssal mud plains of Passchendaele. The war ended for Grieve at the Sambre Canal, where German gunners shot his right leg out from beneath him. How he came to consult for the Inverness-Shire Constabulary in the two years since the war was anybody's guess—rumours were plenteous, facts were few. In the end, the man's results spoke for him, clearly marked in the county police records. When DS Chisolm was stumped, before resigning a case to the ringers from Glasgow, he called for Grieve.

Grieve looked out the window as Kennedy drove, watching the winter-nude countryside crawl past, obstinately puffing on a thorny pipe that filled the cab with stinging, burlap-scented smoke. Grieve was a big man, heavy in the chest and arms, with a thick neck and fiery-red muttonchops and whiskers. A dark flat cap was planted on his head, and he wore a faded tweed suit beneath a wool jacket that draped loosely across his enormous shoulders. Between his knees a blackthorn walking stick was propped, which he held in rough, scarred hands.

PC Kennedy choked in the roiling smoke as he pulled off the high road and onto the gravel drive into the Achnadarag Estate. 'For the love of God, man, open the window...'

Achnadarag Manor sat about a half-mile from Loch Arkaig in a rolling field of old oaks. The house itself was very old, built from ancient, white-weathered stone. Originally, it consisted of a single structure, stretching east-to-west, constructed in the late 17th century. Later, two small wings were added, like the bottom and top feet of a capital 'E,' reaching northward towards the loch.

PC Mackenzie met them as they drove into the circular driveway in front of the sheer south face of the manor. A white medical van was already parked nearby. Above them, the manor house loomed sharp and austere against the cold grey skies.

'Hello Hector,' Grieve muttered comfortably as he climbed from the car, planting his blackthorn stick firmly into the gravel and offering an enormous left hand for a shake. 'Kennedy tells me you've got a murder on your hands.'

'Hello Mr Grieve,' Mackenzie replied, watching his hand disappear into Grieve's gargantuan paw. 'Aye, that we do.'

'Who was killed?'

'The laird, Logan McDiarmid.'

Grieve shrugged and grumbled under his breath, smoke burbling in silky streams from his pipe. 'When did it happen?'

Mackenzie pulled a small watch from the pocket of his dark wool jacket. 'About two hours ago.'

'How many people are we dealing with?' Grieve asked, as Mackenzie turned and led them towards the western corner of the manor house. Grieve leaned heavily against the blackthorn stick with every step of his right leg, which moved stiffly.

'Nine,' Mackenzie said. 'Bella McDiarmid, the laird's new wife of a week. Catherine Ross, his nurse. An out-of-towner, Robert Griffiths—an old friend of Bella's from London, apparently. Then two cooks, a husband and wife; two maids; the head butler; and the gardener, Shuggy MacLeod. Not counting our doctor, and his assistant.'

'And where is everyone keeping, now?' Grieve asked.

'I have them all confined to their rooms. We should be the only ones moving about. Doctor Mulliner's waiting to remove the body once you've seen it.'

'What exactly happened, Hector?' Grieve asked.

Mackenzie turned back as they walked and gave Grieve a strange look. 'I'll give you a summary after you've seen the body,' he said.

They walked along the wall of the manor's western wing. Oaks stretched away from them in the meadowland of the estate, their naked black trunks and mossy boughs dotting the landscape. In the distance, Loch Arkaig lay below the hills, placidly reflecting the overcast skies.

Mackenzie led them away from the manor, towards a large, artificial mound that rose from the earth, breaking the flat landscape.

The Mound had been a facet of Achnadarag for longer than the manor house. Nobody knew its purpose, or who built it. From side to side, The Mound was nearly seventy feet wide, and perfectly circular, rising gently to a height of sixteen feet. For at least a hundred years the McDiarmids had maintained a garden on the feature, bordering its base with shale stones. At the peak, a plateau had been formed, with a small pergola. Boxwood-lined paths spiralled towards this peak, which was crowned with three tall privet hedges, pruned into perfect blocks, triangularly surrounding the pergola like ancient dolmens.

The doctor stood with his assistant at the base of The Mound, smoking cigarettes.

Mackenzie gestured for Grieve and Kennedy to follow. At the base of The Mound, he stepped over the shale border and moved directly up the incline, ignoring the paths by stepping over the boxwoods. Grieve followed him slowly, forced to favour his leg over the low shrubs.

Mackenzie waited for Grieve and Kennedy at the top. 'There he is,' he said as they reached him, pointing into the shadows beneath the pergola.

Puffing on his pipe, Grieve walked into the little shelter, stepping between the towering privets.

Logan McDiarmid was slumped in his wheelchair, leaning slightly backwards in the seat, his head dropped onto his chest,

156

glassy eyes looking sightlessly out across the parkland that stretched away from the manor down to the loch. His right hand had pulled his tartan blanket roughly across his body, dragging it over his lap and dropping it over the right side of the chair. In his left hand was a pipe, the bowl cold and ashen. His cardigan was bunched and twisted around his shoulders, but open across his chest, revealing the bullet hole punched into the white shirt. From the hole, blood had spilled down across his stomach. It was all dry now, hardened and wine-dark.

Grieve leaned in closer to the body, looking at the bullet hole.

'Did he die from this?' he asked.

Mackenzie nodded. 'Doctor Mulliner can't officially declare it yet, of course, but almost certainly. Looks like the bullet struck him just at the base of the left lung. Either drowning on blood in the lung, or blood loss, or internal damage…' Mackenzie shrugged.

'Do we know the caliber?'

'Not yet. Mulliner will take the body when you're done. We'll know tomorrow.'

Grieve took the pipe from his lips and pointed with the stem around the bullet hole. 'This looks like powder burn.'

'I already noted it,' Mackenzie said. 'It appears Logan was shot at point-blank range.'

Grieve blew the lingering smoke from his mouth, and spat into the border of the privets. 'Take this a moment,' he said to Kennedy, handing him his pipe. Reaching out he pulled McDiarmid's pipe from the cold fingers and gently tapped the layer of loose ash from the top. Carefully, he sniffed the remaining tobacco.

'A custom blend,' Grieve said, slowly passing the bowl beneath his nose. 'Heavy on the Orientals, Latakia, some bright leaf…' Grieve carefully laid the pipe on the dead man's lap, with a certain air of melancholy. 'Alright, Hector,' he said, sighing as he turned back around. 'Explain.'

Mackenzie pulled his police book from his pocket. 'This morning, at 11:30, Catherine Ross, Logan's nurse, wheeled him up here to smoke. This was a regular morning ritual. After he was situated, she returned to her room and got a book, which she brought back outside. Come here,' he said, moving to the edge of the plateau, just outside the circle of the privets. 'While she was gone, Shuggy MacLeod

157

rolled up that wheelbarrow you see there, full of shale, and began de-turfing the grass. They're putting in a stone path to The Mound.' Mackenzie pointed to where a wheelbarrow sat abandoned in the grass.

Mackenzie swung his finger to another spot. 'Miss Ross moved to that location, where she spread a blanket, and began to read. It was sunnier, this morning. Now turn this way…'

Grieve and Kennedy moved out of the way for Mackenzie to walk around the plateau, and point to yet another spot in the grass. 'Griffiths, Bella's visitor, had meanwhile walked to that spot, and was standing, facing towards us.'

Mackenzie looked at Grieve. 'Do you see the significance of this?' he asked.

Grieve swivelled around briefly, considering each of the three locations, the smoke from his pipe curling up into the brim of his cap. 'Each person's view of Logan was obstructed, unluckily, by the privets.'

'Exactly,' said Mackenzie. 'However, each person had a clear line of site on the two others. Like the points on a triangle, with The Mound in the middle.'

Grieve nodded.

'Minutes after Ross laid out her blanket and sat down, she heard a gunshot.'

'From The Mound?' Grieve asked.

'No,' said Mackenzie. He moved back across the plateau and pointed towards the house. 'From there.'

'The manor?'

Mackenzie nodded. 'Yes. She said it was unmistakable. So much so that Shuggy immediately stood up and looked towards the manor, and Griffiths came around The Mound from his position, to look as well. After a moment of confusion, they all moved into the courtyard, there, and were met by Bella, who was rushing out of the manor. She said she heard the shot from the house, as well, but coming from the opposite direction, near The Mound. Unsure what to do, they came back to The Mound and found Logan, freshly shot and dying. He expired right there, before their eyes.'

'You say Ross, Shuggy, and Griffiths could all see each other when the shot was fired.'

'Yes.'

'And they all heard the shot coming from the manor. From the side of the courtyard farthest away from The Mound?'

'That is correct,' said Mackenzie. 'There's more. It's the reason we climbed The Mound from the side we did...'

Mackenzie moved carefully back to the side of The Mound facing away from the manor. The ground was wetter there, and the earth on that side was slightly damp. A clear trail of footprints ascended from the grass to the pergola, depressing the ground and in places splitting the boxwoods.

'These prints pass near the place where Griffiths was standing,' Mackenzie said.

Grieve's eyes narrowed. 'But Griffiths saw nobody pass him?'

Mackenzie nodded. 'Yes. And, since he was within view of Ross and Shuggy the whole time, they corroborate his story. In fact, they all corroborate each other. Perfectly.' Mackenzie pulled a small piece of squared paper from the breast pocket of his police jacket and handed it to Grieve. 'Here,' he said. 'I drew this up while I waited for you to arrive, in case you had any trouble visualizing the situation.'

Grieve puffed on the thorny pipe, drawing weaker and weaker plumes of smoke, tamping the ashes in the bowl with his forefinger. The ember in the bowl was beginning to die. With a sigh, Grieve folded the sketch and put it in the pocket of his jacket, removing a box of matches from the same pocket. He struck one across his knee. The match flared as he raised it to the stummel. Gingerly, he sucked the flame down into the bowl, billowing great puffs of smoke that rose and hung in the still highlands air.

'He called it his "morning lunt,"' Catherine Ross said.

They sat in the formal dining room, Grieve, Mackenzie, and Kennedy along one side of a long oak table, Catherine Ross across from them, in a soft white dress and a linen shawl. The dining room windows stretched out behind her. Outside, they could see the courtyard between the West and East Wings of the manor. In the distance, The Mound could barely be seen beyond the edge of the

159

West Wing.

Kennedy typed notes on a small, military-grey typewriter as they spoke.

'His "lunt", you say?' Grieve asked.

'It's an old word,' Ross said. 'Means, 'to walk and smoke.' When he was younger, Mr McDiarmid used to lunt across all these highlands that belong to Achnadarag. After he returned from the war, with his legs, and all… It was a bit of a joke, you see. My wheeling him out in the morning, to sit and smoke, was the closest to his old lunting days he could get.'

'You are Mr Griffiths, correct?' Grieve asked.

'Yes,' Griffiths said. He was a young man, with short cropped hair, lean, wearing a fitted white shirt, beige suspenders, light-coloured trousers and Italian-leather dress shoes. His skin was darkened by sun, and nicked with small scars here and there.

'You served in The War?' Grieve asked.

Griffiths shook his head. 'No,' he said.

'Ah,' said Grieve.

The grandfather clock in the corner softly chimed the half-hour.

'Are you and Bella having sex?' Grieve asked, suddenly.

Griffiths' jaw fell open and for a moment a blank look swept across his face. 'Of course not,' he finally hissed.

'When were Bella and Logan married?'

Griffiths shook his head and shrugged angrily. 'A week ago. I couldn't make the wedding… Business… But they invited me to stay with them anyway, since I would have been a few days late.'

'And you say, Shuggy, you could see both Mr Griffiths, and Catherine Ross, the whole time?'

'Easily,' Shuggy MacLeod said, his Highlands accent thick. He was an older man, bent from years of manual labor, his long white beard yellowed from tobacco. 'Miss Ross is hard to miss, you know, as she cut such a fine picture, there, on the grass, with her book…'

'What exactly was Griffiths doing, where he stood?'

Shuggy leaned back in the chair, and scratched his beard. Finally, he shook his head. 'I canna rightly say, Mr Grieve.'

'He was just standing there?'

'Aye.'

'And nobody moved past him, while he stood there?'

'Nae.'

'Mr Griffiths, when you stood near The Mound, did anyone move past you?'

Griffiths shook his head. 'No.'

'And there is no way you could have missed anyone?'

Griffiths tossed his hands in the air. 'Are you a fool?'

Smoke from Grieve's pipe slowly curled up into the room. 'Please answer the question, Mr Griffiths.'

'There is no way I could have missed someone moving past me.'

'Where did you hear the shot come from, Miss Ross?'

Ross thought for a moment, her eyes moving down into her lap. 'It could only have come from the courtyard.'

'Whereabouts?' Grieve asked.

Ross turned in her seat, and pointed through the windows towards the intersection of the main building and the East Wing. 'There,' she said.

'They came clearly from that side of the manor,' Shuggy said, pointing towards the East Wing.

'*They*?'

'Well, it sounded strange, is all I mean,' Shuggy said.

'How so?'

161

Shuggy shrugged. 'Sounded almost like a double blast. But I might 'ave heard it wrong.'

'I couldn't be sure,' Griffiths grumbled. 'It came from the direction of The Mound, but it was far away. So, I ran around it, and saw Catherine looking to the manor. Shuggy came too. We spoke, then ran towards the house.'

'Did the shot sound odd to you?'

Griffiths shook his head. 'No. Should it have?'

'When you ran to the house, were you worried about Bella?'

Griffiths looked up sharply. 'I'm not a simpleton, Mr Grieve, I know the rumors. They are not true.'

'Then why did you run towards the shot?'

'What else were we supposed to do?'

'Then Mrs McDiarmid came rushing out into us,' Shuggy said. 'Her eyes were wild, they were, and she pointed to The Mound, and said the shot came from that direction. So, we all turned and went back that-a-way. To check on the laird.'

'Miss Ross, how did Bella look when she came out and met you?' Grieve asked.

Ross shook her head. 'She looked right scared, Mr Grieve. She was white as a ghost.'

'Can you think of any reason, Griffiths, anyone here would want Logan dead?'

The muscles in Griffiths' cheeks pulsed in and out, his gaze fixed darkly against the wall behind Grieve.

'Shall I repeat the question?' Grieve asked.

'Now, Miss Ross, I understand this is sensitive…' Grieve took the pipe from his lips and thought for a moment. Kennedy's typing stopped during the pause. 'Were you aware of any relationship between Mr Griffiths and Mrs McDiarmid?'

Ross was very still, and licked her lips before answering. 'No,' she said, clearly and carefully. 'But I was aware of rumours.'

Grieve raised his eyebrows.

Ross shrugged and demurred. 'But I can't tell you if they were true, or not.'

Shuggy coughed at the question. 'I dinna know,' he said. 'I will nae speak ill of the dead…' He leaned forward, and lowered his voice. 'But you've heard the rumours?'

Grieve frowned and shook his head. 'What rumours?'

'Well, just so, you know, that that girl married Logan for his money.'

'Miss Ross, are you aware who will inherit this estate, now that the laird has passed away?'

'Logan left no heirs, Mr Grieve, that I am aware of.'

'Not even by his first wife?'

She shook her head. 'No. He and Mary were quite happy, they were, just the two of them.'

Shuggy shook his head. 'You tell me,' he said. 'I think Logan's only heir is Bella.'

'I don't know,' said Griffiths. 'You'd have to ask Bella.'

Bella McDiarmid sat down carefully, adjusting the dramatic lines of her La Garçonne dress as she slipped into the chair. Her eyes were reddened beneath the soft shadows of her makeup, her shoulder-bobbed hair tousled into a matted mess.

'Bella McDiarmid?' Grieve began.

She nodded. 'Yes.'

'Where were you when you heard the shot?'

Bella sniffed. 'I was in the hall, walking towards the library.' Her voice was deep and mellifluous, even as she spoke softly.

'And where might 'the hall' be?'

She turned and pointed. 'Right there. It moves behind the dining room, here, into the house. The library is there.' She pointed out the windows, towards a set of French doors in the West Wing.

Grieve nodded. 'Were you a singer, by any chance?'

Bella raised her eyebrows. 'Yes, I was. I sang, during the war, and a little before. How did…'

Grieve smiled, and shook his head. 'You have a very musical voice.'

'Oh.'

'So, you were in the hall, and heard the shot?'

'Yes,' Bella said. 'I had just moved past the open doors to the courtyard, and heard it coming from across the lawn.'

'Can you be sure of the direction?'

Bella nodded. 'Yes.'

'Had anything upset you, before that?'

Bella was silent, save the snapping of her fingernails as the dug them against each other beneath the table. 'No,' she said.

'Bella, I don't mean to be impertinent, but are you aware that you'll inherit now Logan is dead?'

164

Bella kept her eyes averted, and nodded slowly. 'I am,' she said.

Grieve turned and looked at Mackenzie and Kennedy, a wry smile curling around the thorny pipe.

'Again, Bella, I don't wish to offend…but what of the rumours concerning you and Griffiths?'

Bella shrugged. 'We grew up together, years ago. We've always kept in touch. I know Griffiths can be…' she shook her head, searching for the words, '…abrasive at times. But he's really very sweet, and kind, if you get to know him.' Bella looked up suddenly, locking eyes with Grieve. 'He would never allow me to fall prey to such an unsavoury practice as adultery.'

'If I may,' asked Grieve, 'how much older was Logan?'

Bella sighed. 'He was forty years old, Mr Grieve. I suppose, considering that, I can at least understand the rumors, even if I can't sympathize with them.'

The housemaid sat pertly, smoothing her white apron across her starched black dress.

'Don't worry, my dear,' Grieve said. 'We only have a few questions for you.'

The girl nodded briskly, her eyes lowered to the shining polish of the walnut dining table.

'Your name is Mary Jones?'

Jones nodded. 'Aye, sir.'

'You were in the kitchen, when the shot was fired?'

'Aye, sir.'

'Did you see, or hear anything else after that?'

'Only Mrs McDiarmid, sir.'

'You saw Bella McDiarmid?'

'Oh, aye. A few moments after the shot, she came rushing past the door on her way out to the courtyard. Sir.'

'Was there anything unusual about her?'

Jones nodded, looking up and easily meeting Grieve's gaze. 'Aye, she looked like she'd seen that ghost again.'

'I see…' Grieve began to speak, but stopped. 'You say, she looked like she'd seen that ghost, again?'

'Aye, sir. Looked pale as a sheet she did, just like the night the ghost appeared in her room. Did she nae tell you that? Did I say something I wasn't supposed to say?'

'No, no, Mary, you've done well. Tell me about this ghost.'

'Well, there isn't much, really. There were always stories, you know. About ghosts that walk among the oaks under the full moon, or a blood moon. And this part of the house, the old part...' she raised her eyes up towards the shadows of the ceiling above her. 'They say there are ghosts here as well.'

'What about Bella's ghost?'

'Well, five days ago, old Shuggy saw a pale figure disappear into the Oaks, at dead of midnight, and when he went to find it, the thing was gone. I myself have heard steps outside my chamber door.' Jones sat up a little straighter. 'I don't believe in ghosts, though, Mr Grieve. So, I put my head right out, I did, when I heard the steps.'

'And what did you see?'

She shrugged. 'There was nothing there.'

'Bella,' Grieve said as the young woman sat down again, 'what happened in your room, three nights ago?'

'What? Who told you?'

Grieve smiled and shook his head. 'It doesn't matter, does it? Why didn't you mention it earlier?'

Bella shrugged. 'I didn't think it was important... And, I didn't want you to think... I was a...'

'Never mind about that,' said Grieve. 'I think you'll find me very open to any possibility. Tell me. What happened?'

'Logan and I were asleep. It must have been two, or three, in the morning. I suddenly woke, and had the feeling there was someone there, so I turned, and saw a shadow, moving along the window, towards me. I screamed, jumped from the bed, and reached for the lamp. By the time I'd turned it on, whatever it was had vanished.'

Grieve frowned. 'Did Logan see it too?'

Bella shook her head. 'No. I'd nearly scared the poor man to...' she stopped herself, looking up sharply at Grieve. 'I scared him awake. He'd pulled himself up in bed, and was trying to see what

166

was wrong.'

'Could whoever it was have simply used the door?'

Bella shook her head. 'No,' she said. 'It was always locked. Logan hated to sleep in an open room, ever since he returned from the war.'

'The windows…'

'We slept on the third floor up, Mr Grieve. And I checked. All the windows were still latched.'

'How long did it take you to turn on the lamp?'

'It couldn't have been more than a few seconds.'

'Well, Dougal, what do you make of it?' Mackenzie asked, as he returned from seeing Bella out of the room.

Grieve frowned, running his fingers through his thick muttonchops. 'My first thought was a sniper.'

'But the powder burns,' Mackenzie said, sitting back down.

Grieve nodded. 'Exactly. Then, I wondered if Logan could have been killed earlier.'

Mackenzie shook his head. 'Shuggy, Ross, Griffiths, and Bella all agreed, the blood was flowing when they found him in his wheelchair. And if he was killed earlier, then Ross must be lying. Does she strike you as the duplicitous type?'

Grieve frowned, the smoke slowly curling upwards into the room. 'No, Hector, she certainly does not. Of course, another option is that they are all lying. But I find that equally difficult to stomach. They each have such different reasons for being here. They each seem to have viewed the laird and his wife…wives…so differently.' Grieve shook his head. 'If they are in it together, I couldn't guess what the common denominator would be. Also, if Bella was truly involved, why would she admit so freely that she is the heir of the estate?'

Mackenzie shrugged. 'Misdirection?'

'Possible,' Grieve muttered. 'Speaking of Bella, do you think she's lying?'

Mackenzie thought a moment. 'Yes,' he said. 'But I'm not sure what about.'

'I agree,' said Grieve. 'On both accounts… When should we

167

expect the detectives from Glasgow?'

Mackenzie turned to Kennedy.

'Scheduled for tomorrow afternoon, sir,' Kennedy said.

They all sat, silently, listening as the grandfather clock quietly counted the passing time in the corner.

'I'm staying here tonight, Mackenzie,' Grieve said suddenly. 'Removing the possibility of a sniper, removing the possibility of the entire manor being in league with each other for murder, and assuming Bella had no actual opportunity to kill the laird for his money... There's only one option left.'

'Such as?' Mackenzie asked.

'The ghost,' said Grieve.

Grieve caught Kennedy as Mackenzie left to arrange a telegram to DS Chisholm at Inverness.

'Listen, Kennedy,' said Grieve. 'The more I consider this problem, the more there is one thing I would like to know. Something I can't learn from here.'

Kennedy nodded. 'Sergeant Chisholm said expressly I was to make sure you had whatever you required.'

'It may require a trip to Glasgow... Tonight. Could you pull that off, if necessary, and return before the detectives, tomorrow afternoon?'

Kennedy thought a moment. 'Perhaps, Mr Grieve. But it depends on the nature of the errand.'

Kennedy left Achnadarag quickly, without speaking to Mackenzie. When Mackenzie queried Grieve, Grieve seemed reticent to explain. Mackenzie accepted it with poise, having experienced Grieve's methods before.

And so, the evening fell over Achnadarag.

A sombre dinner was served at eight. Bella dined alone, in her room. Very little conversation graced the table. Outside the dining room, the skies had already darkened, draping the oaks in damp shadows.

After dinner, Griffiths retired to the sitting room and poured himself a large snifter of brandy. Mackenzie and Grieve stayed behind, in the dining room. Mackenzie lit a small cigar, Grieve his pipe.

When the grandfather clock chimed the hour, Mackenzie excused himself, leaving only Grieve. When the clock chimed the half-hour, Grieve repacked his pipe, lit it afresh, and rose from the table, walking over to the courtyard door.

The night was frigid and wet. Grieve pulled his jacket collar closer around his neck, and set off into the field.

Above him, a few lights in the manor glowed from stone casements. Grieve stopped, and turned. Three stories up, he could make out the light from Bella's room. There was no drain-pipe anywhere near the windows, nor ledges, nor any easily perceivable hand holds by which an intruder could reach them.

Grieve's eyes moved across Achnadarag Manor, stopping on the West Wing; he walked back towards it. Inside was the library. One of the French doors was unlocked. He entered, found the switch, and turned on the lights.

The library was long, narrow, and windowless, opening into the courtyard by the set of French doors. At the far end, a single door was fixed in the library's western wall. A third door connected to the manor, in the middle of the room, sunk into the towering bookshelves that lined the walls. A few chairs, a settee, and some small tables were arranged around the space haphazardly.

Turning, Grieve inspected the French doors. After a moment of fiddling, he unlatched the locked door, and opened them both fully. The opening was prodigious. He closed them again, and walked back into the night, away from the house.

At the border of the trees, Grieve stopped, his eyes slowly scanning the darkened trunks. In the stillness he could hear the wind, a soft rain beginning to touch the grass around him, the creaking of the boughs overhead.

He turned back towards the manor. It cast a ruddy glow across the field.

The snapping was brief, but he clearly heard it. Something

169

moving, quickly, behind him.

Grieve spun around on his feet.

But there was nothing there, save the darkness, and the wind, and the oaks.

Kennedy returned early the next morning. His hair had been smoothed across his head instead of brushed, and his eyes bore the red bleariness of a night without sleep. Yet there was a spring in his step as he looked for Dougal Grieve.

He found him in the dining room, drinking his morning coffee and leisurely staring out the windows, watching a flock of sparrows bouncing and bobbing in the courtyard grass. Mackenzie sat across from him, silently paging through his notebook.

Grieve stood up quickly when Kennedy entered, leaning against the table to support his bad leg. Kennedy handed him a large envelope. Grieve tugged it open and pulled out a small stack of papers. 'Splendid,' he muttered, glancing through them quickly, nodding his head as he read.

When he finished, Grieve stuffed the papers back in the envelope, and snatched his blackthorn from where it leaned against his chair. 'Gather Ross, Shuggy, Griffiths, and Bella, and take them to The Mound,' he said.

Mackenzie stood up, pointing towards the envelope. 'Now wait a minute,' he began, but Grieve was already out the door to the courtyard, scattering the sparrows. Mackenzie and Kennedy watched the man limp quickly across the courtyard, towards the library in the West Wing.

'What the devil did you bring him, Kennedy?' asked Mackenzie.

Kennedy stammered for a moment, but Mackenzie shook his head and raised his hand. 'No. Never mind,' he said. 'If he'd wanted me to know, he'd have told me himself. I'm sure I'll find out soon enough.'

The morning was cold and wet, like the night before. Catherine Ross and Bella McDiarmid stood, wrapped in shawls, at the base of The Mound. Shuggy MacLeod ambled in a dirty overcoat, stained with mud, hands planted in his pockets, scratching at the shale border with the hobnails of his boots. Griffiths paced slowly back and forth, a cigarette smouldering half an inch from his grimaced lips. Kennedy and Mackenzie stood a few feet farther off.

'Do you know what he has planned, Kennedy?' Mackenzie asked in a quiet voice.

Kennedy shook his head. 'No,' he said. 'But if I were to guess—'

The first shot rang out, crisp like the crack of a whip. Its report came at them sharply from the area around the intersection of the East Wing and the manor house. As sharp as the report was, it had a strange doubled quality.

Mackenzie leapt forward, but stopped. He turned, and looked at the group assembled next to him. They all gazed in dumb silence towards the East Wing.

Another shot broke the silence, just as clear as the first, and with the same doubled report.

'Good God,' Bella said as her knees buckled from beneath her. She fell heavily into Ross, who grabbed her, carrying her down to the ground. Bella's face was white as a sheet. She put her hands down into the wet grass, closed her eyes, and lowered her head.

'Did you catch that?' Grieve asked suddenly, from where he'd emerged from the library door set in the western wall, in full view of The Mound. He replaced a small, snubbed revolver in the leather holster beneath his right armpit, and draped his jacket back across it.

'I don't understand,' Mackenzie said as Grieve slowly approached, streams of smoke trailing behind from his pipe.

Grieve stopped before Bella and Ross. He looked down, his face covered by the shadows of his cap, looming tall above them. 'Let me tell you a story, Bella' he said. 'You stop me if I get anything incorrect.'

Smoke curled from Grieve's pipe as he spoke, disappearing into the morning mist that draped the field. 'Four years ago, Logan McDiarmid was drafted,' he said. 'He was old, for the war, and married, but by 1917 there he was, heading off to France. Logan's final battle was at Arras, when the British assaulted the Hindenburg

171

Line. Logan's company was decimated. Only a few survivors. Logan's legs were shot out. At least, so he told the field doctor.'

Grieve pulled out the envelope from Kennedy, and held it towards Mackenzie. A soft rain began to patter off it. 'That field doctor was originally sceptical,' he said. 'Here are McDiarmid's war records. Kennedy was kind enough to retrieve them, from Glasgow, yesterday. They're quite interesting. Apparently, the doctor was under the impression Logan's legs were, in fact, not damaged. He suddenly changed his tune, however, and reported Logan as suffering from battle fatigue, that left his legs immobile. I can only imagine money must have been involved.'

Mackenzie took the envelope. 'Are you saying... All these years, Logan McDiarmid could walk?'

Grieve shrugged. 'Yes. And I suspect Dr Mulliner's autopsy, if directed in that way, will prove the laird's legs show less atrophy than they should if he was truly paralysed since 1917.'

Griffiths broke in. 'That is ridiculous,' he hissed. 'Are you seriously suggesting Logan faked his injuries for three years?'

'I am,' said Grieve. He turned back to Mackenzie. 'He was sent home, Hector. He was sent back home.' Grieve shifted his weight against his blackthorn stick, and chewed for a moment on his pipe. 'He faked it,' he said, finally, 'because if he was discovered, he risked being sent back to Hell.'

Grieve turned to Bella, still collapsed upon the grass. 'Logan's first wife died; she probably knew his secret. Then he met you. I suspect he actually loved you. I can only guess your motives. You were married. A week ago. He probably meant to tell you... But then...' Grieve raised his eyes to Griffiths.

'This is ridiculous,' Griffiths said again, spitting the cigarette butt into the mist. Bella began to cry.

'The truth often is, Mr Griffiths,' said Grieve.

After a moment, Grieve continued, speaking to Griffiths. 'Your relationship with Bella was anything but innocent,' he said. 'And you thought there was no way Logan could ever find out. But you were both wrong. He was watching, all the time, of course. Shuggy almost caught him one night among the oaks. And you, Bella... You saw him moving about that night, in your room. But you never guessed it could be him. When you screamed, and turned to reach

172

for the light, Logan simply leapt back into bed, and so you saw what you expected to see—your husband, laying in tousled covers, out of breath for fear.'

'I'll be damned,' Kennedy murmured.

'But what about the shot?' Ross asked. 'And the footprints?'

Grieve turned to Ross. 'Logan had already made his plan, my dear, when you rolled him out for his...lunt.'

Ross sucked in her breath, sharply. 'My God,' she said. 'To walk and smoke...'

Grieve nodded. 'Yes. It was a joke. Just not the one you believed it to be. You wheeled Logan to The Mound, and then you left. He simply got up and walked down the east side of The Mound, the dry side, and into the library by its western door. Shuggy and Griffiths came shortly after Logan left The Mound. From here, I must deduce a bit. But, Bella, correct me if I get anything wrong.'

Bella broke in, suddenly. 'He was hiding, crouching behind a chair. You're right, Mr Grieve, it's all true...'

'Bella!' Griffiths snapped, stepping forward. Kennedy gripped the man by the arm.

Bella shook her head. 'No, there's no hiding it now. Grieve knows... He knows about the gunshot. Griffiths and I were to meet that morning, in the library. That was why he stood, waiting, by The Mound. But when I entered, so help me, Logan came out from behind the chair. The minute I saw him, I knew what he meant to do. It all dawned on me then, that he must have seen us, that he was the ghost... I tried to scream, but before I could do anything he pulled out an old revolver. I jumped at him and grabbed the gun, and we struggled.'

Bella looked up, her hair laying in wet strings against her face.

'I didn't pull the trigger, Mr Grieve... God help me, as my witness, I didn't!'

The smoke slowly curled around the brim of Grieve's cap. 'You've already lied to me once, Bella,' he said. 'Whether or not you pulled the trigger... That will be for a jury to decide.'

'But the footsteps?' Mackenzie asked. 'And why was the body found on The Mound?'

'Logan realized he'd been shot,' said Grieve. 'He realized he was done for. He'd failed. So, he turned and went back the way he'd come. Everyone had run towards the sound of the shot, away from The Mound, towards the East Wing. He simply stumbled out that door,' pointing to the nearby west door to the library, 'and around The Mound, to the damp side. He must have been disoriented, because he walked part way around the base before climbing. McDiarmid returned to his chair. The footprints were his own.'

'But why?' Kennedy asked.

'The only one who knows for sure, is Logan. But if I were to guess...' Grieve stopped speaking, puffs of smoke rising from the bowl of his pipe. He closed his eyes, savouring the flavour as the rain dappled the shoulders of his jacket. 'If I had to guess,' he repeated, 'it would have been to try and finish his last pipe.'

The grandfather clock quietly chimed the hour as Grieve and Mackenzie sat down at the dining table. An old service revolver lay on the table between them. It had been retrieved from the library, where Bella told them she'd hid it, when she returned after the body had been discovered.

'I still don't understand,' Mackenzie said. 'If the gun was fired inside the library in the West Wing, how was the shot heard coming from the East Wing?'

'It's simple, Hector,' said Grieve. 'Here,' and he pulled out the sketch Mackenzie had given him. He leaned over it for a moment, scratching out a few lines with his fingernail and making a few new lines with his pen. Then he slid it across the table.

(Note to Reader: Sketch on page 176)

'It was all in the way sound travels,' Grieve said.

'Well, I'll be double damned,' Mackenzie muttered under his breath.

'The library walls are thick,' said Grieve. 'Easily thick enough to insulate the sound of a shot. The French doors were open; the sound left the room in the only direction it was given. Of course, the path of an echo isn't perfect. Even moving at the speed of sound, a clever ear could detect something was off. Shuggy, of course, has been around firearms his whole life. It's little surprise he recognized the 'double' blast, as he put it.'

'And Bella, I suppose, simply fled?'

Grieve shrugged and sighed. 'That's the question, isn't it? She ran through the manor, but then turned back into the courtyard, and directed everyone to The Mound. I think there are only two possibilities. One, she believed she was misleading the group, buying time to deal with the body she thought was in the library. Or, two, she saw Logan as he climbed The Mound, behind her friends who were approaching, and attempted to help him without implicating herself.'

Mackenzie thought for a moment, chewing on the tip of his pencil. 'Which do you think it was?'

Grieve struck a match and raised it to the blackened, thorny stummel, sucking the flame down into the bowl. Slow, silvery trails of smoke curled up into the room as he decided how he'd answer the constable's question.

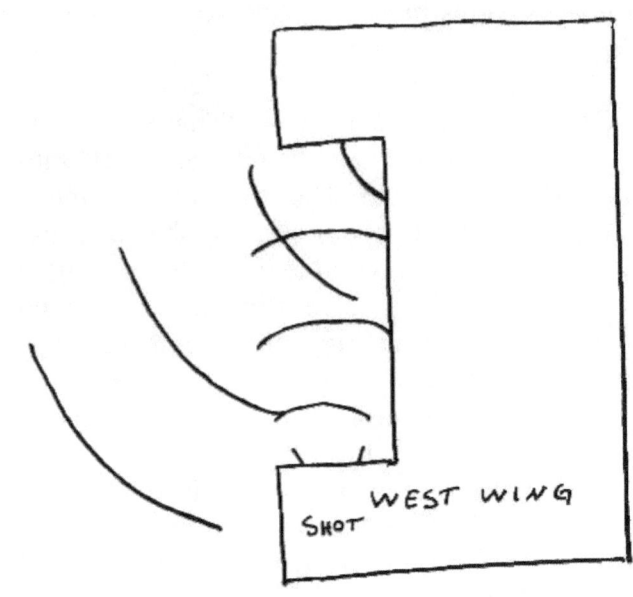

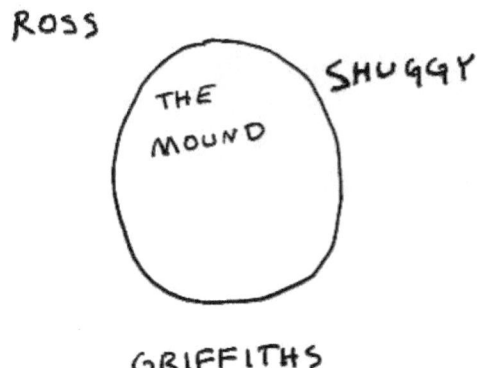

ROSS

SHUGGY

GRIFFITHS

The Adventure of Woodbury Barrow
Cameron Trost

Andrew Bellingham was waiting for Oscar Tremont, Investigator of the Strange and Inexplicable, in the hall of Oxford Station. Oscar recognised his client immediately upon stepping in from the platform. He looked the same as he had just two weeks earlier when Oscar passed the test set for him at Rose Grove with flying colours. His face was a tad paler perhaps, but that vaguely bewildered look hadn't disappeared from it.

'Good to see you again, Oscar. Welcome to Oxford. Not your first time, I take it?'

'Only the second. I'd like to take in a few of the sites again and visit a couple of addresses I didn't make it to last time once I've solved your mystery.'

'That's the spirit! Once it's all wrapped up with a nice little bow. I like that attitude, and I have every confidence in your talents. I'd be only too happy to be your guide—with immense pleasure. First things first, being Friday evening, I'll drive you to my humble abode, give you a tour, and we can enjoy a nice whisky before dinner.'

'The best way to start any investigation,' Oscar replied with a suitable wink.

It was a short walk down the street and across Osney Bridge to where Andrew had parked his burgundy Jaguar XJ. The drive, on the other hand, was long and a rather luxurious one for Oscar, used to the jolts and shudders that were part and parcel of driving a classic Peugeot 403. The countryside was lush and homely, and Oscar knew exactly where he was being taken and had a good idea which towns they were passing along the way. He had, of course, thoroughly researched Woodbury Manor and its place in local history prior to leaving his home in Brittany. He knew that it had passed through the

177

hands of many grand families over the centuries and been renovated several times, with major reconstruction taking place after it was all but razed by Cromwell's New Model Army. The Bellinghams were relative newcomers in the property's history. There were still a few gaps to be filled, but Oscar was sure Andrew would provide further insight during the tour and answer some of those questions that were already beginning to nag.

It was almost seven o'clock, after a forty-minute drive, when Andrew Bellingham turned right onto a long gravel drive leading gently uphill past flanks of Wellingtonia trees. The manor stood atop the rise, which could hardly be termed a hill considering the subtlety of its contours and the fact that nearby mounds rivalled its height. Between them, the evening gloom had gathered, making them seem to float like islands. Only the tips of the five highest chimney stacks, glowing like beacons above the gabled roof of the third storey, felt the last warmth of the setting sun.

The Jaguar sailed up to a gate in the garden wall extending from the manor's east wing.

'I use the back entrance in general, for the sake of convenience,' Andrew explained as he opened his door. He then took Oscar's suitcase from the boot.

'Do you have a large staff?'

He laughed as Oscar followed him to the gate. They stepped inside the garden and Oscar admired the meandering paths leading between shrubs, conifers, and climbing roses on trellises. There was a small white gazebo in the middle with a wheelbarrow against which a spade was leaning parked to one side.

'You've been watching Downton Abbey, have you?'

'I assure you I haven't. I am, however, guilty of reading too much Agatha Christie.'

'Those days are long gone. Well, they never were for the *nouveau riche* like myself. I don't think anyone who's not nobility has help nowadays. Not really a matter of expense either. It's just no longer the thing to do, you know? And I quite agree.'

'Your great-grandfather bought Woodbury?'

'That's right. He made a good living as a haberdasher before branching off into women's fashion. He hired a talented designer on generous terms and was smart enough not to interfere in his work.

That's how he made his fortune. He eventually bought Woodbury, left Oxford to live here, and promptly passed on. That's the long and the short of it.'

'The business remains yours today?'

'Precisely. My younger brother takes care of it in London, and spends a good deal of time in China and Pakistan. He has a good head for business. I'm stuck in the past. We accept and appreciate our differences, so we have a bit of a deal. While he looks after the nuts and bolts of finances, I take care of the manor, keep up family tradition, and maintain local relations. He gets more out of the deal financially, but it suits us both to a tee.'

Oscar nodded while he surveyed the surroundings.

'The garden is gorgeous.'

'Thank you. I spend a good part of every week tending to it. We believe it has been here, certainly in varying states of glory and disrepair, since the Elizabethan era. I'll show you around in the morning.'

'You attend to the entire property personally?'

'I do.' Andrew unlocked the back door and flicked the light switch, bringing to life a kitchen that Oscar immediately recognised as retaining several Edwardian features, from porcelain and copper pans to the lamps and cooking range. 'I don't cook here. This is for show and only used on the odd special occasion, such as fundraising events. There's a modern kitchenette upstairs that meets my daily needs.'

Oscar followed him across the kitchen and to the foot of the stairs in the entrance hall. There, Andrew stopped and looked his guest in the eye. 'You see, I'm an old bachelor, Oscar. I live here alone most of the time. It can be lonely at times, but I have plenty of family and friends who come to stay. It's rare that I don't have company for the weekend. Mind you, you're the first private investigator to set foot here.'

He continued up to the first floor, and Oscar admired the portraits watching them from the walls as he followed.

'I do hope you'll like your room.'

Oscar smiled as he stepped inside, flicking his flat cap from his head.

'No surprises under it today?'

'What's that? Oh, my flat cap. I'm afraid not.' Oscar laughed, lowering his shaved head towards his host. 'You liked that little touch at Rose Grove?'

'You know I did. It bowled me over!'

Oscar performed a theatrical bow.

The bedroom was small but stately, a mock Tudor affair of wattle and daub with matching dark bed, dressing table, and wardrobe. 'It's very charming. I suspected a hint of understatement when you referred to it as your humble abode.'

The host placed the suitcase on the bed. 'It's not as ostentatious as some of the grand homes in the area, but I'm glad you're impressed. I do hope you'll feel the same about my whisky. You must think me terribly rude though. Do you need to rest for a minute?'

Oscar shot him a mischievous look.

'Not a problem, my boy. I assure you.'

'In fact, I was thinking quite the contrary. Is it around this time of night that the scratching occurs?'

'I take my walk a little earlier. Just before dusk. But I daresay it could be happening at this very moment. I was rather hoping you'd want to jump right into it, I must admit. You'll need your wellies.'

Oscar unzipped his suitcase and pulled a pair of knee-high green wellies out of a plastic bag inside it. 'How muddy is it?'

'If you walk behind me and don't put a foot wrong, the mud shouldn't go over the top of your boots.'

'*That* bad,' Oscar took his Doc Martens off and slipped the wellies on. 'I'll tailgate you then. Lead the way!'

They returned through the kitchen and out the gate to where the Jaguar was parked in the deepening gloom. Andrew turned left and led Oscar downhill along a track worn hard by years of trampling. But as they descended into the misty vale, the brambles crowding in on either side grew higher and thicker, and the ground changed from solid to spongy.

'It's so quiet here,' Oscar practically whispered.

'That's why the scratching is noticeable. Apart from birds, there's not much to hear around here. Gunshots during hunting season, of course. Watch your step—it gets muddy for a while here until the land rises again just before we reach the barrow.'

They made their way slowly through the evening mist, and the squelching of the sodden ground under their boots was the only sound to disturb the silence of that timeless landscape. As the land rose again, Oscar could feel it growing more solid.

When Andrew raised a hand and stopped, he knew they must have arrived at the barrow, but he couldn't see anything.

'Listen,' Andrew whispered.

Oscar did, and he could hear it—a muffled scratching coming from within the earth.

'Where's the barrow?' he asked quietly.

Andrew pointed in front of him.

Oscar took a step forward. It was so dark now that it would have been difficult to make out much at all even without the mist. There was a sharp rise in the land, ending slightly higher than Oscar himself, and when he followed it—walking clockwise—he soon understood that this was it, the Woodbury barrow. There wasn't much to it really, which shouldn't have surprised him, but did for some reason. Twenty-odd strides around the base of the protrusion and he was back with Andrew, who was standing still like a lost ghost in the otherworld.

The stifled noise continued—each scratch and subsequent pause a different length. Oscar made a circling motion with his index finger and went on to circle the barrow a second time.

'What do you think?' Andrew asked in a hushed voice.

'I think there's someone in there,' Oscar answered matter-of-factly.

'That's impossible,' Andrew gasped.

Oscar shrugged. 'You'd think so, and yet, it's the most likely explanation. I can't imagine it being an animal, and the scratching is too irregular to be mechanical. In fact, I'd say it was more a matter of scraping than scratching.'

'Yes,' Andrew said. 'I agree. Quite like a spade.'

Oscar clicked his fingers. 'Just so, isn't it? A small spade, or even a trowel.'

'You don't believe in—well, you know?'

'Ghosts?' Oscar asked, studying his client's face as best he could in the gloom. 'No. But I could be wrong. It has been known to happen.'

Andrew frowned. 'Hauntings, you mean?'

'Being wrong, my good man. It happens to us all. I'm not infallible.'

'Oh, indeed.' Andrew grinned. 'Of course.'

'And yet,' Oscar went on, 'that would be a much simpler explanation than trying to fathom why a human is in there.'

'Why—and how?'

'Have you ever climbed up top?'

'The first time I heard it,' Andrew said. 'I clambered up there and had a good look but didn't see anything out of place.'

Oscar nodded and glanced at the top of the mound.

'Do you ever come down here during the day?'

'Rarely. I have done on occasion, but I only hear the noise in the evening.'

'As I suspected,' Oscar said. 'Well, let's head back.'

Andrew didn't move, and it took Oscar a moment to realise he was staring at him wide-eyed.

'What's wrong?'

'You're not going to try to find the entrance?'

'Believe me, I want to, but what if I end up giving myself away. Whoever is in there doesn't know that we know. I'd rather keep it that way until I can work out what's going on.'

'I see,' Andrew said, but the hesitation in his voice indicated that perhaps he didn't really.

'Can we talk about it inside?'

'You're running the show,' Andrew conceded. 'Let's clean up and have a whisky.' He took a torch from his pocket and used it to help them retrace their steps through the dark, all the way back to Woodbury Manor.

'Wait a minute,' Oscar said once they'd reached the Jaguar. 'Where's the nearest road to the barrow?'

'Without passing by here, probably a good five hundred yards from the barrow. There's a dirt road on the other side of the property.'

'It might be worth going for a quick drive.'

'You're thinking there might be a vehicle parked nearby?'

'There's a very good chance.'

'My keys are inside,' he said. 'Wait here. I'll bring your boots down for you.'

Oscar looked at his muddy wellies and then back to Andrew. 'I suspect the Jag would appreciate me changing back into my Docs.'

The drive around the property took no time at all. Oscar studied every conceivable spot where a car could be discreetly parked while Andrew drove, but they made it back to the manor without having spotted another vehicle of any kind.

'How far is the nearest town on foot?' Oscar asked as they got out of the car and entered through the gate.

'A short walk,' Andrew said, putting their wellies by the kitchen door.

Oscar hummed. 'I'll take a close look at the barrow first thing in the morning. It's imperative that I do it carefully, without leaving so much as a footprint in plain sight, so that no suspicions are aroused when our nocturnal visitor returns in the evening.'

'I'll let you get on with it in that case. You know the way now. In the meantime, let's get ourselves cleaned up for the evening.'

Andrew showed Oscar to the bathroom nearest his bedroom. A freestanding porcelain bathtub took centre stage and fluffy white towels hung from a rack beside it.

'Take your time. I have another bathroom of my own. I'll meet you in the drawing room. I didn't show you where it is though, did I?'

'I think I caught a glimpse of it coming from the kitchen to the stairs.'

'Of course, nothing gets past you, does it?' Andrew chuckled.

'What slips past, I don't know about,' Oscar replied with a wink.

Andrew left his guest to it, and Oscar got the right balance of hot and cold water running before returning to his room to fetch a clean pair of corduroys and a shirt. When he got back to the bathroom, he dipped a hand in the water and smiled to himself. He undressed and got into the tub, but as his body slid down into the warm water, his mind buried itself in the cold barrow.

'A fine drop indeed,' Oscar agreed, closing his eyes and resting his head against the back of the Chesterfield armchair. 'The peat pulls you down into the earth.'

'It does,' Andrew mused. 'No peat in these parts, mind you.'

'No, but there's clearly something buried here.'

'You think so?'

Oscar held the glass to his nose and inhaled before taking another sip.

'There must be, Andrew,' he went on. 'Whoever is going to the trouble of scratching away every evening is in search of something important. No other explanation would make an ounce of sense.'

'That was the first thought that crossed my mind, I must say—someone digging in, or out,' Andrew said darkly, then drained his glass.

Oscar followed his host's lead, eager to sample the next delicacy from his collection.

'Out?' Oscar repeated, shaking his head. 'The universe holds secrets mankind may never discover. I grant you that. But there are no ghosts behind this mystery. A living human being is at the heart of the matter. Mark my words.'

Andrew took another bottle from his whisky cabinet and held it ceremoniously for Oscar to see before pouring.

'The colour is heavenly.'

'Quite.' He poured the drams. 'And the taste?'

Oscar inhaled, his eyes closed. 'It's silky smooth, I'd say.'

Andrew nodded. 'This one is velvet.'

They drank, smiled, and remained silent for a long moment.

'Exquisite,' Oscar whispered eventually.

'What could be in there?' Andrew asked, and it took Oscar a second to realise he was talking about the barrow.

'That's the big question. The excavation was documented?'

'Naturally. Oh, I quite forgot—there's a section about it in a book I have on Oxfordshire archaeology. I'll fetch it for you. Won't be a second.'

While he waited, Oscar sipped thoughtfully. Time was on his mind. Thousands of years had passed between the barrow's completion and its unearthing. A much shorter period of time separated the excavation from the present. All the same, well over a century later, why would anyone suddenly have cause to doubt the thoroughness of the excavation to the point of undertaking a clandestine dig on private property?'

Andrew returned with the book and handed it to Oscar. 'A spot of bedtime reading for you.'

'It may shed some light on the affair.'

'Not too hungry yet?'

'Not particularly. I had a sandwich on the train. Don't go to any trouble.'

'I had my dear friend, Helen Edwards, prepare her delectable chicken and ale pie for me.'

'That does whet the appetite,' Oscar admitted.

'Another dram while I put the oven on? I have a delightful Speyside you probably don't know.'

'With pleasure. One last drop. I want to have a look through this book before I go to sleep, so best keep a clear head.'

'Right you are. I hope it proves useful.' Andrew poured their drams and looked at Oscar, his brow furrowed, as he handed him his glass. 'I don't know how it's possible. I really don't.'

'That someone can be inside a barrow that was excavated and filled in again over a century ago without any external sign of disturbance. Is that what you mean?'

'Precisely.' He raised his glass. 'Cheers.'

'*Slàinte mhath*,' Oscar replied, and he smiled to himself as he savoured the delicate aroma with a hint of toffee to it. 'There's another way of looking at the problem.'

Andrew remained silent for a while, then slowly parted his lips to speak. 'That no other solution is possible.'

Oscar sipped, closed his eyes, and answered his host with a single nod.

Andrew slipped away to the kitchen—no less confused than he had been before—leaving the investigator to his thoughts.

When Oscar opened his eyes, he took another sip and opened the book. He ran a finger down the table of contents and flicked to the relevant page. The section dedicated to Woodbury Barrow was short but detailed. It didn't really contain any information he hadn't already found on the subject. Excavated by Sir Henry Wheeler in 1892 using local labour. The barrow was round; fifty feet in circumference by seven high. Excavation ceased when Sir Henry discovered the site had been previously plundered. The barrow was filled in.

'Interesting,' Oscar said to himself. 'Such an unremarkable site.'

He closed the book thoughtfully and placed it beside the bottle of Speyside. The barrow had been included for no other reason than to ensure the book was a complete survey of Oxfordshire digs, and yet, for a reason he couldn't put his finger on, its insignificance made it all the more fascinating.

'It's going to be delicious,' Andrew said, reappearing in the drawing room. He stopped short and shot Oscar a quizzical look. 'You've had a flash of inspiration, haven't you?'

Oscar met his gaze. 'I believe I have—just this very instant.'

'Well?'

'It's no more than a vague suspicion at this point.'

'Promise me it's all very rational, at least. No family curses or the like.'

'All perfectly rational, my dear fellow. This business has nothing to do with your family at all.'

'The previous owners then?'

'I don't think so.'

Andrew sat and sipped his whisky, contemplating the enigmatic man in front of him.

'Will we know more this time tomorrow?'

Oscar leaned forward, raised his glass, and looked Andrew in the eye. 'This time tomorrow, I plan on having the case all wrapped up, but that depends on what I discover when I inspect the barrow in the morning.'

It was still dark when Oscar's mobile phone vibrated on the nightstand. He gave himself a minute to collect his thoughts before getting up and donning the forest green clothes he'd brought with him. He already had a torch and compact binoculars in the pockets of his utility vest, as well as a Swiss Army knife. In his backpack were his camera, a camping shovel, and a hammer. Certain he had everything he needed, he put his ubiquitous flat cap on and left the bedroom quietly, not wanting to disturb his host. With the aid of his torch, he negotiated the stairs under the watchful gaze of the portraits and passed through the kitchen, closing the door gently behind him. He wriggled his feet into his boots and headed down to the barrow, arriving just as dawn was breaking.

Oscar wasn't really sure why he'd felt the need to get such an early start, but standing there in front of that otherwise unimposing mound of earth—one that most people wouldn't recognise as a Neolithic barrow at all, he suddenly understood. It was as though his unconscious had guessed it and compelled him. For at that moment, Oscar was no longer on the Woodbury estate, but in the otherworld. The morning mist hugged the rise and fall of the land, making the barrow an island in a fjord, and the rays of the rising sun reached down until they eventually touched the top of it—nature's golden crown. It seemed to Oscar that the birdsong intensified at that moment in celebration.

He took a deep breath of crisp morning air and indulged himself, but then he brushed magic aside and turned once again to reason. The mat of long grass on top of the barrow was glowing softly—beckoning him. Oscar climbed up there, carefully choosing the firmest footholds and making sure not to leave prints. He walked around the top at a snail's pace, studying the surface, which was almost flat. There were clumps of damp grass interspersed with weeds and fallen leaves. It was rocky around the edge but less so in the centre.

He paused for a moment and raised his eyes to the clear sky, as though seeking an answer there, and perhaps it did just the trick, because when he looked down again, he noticed a faint but undeniable trace of fresh earth. It wasn't much and didn't even constitute an unbroken line, but to the investigator's keen eye, it was a giveaway. This was dirt that had spilled from a suspended receptacle in motion. Looking more closely, he detected others like it, but not so clear and fresh. Starting from where the faint trail disappeared at the edge, or rather became fainter in the mist still gathered around the barrow, Oscar followed it towards the centre until there was no longer any trace of it. He dropped to his knees and started feeling around in the largest mat of damp grass, and a smile made his moustache twitch as he fingers touched metal. He shuffled his fingers further along—a ring! He looked to his left, where there was another large clump of grass, and dug the fingers of his left hand into that one.

'Brilliant,' he whispered, and he pulled on the iron rings, lifting the camouflaged trapdoor clear. He placed it delicately to one side and reached into the pocket where he'd put his torch.

He saw exactly what he'd been expecting in the hole. It was no deeper than four feet and in it sat a metal bucket containing an electric lamp, trowel, hand spade, and short digging bar. That was it. He leaned in closer, sweeping every inch of the hole with his torch and shining it into the bucket, but there was nothing else to be found

He replaced the trapdoor, making sure that every blade of grass lay naturally. A single blade jammed in the gap risked setting off alarm bells. It was a work of art, no less, and a wily mind was behind it. They say there's no honour among thieves, but Oscar Tremont had no qualms about entertaining a feeling of admiration for worthy opponents in the game of subterfuge. He walked to the edge of the barrow where the trail of soil led, looked back to make certain he'd left the scene exactly as he'd found it, and descended into the thinning mist. He walked over to the nearest tangle of brambles and peered behind it to find not a pile of earth but a broad patch spread out across the ground.

He pinched the brim of his flat cap between thumb and forefinger in a gesture of respect.

'Challenge accepted.'

While he walked back to the manor, Oscar weighed his options. He was often given the opportunity to pounce upon unsuspecting prey in the course of his work, but there were pitfalls to that approach—you never knew how tight-lipped they would be, and this was particularly a problem in a case that didn't involve and most likely wouldn't interest the police. Having the facts of the case worked out in advance ensured a position of strength for any eventual negotiation or pressure that may be—and usually was— required, and this was especially so when the adversary in question was evidently a clever one. But, of course, it was also a matter of personal satisfaction. Solving a seemingly inexplicable puzzle is a mental wrestle, not a physical one. Oscar couldn't be truly satisfied with the outcome of an investigation unless he cracked every aspect of it through pure reasoning, backed up by solid detective work.

By the time he'd reached the kitchen door, where his client was standing with a mug of steaming tea, he knew precisely what steps he had to take.

'Don't keep me in suspense,' Andrew chided as Oscar removed his boots.

'Suspense is my milk and honey. Let me lap it up.'

Andrew laughed, making sure he didn't spill his tea. 'Come and have a cuppa. That'll loosen your tongue.'

'I suspect it will. You don't happen to have herbal tea, do you?'

'I'm afraid not. You don't drink Earl Grey?'

'The Earl will do nicely. Thanks.'

'I can get some in town this morning.'

'As a matter of fact,' Oscar said, 'I was wondering whether we could go for a little drive.'

Andrew grinned. 'Is this business or have you fallen in love with my Jag?'

'I assure you it's a healthy mix of both.'

'Milk? Sugar?'

'Milk, please.'

'Where are we going then?'

'Hook Norton.'

Andrew raised his eyebrows. 'Not much to see there, apart from the brewery.'

'Well, if a celebration's in order—why not? I try to make a point of never refusing a pint. The first stop, however, shall be the village museum.'

'You're enjoying this.'

'I most certainly am,' Oscar admitted, and there was twitching of the moustache again.

Andrew shook his head and handed Oscar his tea. 'Let's rewind a little here. What did you discover at the barrow?'

'A trapdoor camouflaged to look like normal grassy terrain.'

'Good Lord! On top of it?'

'Yes. Top-centre. Our nocturnal visitor has dug about four feet into the barrow. The excavation is being carried out extraordinarily slowly and meticulously so as to avoid arousing suspicion.'

'A one-man job?'

'Most probably. One man, or woman perhaps.'

'But why?'

'That's what I'm counting on discovering at Hook Norton.'

'Who lives—oh, I see—that's where the excavator lived. Sir Henry Wheeler was from there.'

Oscar shot him a wink.

'He's the key to this?'

'Who else could be? No one in his right mind would go to so much trouble to excavate a barrow singlehandedly and in complete secrecy without a very good reason, and that reason has to be connected to the man who undertook the dig. What do you say?'

'Simple logic when you put it like that.'

'I've done my research into Sir Henry Wheeler. We know that he was a dedicated and respected archaeologist whose career remained undistinguished because he never made an important discovery. Your barrow was one of his last digs, and it was a disappointment. Not long after, he died in a riding accident.'

'That's right,' Andrew said.

Oscar sipped his tea thoughtfully.

'You believe there's more to it?'

'Undoubtedly. There simply has to be more to it—and I can guess what happened.'

'For crying out loud man, tell me!'

'But I might be wrong.'

'This is no time for self-doubt or hypocritical humbleness.'

Oscar looked wounded, but it soon passed and he shot his client a cheeky smile, the kind that made the ends of his moustache twitch.

'No, it's not, is it? Right, Andrew—fire up the Jag!'

Hook Norton wasn't exactly a hive of activity, but it wasn't without its charms. Honey-coloured houses lined the streets, and the old church with its timeworn graveyard stood watch along the High Street. The village museum was a far cry from the Pitt Rivers in Oxford but Oscar was relieved to see it was open. Andrew parked outside and immediately got the attention of the elderly ladies chatting inside.

'Good morning. Are you gentlemen lost?' the one with half-moon glasses and a blue shawl that matched her eyes asked.

'If this is the Hook Norton Village Museum, then we are where want to be,' Oscar announced grandiloquently.

It did the trick, getting a chuckle out of them.

'It's just that we don't get too many visitors from out of town, do we, Martha? Not at this time of year.'

'We do not, Betty.'

'My name is Oscar Tremont and this is Andrew Bellingham,' Oscar offered, deciding to play an open game.

'How can we help you?' Betty asked, straightening her back as best she could and cocking her head to one side. Her hair was short and grey and exuberant silver earrings dangled from her ears. She'd clearly been a coquette all her life and wasn't planning on stopping any time soon. Oscar loved it.

'We're interested in the work of an archaeologist who lived in Hook Norton; a man who never received the attention he deserved.'

Martha took her glasses off and smiled tenderly. 'Sir Henry Wheeler.'

'That's him,' Andrew said.

'We don't have any artefacts he unearthed here, I'm afraid.'

'That's a shame,' Oscar replied, turning to Andrew with a look of immense disappointment. 'We've come all this way for nothing then. I should have called first, I suppose.'

'I'm terribly sorry,' Martha said.

'It can't be helped. I don't suppose you can tell us where he lived? We'd very much like to take a selfie in front of his house.'

'You can do that, naturally, but you won't be able to go inside,' she said, her voice apologetic. 'You could have done until a couple of years ago. Friends of mine lived there before selling up and moving to a retirement village. A young family lives there now.'

'I understand,' Oscar replied. 'In any case, it probably looks nothing like it did back in his day.'

'I dare say it's altogether different now. They've just finished renovating it, you see, although quite tastefully, wouldn't you agree?' She turned to Betty.

'Oh yes, as far as I know. It looks much the same from the outside but I'm told they've done up the interior. All the modern conveniences a young family needs. The wallpaper was old and stained and the floorboards rather wonky.'

'Good for them,' Oscar said, hiding his excitement. 'I'm sure it

191

was quite a find. All the same, we'd like to take that selfie.'

'No harm in that,' Martha said. 'I'll jot the address down for you. I'm not very good at drawing maps though.'

'Not a problem. We can enter the address in the satnav.'

Martha jotted it down on a museum flyer and handed it to Oscar.

'Thank you, ladies.'

'The same to you both.'

The men took their leave, and no sooner had they stepped outside than Andrew turned to Oscar with a conspiratorial gleam in his eye. 'I understand now.'

Oscar grinned and nodded. 'You have a choice, Andrew.'

'I do?'

'Wait until we're in the car.'

They climbed in and Andrew entered the address in the satnav.

'Not far at all,' Oscar observed.

Andrew pulled out and followed the directions to the house. Once outside, he stopped so Oscar could have a good look. It was a two-storey townhouse made of the same stone as almost every other edifice in Hook Norton. The window frames were immaculate white.

'This choice I have?'

'Yes,' Oscar said. 'There are two paths. I must choose one. I can either enter the house illegally, thereby breaking yet again a promise I've made to my wife on several occasions, or we can assume what we both think happened did indeed happen and skip straight to the setting of the trap. We know where our prey lives, and so the ball is in our court.'

'I don't want to be responsible for you breaking any promises to your wife. I'll take the second option.'

'Very well. Thank you. I could do with the exercise after all.'

Andrew raised his eyebrows. 'Tomorrow?'

'Yes. I'll need to start at daybreak. This evening, I'll find a good spot overlooking the barrow and do a little wildlife photography.'

'Is this worth celebrating?'

'Guesswork verified by facts?' Oscar nodded. 'That constitutes a small victory.'

'Jolly good! In that case, let's try a Hook Norton brew! It's my shout.'

After a pint of real ale, they returned to Woodbury Manor for lunch and played a couple of games of chess, and when Andrew went into town to run errands and fetch some herbal tea for breakfast, Oscar found a hiding spot overlooking the barrow. He took a few shots of the barrow to make sure his zoom was set, then he sat back to wait. His mind wandered back home, and he wanted to send a message to Louise, telling her the case was progressing well and to give the boys a hug, but he had no signal where he was. Instead, he made himself as comfortable as he could on the old blanket Andrew had given him and asked himself what exactly it was that Sir Henry Wheeler had kept from the world. Oscar knew from his own interest in the subject that Neolithic barrows rarely held items of great monetary value. Their importance lay in the insight they provided into early architecture and social systems. What had he been hiding?

The sun was setting when the figure appeared from behind a copse of elms to Oscar's right. It was then that he realised the perpetrator was indeed in the habit of parking in town and walking to the barrow. For all he knew, Andrew may have crossed paths with him unwittingly mere minutes earlier. Although the head was hooded and Oscar was looking down at an angle, it was clear from the gait that this was a man. He was of medium build and rather unremarkable in his black hoodie and tracksuit bottoms. If Oscar didn't get a decent shot of his face once he reached the top of the barrow, he wouldn't get much at all. He had to hand it to him, Oscar admitted—he was going about it all very cleverly. If Oscar had found himself in his shoes, would he have gone about it any differently? Would he have done it at all?

He smiled to himself as he took a shot of the man clambering up the barrow, and he kept his finger poised over the shutter release, waiting. The instant the target crouched down and looked all around to make sure no one was near, Oscar took a volley of shots.

'Got you,' he mouthed silently.

The trapdoor was lifted, the man entered, and the trapdoor was closed again from the inside.

Oscar took a deep breath and shook his head in admiration as he released it. This was no murderer or rapist, but merely a man who was grasping what Fortuna had laid at his feet, and he was working bloody hard to get it.

Oscar couldn't help but feel a pang of guilt, but he brushed it aside. Andrew Bellingham was his client and a friend of a dear friend, and this was his land after all. Whatever was buried there belonged either to him or the British public if it fell under the umbrella of the Treasure Act. That, however, was not Oscar's concern. He'd been hired to solve the mystery—nothing more and nothing less. Andrew no doubt knew a solicitor who could handle the boring administrative aftermath.

Oscar put the lens cap back on his camera, stretched his legs, and got up. There was no point sitting there all evening. Even if the treasure was unearthed that night, it was unlikely it could be carried back to town, unless it was very small. No—Oscar was going to need a good night's rest, because the morning had a mammoth workout in store.

'So, this is our man,' Andrew Bellingham mused, squinting at the camera screen. Oscar zoomed in on the face.

'Not what you were expecting?'

'I don't know what I was expecting. I'm just glad it's a human being and not some Neolithic ghoul.'

Oscar tutted. 'I suppose living alone in a home the likes of this one does terrible things to a man's mind.'

'You're probably right,' Andrew admitted. 'In any case, this chap doesn't come across as the hardened criminal. Once again, it looks like you've hit the nail on the head.'

Oscar put the camera down and leaned back in his armchair. 'Yes, quite so. I hit the nail on the head, as you say, and this character—?'

Andrew realised Oscar wanted him to fill in the gap. After a moment's reflection, he grinned, and said, 'Well, he hit the jackpot, didn't he?'

Oscar nodded and stroked his moustache. 'We'll know for sure tomorrow!'

'Whisky?'

'With pleasure.'

Andrew walked towards the drinks cabinet, but he was moving slowly and Oscar could tell there was something on his mind. It was when he returned with two crystal glasses and a bottle of Highland Park that he spoke his mind. 'What are we to do with him?'

'That's your call, Andrew. You hired me to solve a mystery, and I thank you, both for that and your wonderful hospitality—I'm tempted to say "friendship"—to be honest.'

Andrew placed his hand over his heart. 'I should certainly hope so.'

'It is one of the most intriguing cases I've had in quite some time, even though somewhat less convoluted than the one I solved at Rose Cottage.'

Andrew laughed as he passed Oscar his glass. 'More authentic, perhaps.'

Oscar winked. '*Slàinte mhath.*'

Andrew returned the highland toast.

'If tomorrow proves me right and the mystery is solved, my job will be done. I'll certainly offer my advice if requested, but it will ultimately be up to you to take a decision. Depending on the nature of the find, if indeed there is one, you will have legal considerations to take into account. That is your business. Of course, our trespasser may take it upon himself to go public if he suspects you fail to declare a significant archaeological find, even though we can be quite certain he wouldn't have done so in your place.'

Andrew sipped his whisky. 'What is the legislation on the matter?'

Oscar took his smart phone and looked up the Treasure Act for his client's benefit. He read out the stipulations of the act, explaining the conditions under which artefacts may be considered treasure.

'I suspect that Wheeler discovered an object he wasn't expecting to find in the barrow and was stowing it away for a rainy day. After all, is there a better place to hide a treasure than in a Neolithic barrow that you have the authority to declare void of interest, especially when it was already hidden there to begin with?'

'It's perfect,' Andrew agreed. 'And yet, we still have no idea what it could be.'

Oscar sipped his whisky, hoping that would hide his smirk, but it didn't.

'You know!'

'I have an idea. This afternoon, after lunch and chess, I strolled through your library and browsed the shelves before heading down to the barrow.'

'Yes?'

'There was one book that caught my attention. It's on the same shelf as all the other local history books, including the one you showed me yesterday evening. The title is *The Civil War in Oxfordshire*. Now, we both know what turmoil the civil war caused and the wave of fear that shook the land.'

'It was a time of terrible violence and upheaval,' Andrew said, and then understanding dawned. His eyebrows arched. 'You don't think—?'

'It's only a guess, but as good a one as any.'

'A find of that nature would fall under the Treasure Act beyond a shadow of a doubt.'

'I'm afraid it would.'

'I can't bear not knowing,' Andrew said. He took a long sip and closed his eyes. 'Dawn won't come soon enough.'

'I don't think I'll sleep soundly tonight,' Oscar said. 'But I will have to try.'

'Early dinner and early to bed?'

'I think that would be for the best.'

'A second dram all the same,' Andrew said quietly, producing another bottle.

'Glenkeir Treasures,' Oscar read aloud. 'With a name like that and such a wonderful golden glint, it would be bad luck not to partake.'

Oscar was up before dawn for the second day in a row. Knowing he wouldn't go back to sleep, he cancelled his phone's alarm and gave himself a minute before climbing out of bed. He'd slept surprisingly well, but the excitement was kicking it now.

He crept out of the house again, not wanting to disturb Andrew unnecessarily, but he took a bottle of spring water from the kitchen this time and grabbed the spade he'd spotted by the gazebo when he arrived at Woodbury. He took his hand spade as well, but the time for subterfuge had passed and the full-length one was more likely to help him get the job done without killing himself in the process.

It was still misty, but he had the impression there was a change in the air—for better or worse? In any case, no rain was forecast. That sense of entering the otherworld had by no means dissipated, and Oscar felt as though his body was gathering strength and energy from the very air around him.

'Fresh air and increased oxygen levels in my blood,' he told himself. 'Purely rational. A good dose of adrenaline on top of that.'

Nevertheless, once he'd removed the trapdoor and bucket from the barrow and stuck the spade into the earth at the bottom of the hole, the grating sound it made rang out sacrilegiously, making him look around nervously for an instant. He drew the soil out carefully and dumped it to one side, then thrust the spade in again. This time, the spell broke and Oscar set about his task, digging rhythmically and stopping only to catch his breath and drink a little water.

Less than an hour later, Andrew brought him a pot of herbal tea and toast with marmalade. He stayed with Oscar for a few minutes, but his eagerness to get to the bottom of the mystery was all that was on Oscar's mind. He drank the tea, ate one triangle of toast, and told Andrew he wanted to get on with it, refusing his offer of assistance. It was a job best done alone.

Oscar lost track of time after that, but the pile of dirt beside him rose ever higher like the sand at the bottom of an hourglass, and his hands grew sore. The sun was high in a clear sky and the effort made it feel like a warm summer's day.

It was the first thrust of the spade after removing his jumper that sent of shiver of hope through his body. He cast the spade aside, grabbed the hand spade, and jumped into the hole—which was almost up to his armpits. He'd had to make it considerably wider than he'd wanted to in order to have enough room to dig with the long-handled spade. After five long scrapes with his hand spade, however, he gasped. He'd exposed the contours of a wooden container, and despite the unkindness of time, its quality remained obvious—fine polished wood with iron straps.

'Oscar?'

'I'm in here. Your timing is impeccable.'

Andrew peered into the hole to find Oscar scratching away the last layer of soil to expose the curved lid of small box no larger than a modern toaster. It lay quite close to the centre of the hole.

'You found it!'

'I dug the last stretch to it,' Oscar corrected him, 'but I'm not the one who brought its existence to your attention.'

Andrew smiled faintly. 'This is true.'

Oscar looked up at him and nodded.

'Can you open it?'

He dug away at the front of the chest until a lock was exposed in the ironwork. 'Best lift it out first. I wonder how heavy it is.'

Once the earth had been removed from all sides down to the base of the box, Oscar placed a hand on either side and wiggled it gently. It took some effort to move it, and as he lifted it, its weight and the jingling inside told him he'd guessed correctly.

'Civil war coins?' Andrew asked.

'Unless this is another test of yours—one which I have failed.'

'Not on your life, Oscar Tremont. If this is a trick, we've both been played for fools!'

'Are you ready?'

'I am,' Andrew said, reaching out to take the box. He put one hand under it and pressed the other against one side. After placing it on the ground, he reached out to help Oscar out of the hole.

Oscar tried to lift the lid but it didn't give. 'This is a seventeenth-century money chest—a treasure in its own right.'

'You can't unlock it?'

'As much as I'd love to try, I'd never forgive myself if I damaged it.' Oscar looked at his client meaningfully. 'I don't want to break the lock mechanism.'

Andrew gently tried the lid but to no avail. 'Sealed tight.'

'Hold it up for me,' Oscar instructed, and as Andrew did so, he craned his neck to peer at the underside. 'There's a slight chance. I can see a split in the bottom. Do you have a pair of tweezers?'

'In my bathroom.'

'I might be able to pull a coin out.'

'We have to try,' Andrew replied. 'Then, we'll have to take a decision. I think we ought to break the news to our twilight excavator and see how he takes it. If he's as smart as his actions have led us to believe, he'll come to terms with the fact that the game's up and accept my invitation to join us as equal partners—all three of us—when we present our find to the district coroner. What do you think, Oscar?'

'I think, my friend, that this is the wisest and most honourable course of action, and it reassures me to know that I was right about you.'

Andrew placed a hand on Oscar's shoulder. 'There are two gentlemen involved in this affair. Of that we should be thankful.'

'This is true, Andrew. As for the third participant—the original, if you like—how are we to consider him?'

'Not harshly. There's no resentment towards him in my heart. He has given me a bit of a turn but done no real harm, has he?' Andrew looked around for a moment and took a deep breath. All was quiet except for the birdsong. 'It's been an adventure the likes of which I'll never forget,' he said eventually, 'and for that I'm almost grateful.' He paused. 'I must sound mad.'

'Not on your life,' Oscar replied. 'I completely understand.'

'That's hardly reassuring coming from you. You're as mad as you are brilliant, Oscar Tremont.'

They laughed.

'You're probably right,' Oscar admitted. 'In that case, we come back here before dusk and wait for him to arrive.'

'And then?'

'We compare notes if he's willing to do so,' Oscar said with a shrug. 'If he's not willing—that's his loss.'

'As simple as that?' Andrew wondered.

'There's only one way to find out. The adventure's not over just yet.'

He arrived on scene from behind the copse of elms just as he had the previous evening. Oscar and Andrew watched as he climbed the barrow and bent over to remove the trapdoor. No sooner had he taken it away than he froze, hooded head bowed as he stared into the hole. By the time he'd dropped the trapdoor and started looking all around—panic etched on his face—Oscar was jogging down the slope with his client stumbling after him.

'Who are you?'

'Who are *you*?' Andrew countered. 'This is *my* land.'

The man slid his hood back and his shoulders slumped. He wasn't going to run and he wasn't going to lash out.

'You're a long way from Hook Norton,' Oscar said.

The look of surprise on the man's face was priceless.

'My name is Andrew Bellingham and this is Oscar Tremont, my private eye.'

'Trevor Brooks,' he conceded. 'How do you know where I live?'

'Henry Wheeler told us,' Oscar said.

Trevor stared into the hole and frowned. 'You found the gold?'

'We did.'

He sighed. 'You've called the police?'

'No,' Andrew replied. 'We haven't.'

Trevor looked up. 'You haven't?'

'No, not yet. I'm a reasonable man, Mister Brooks,' Andrew said. 'Without you, the treasure would have stayed right where it was—and no one can say for how long.'

'It was under the old floorboards?' Oscar asked.

Trevor turned to Oscar and raised his sandy eyebrows. When he looked at Andrew again, he said, 'You certainly found yourself a good detective.'

'The best,' Andrew assured him. 'The very best.'

'Please let me see it,' he pleaded. 'Can I at least hold a coin?'

Andrew turned to Oscar and smiled. Oscar, in turn, reached into a pocket and removed a square of cloth which he unfolded and held out.

Trevor took the coin and examined it, then covered his mouth with a hand and closed his eyes.

'Do you feel unwell?' Andrew asked.

'I—this is terribly embarrassing, isn't it? I feel awful.'

'To be honest, I might have done the same under the circumstances,' Oscar said. 'I can imagine how thrilling it must have been when you read Wheeler's journal—if that's what it was?'

'That's precisely what it was,' Trevor replied, handing the coin back. 'It really is a Civil War coin?'

200

'I'm no numismatist, but it looks like a Triple Unite.'

'A what?' they both chimed.

'The highest denomination produced at the mint of King Charles I in Oxford. Most of the coins inside will be of a lower denomination, but even so, we're looking at a very handsome reward.'

No one spoke for a moment.

'Andrew?' Oscar asked.

'We'll go to Oxford together with our find—the three of us. What do you say?'

Trevor was speechless, and for a moment, Oscar thought he was on the verge of tears. He wished more of his cases could end this way.

'I don't know,' Trevor said.

'What don't you know?' Andrew pressed him.

'We played a game and I lost. That's what it boils down to. I don't deserve your pity—and I don't want it.'

'This isn't a question of pity. Without you, there wouldn't have been a game at all,' Andrew said. 'That's how we see it.'

Trevor looked from Andrew to Oscar, hardly able to believe how understanding they were about what he'd done, and yet, he knew they were right—the treasure would never have been discovered if he hadn't bought Henry Wheeler's old house and started renovating it. He'd been the key player in the game.

'Andrew owes me a tour of Oxford and I'd very much like you to join us. I want you there with us when we find out how much this treasure is worth. You started the game and you owe it to us to keep at it all the way to the end.'

'What do you say?' Andrew asked again.

'I say I'm in!' Trevor told them.

They shook on it, those three men standing on top of Woodbury Barrow, and Oscar Tremont looked to the west and beamed at the sky, where clouds reflected the day's last rays of golden sunlight.

Author Biographies

Cameron Trost is an author of mystery, suspense, horror, and post-apocalyptic fiction best known for his puzzles featuring Oscar Tremont, Investigator of the Strange and Inexplicable. He has written three novels, *Flicker*, *Letterbox*, and *The Tunnel Runner*, and three collections, *Oscar Tremont, Investigator of the Strange and Inexplicable*, *The Animal Inside*, and *Hoffman's Creeper and Other Disturbing Tales*. His short fiction has appeared in numerous anthologies and magazines in Australia, the United Kingdom, the United States, Canada, and France. Originally from Brisbane, Australia, Cameron lives with his wife and two sons near Guérande in southern Brittany, between the rugged coast and treacherous marshlands. He is a registered heritage tour guide (guide-conférencier) and runs the independent publishing house, Black Beacon Books. He is also a lifetime member of the Australian Crime Writers Association. *camerontrost.com*

Edward Lodi draws much of the inspiration for his fiction, poetry, and nonfiction from his experiences growing up and working on cranberry bogs on Cape Cod. He has written and edited more than thirty books, including six *Cranberry Country Mystery* novels featuring feisty septuagenarian Lena Lombardi. In his responsible years he was a college English instructor, a social worker and trainer of social workers, and a publisher and editor. In his irresponsible years he was a hippie and a bum. He lives with his wife, Yolanda, in Hingham, Massachusetts.

Robert Petyo is a Derringer award finalist whose stories have appeared in small press magazines and anthologies, most recently *Stonewall Detectives*, *Strictly Off the Record*, *More Groovy Gumshoes*, *Unnerving*, *Matrimony*, *Murder and Mayhem*,

Crimeucopia: Boomshakalaking, and *Malice*. Though he mainly writes crime fiction, he has published science fiction in small press magazines, and in the deep dark past he wrote three science fiction novels under three different names. X and Facebook *@RobertPetyo*

Karen Keeley writes mostly speculative and crime fiction. Her short stories have appeared in anthologies published by Thalia Press, Outcast Press, Last Waltz Publishing, Wolfsinger Publications, Black Beacon Books, and many others. She is a member of the Short Mystery Fiction Society (SMFS) and has attended many writers' workshops, seminars and conferences. A former Communications Analyst with the Yukon government, she is now retired, and makes her home in Calgary, Alberta, Canada where she divides her time between family, friends, the outdoors, and writing. Visit her at *karenmkeeley.blogspot.com*

Jon Matthew Farber is a recently retired pediatrician from Northern Virginia and a member of the Mystery Writers of America. He has published stories in *Ellery Queen* and *Black Cat Mystery Magazines*, among others, as well as in *The Black Beacon Book of Mystery*. His first (and probably only) novel, co-written with Daniel Reinharth, is the whodunit *Do Not Resuscitate*, available on Amazon. Much of his now extensive spare time is spent travelling and hiking with his wife, and playing (and writing stories about) bridge.

Christina Hoag is the author of noir novels *Law of the Jungle*, *The Blood Room*, *Girl on the Brink* and *Skin of Tattoos*. Her short crime fiction has appeared in *Black Cat Mystery Magazine*, *Mystery Tribune*, *Black Cat Weekly*, *Shotgun Honey*, and *Guilty Crime Story Magazine*. She was longlisted for The Commonwealth Foundation's Short Story Prize 2024, placing in the top 3% of 7,359 entries. A former journalist and Latin America correspondent, she lives in Los Angeles where she has taught creative writing to lifers in prison.

Teel James Glenn's writing has been published in dozens of novels and his poetry and stories have been printed in over three hundred magazines including *Weird Tales, Mystery, Black Cat Weekly, Tough, Pulp Adventures, Mad, Cirsova, Silverblade, Heroic Fantasy,*

Blazing Adventures and *Sherlock Holmes Mystery*. His novel *A Cowboy in Carpathia: A Bob Howard Adventure* won best novel 2021 in the Pulp Factory Award. He is also the winner of the 2012 Pulp Ark Award for Best Author. His novel *Callback for a Corpse* was a second place winner in the CWR Poll as best mystery. His website is *TheUrbanSwashbuckler.com*

Chris Hook is a journalist living in inner Sydney with his partner, their small, round cat and various backyard guests including possums, flying foxes and brush turkeys. He has spent years covering crime and carnage and now enjoys creating neater mysteries than those offered by real life. This is his first story to be published, but there are more Frankie Ross adventures on the way. Find him *@chrishook.bsky.social*, on X *@MrChrisHook7ND* and on Instagram *@MrChrisHook*

Ron Fein is a Boston-area public interest lawyer who, in his copious free time, writes science fiction, fantasy, horror, mystery, and comedy. His work appears in *Nature*, *Factor Four*, *Daily Science Fiction*, *Nonprofit Quarterly*, *MetaStellar*, *NoSleep Podcast*, *Mystery Tribune*, and *McSweeney's Internet Tendency*, and has been translated into Croatian and Romanian. Find him at *ronfein.com*

S. B. Watson lives near the coast of rainy Oregon, where he writes tales of crime, mystery, suspense, and the macabre. His works have appeared in *Spinetingler*, *Punk Noir*, *Mystery Tribune*, and *Mystery Magazine*, as well as various anthologies, including *The Black Beacon Book of Pirates*, *Crime Wave*, and *Crimeucopia: Through the Past Darkly*. For more information, visit *SBWatson.com*

Also Available from Black Beacon Books

An edge-of-your-seat anthology of new fiction inspired by the classic films of Alfred Hitchcock, the Master of Suspense!

For news, reviews, competitions, author interviews, and exclusive excerpts

Visit our website
blackbeaconbooks.com

Like us on Facebook
facebook.com/BlackBeaconBooks

Join us on Twitter
@BlackBeacons

Find us on Instagram
instagram.com/blackbeaconbooks

Subscribe on Patreon
patreon.com/blackbeaconbooks

Discover All our Social Media Links
https://linktr.ee/blackbeaconbooks